BLACK GOLD

Matt Braun

St. Martin's Paperbacks

BLACK GOLD

ISBN: 0-312-98174-0

Printed in the United States of America

St. Martin's Paperbacks edition / January 2004

St. Martin's Paperbacks are published by St. Martin's Press, 175 Fifth Avenue, New York, NY 10010.

10 9 8 7 6 5 4 3 2 1

PRAISE FOR MATT BRAUN

"Matt Braun is one of the best!"
—Don Coldsmith, author of *The Spanish Bit* series

"He tells it straight—and he tells it well."
—Jory Sherman, author of *Grass Kingdom*

"Braun blends historical fact and ingenious fiction. . . .
A top-drawer Western novelist!"
—Robert L. Gale, Western Biographer

ST. MARTIN'S PAPERBACKS TITLES
BY MATT BRAUN

BLACK FOX
OUTLAW KINGDOM
LORDS OF THE LAND
CIMARRON JORDAN
BLOODY HAND
NOBLE OUTLAW
TEXAS EMPIRE
THE SAVAGE LAND
RIO HONDO
THE GAMBLERS
DOC HOLLIDAY
YOU KNOW MY NAME
THE BRANNOCKS
THE LAST STAND
RIO GRANDE
GENTLEMAN ROGUE
THE KINCAIDS
EL PASO
INDIAN TERRITORY
BLOODSPORT
SHADOW KILLERS
BUCK COLTER
KINCH RILEY
DEATHWALK
HICKOK & CODY
THE WILD ONES
HANGMAN'S CREEK
JURY OF SIX
THE SPOILERS
MANHUNTER
THE WARLORDS
DEADWOOD
THE JUDAS TREE
BLACK GOLD

Author's Note

Black Gold is based on a true story.

In 1923, oil production soared to record heights in Osage County, Oklahoma. Unlike other Indians, members of the Osage tribe jointly owned the mineral rights to the land that once comprised their reservation. By law, when the tribal rolls were closed, only 2,229 people qualified as Osages. The oil royalties were shared equally, and the Osages quickly became rich beyond imagining. Every member of the tribe, by today's standards, was a multimillionaire.

White men had preyed on Indians for hundreds of years. Nothing was more natural than for the unscrupulous to engineer a dizzying array of schemes to rob the Osages. Yet some men, greedier than others, visualized a way to steal not just part, but all. The means was violent and bloody, a conspiracy involving white law enforcement officials, and therefore foolproof. They began murdering the Osages.

The Osage Tribal Council sent an urgent appeal to officials in Washington. President Warren G. Harding, at the behest of the Bureau of Indian Affairs, ordered the U.S. Bureau of Investigation into action. Special Agent Frank Gordon was assigned to the case, and organized an undercover operation in Osage County. What he uncovered was wholesale murder, orchestrated by the ringleader of a band of cold-blooded renegades and killers. Gordon found himself pitted against men who were soon determined to kill him.

Black Gold is fiction based on fact. As with any fictional account, literary license has been taken with certain historical characters. Yet the tale is true to the time when Osages were being murdered.

All else is a storyteller at work.

Chapter One

A crowd of several hundred men was gathered in front of the courthouse. There were no hoods or white robes, no fiery crosses ablaze on the lawn. Yet everyone knew who they were and their reputation for brutish violence. They were Klansmen.

Their purpose on that bright April morning was to intimidate the grand jury. A recent Klan flogging was the latest in a rash of atrocities across the state. The incident was particularly brutal, leaving a Negro farmer near death, and the governor had finally declared war on the secret brotherhood. Through the attorney general, he had ordered a grand jury impaneled at the Okmulgee courthouse and demanded indictments against known Klan leaders.

Okmulgee was some ninety miles east of Oklahoma City, the state capital. The rumor was out that Governor Martin Trapp intended to appear before the grand jury and deliver his demands in person. Whether true or not, the mere suggestion had brought out the Klan in force, and they began assembling early that morning. There was rumor as well that Klan leaders meant to make a stand, to block the governor from entering the courthouse, to show him who ruled Okmulgee County. A sense of impending violence hung in the air.

Frank Gordon stood near the front of the crowd. He

wore bib overalls, a faded denim shirt, and a crushed fedora covered with dust. Ganged around him were five men, similarly dressed as hardscrabble farmers, their eyes alert and watchful. All of them were armed, pistols secreted in their overalls, and they carried badges identifying them as agents of the U.S. Bureau of Investigation. Their mission today was to arrest Cullen Horner, a ranking official of the Klan. They waited for Gordon to make the first move.

The operation was meant to strike a blow at the Klan. A mood of isolationism had swept over the country after the World War and with it a resurgence of bigotry. Just three years ago, during the Great Red Scare, some seven thousand suspected Bolshevists had been jailed without warrant, and many deported without judicial process. A year later Congress enacted a bill to protect the racial purity of America.

The immigration of Europeans was limited severely, and banned altogether for Asians. This hotbed of jingoism, fueled by evangelical preachers, provided a fertile climate for the rebirth of the Ku Klux Klan. In keeping with antics of the Roaring Twenties, the KKK flaunted itself with bold provocation. Yet for all its bizarre regalia and absurd rituals, the movement expanded rapidly across America. By 1923, the membership was estimated at five million, with one hundred thousand members in Oklahoma alone. The political apparatus of at least seven states was dominated by the Klan.

Oklahoma had thus far kept the State House free from entanglement. But the Klansmen controlled many rural areas, justifying their methods with a call to patriotism. Okmulgee was one among many such towns, where the Klan was the bastard child of weak law enforcement and law-abiding citizens fearful to speak out. By appearing personally, Governor Trapp would demonstrate that neither he nor Oklahoma could be intimidated by hooded thugs. That would be the message he delivered to the grand jury.

Frank Gordon planned to underscore that message. A Special Agent with ten years' service, he normally worked out of the Dallas office. But he'd been temporarily assigned to the Oklahoma City office by Director Forrest Holbrook, head of the Bureau. Over the years he had been placed in charge of several undercover operations, most notably a case involving Mexican terrorists and German spies on the Rio Grande. His experience made him the logical choice to investigate the Klan.

For the past three months, Gordon had operated an undercover ring in Oklahoma. There were five agents under his supervision, and they had managed to infiltrate the Klan in several counties across the state. The target was Cullen Horner, trusted lieutenant for the Grand Dragon of the Midwestern region. A fiery rabble-rouser, Horner traveled from state to state, holding recruiting rallies and inciting violence. He was constantly on the move, his whereabouts known to only a few Klan leaders. Today, he was in Okmulgee.

Gordon had summoned his agents from around the state. Their best intelligence was that Horner would be in the crowd outside the courthouse, leading the demonstration. One of the agents, Jack Spivey, had seen Horner without his robe and hood after a rally in the town of Lawton. Identifying Horner was critical to an arrest, so in that respect, Spivey had distinguished himself from the other agents. He nudged Gordon now, indicating a small group of men near the courthouse steps. He kept his voice low.

"That's our boy," he said. "The skinny gent with the mustache."

The group of men was somewhat separated from the crowd. Gordon studied them a moment; from their air of authority, he assumed they were Klan leaders. Three of them had mustaches, but only one was tall and lanky, and he knew he was looking at Horner. He nodded to his agents.

"Just like we planned," he said softly. "Wait and see how it plays out with the governor. Follow my lead."

Shortly before ten o'clock a caravan of five cars rolled to a halt at the curb. State troopers piled out of the vehicles to the front and rear, and quickly formed a protective wall before the center car, a four-door Buick sedan. The troopers carried Winchester pump-action shotguns, held at port arms, and they stared at the crowd with hard eyes. Governor Trapp, accompanied by his personal bodyguards, stepped from the Buick.

The men gathered on the courthouse lawn abruptly turned from a crowd to a mob. A dark, muttering growl erupted, and then their voices were raised in shouts of rage. The troopers immediately formed a wedge, the governor safely positioned in the center, surrounded by his inner ring of bodyguards. The troopers bulled a path through the mob, roughly cracking those who failed to step aside with the butts of their shotguns. The governor's party made it to the worn marble steps of the courthouse, and a moment later disappeared inside. The Klansmen, outmaneuvered and furious, were left staring at the door.

Gordon and his agents, unnoticed during the commotion, moved closer to Horner. Gordon's plan was to wait until the crowd was distracted, their attention turned from the courthouse when the governor came back down the walkway. The diversion, with everyone looking toward the street, would provide just enough time to effect the arrest. He thought they could take Horner without anyone being hurt.

Some thirty minutes later the courthouse doors swung open. The troopers, again formed in a tight phalanx, emerged with Governor Trapp in the middle. They were greeted by a strident chorus of catcalls and jeers, for it was apparent from the governor's confident expression that he'd delivered his message to the grand jury. The crowd surged forward, jostling and shoving, screaming obscenities. Clenched fists were raised in threat.

The troopers leveled their shotguns. The Klansmen split apart as if cleaved in half, and the troopers hurriedly led the governor down the walkway. A roar went up from the crowd, even more clamorous than before, their attention fixed on the governor as the troopers hustled him toward the cars waiting at curbside. The mob followed along, shouting and cursing, still wary of the shotguns. Their eyes were trained on the street.

Gordon intercepted Horner and the three Klan leaders. He pulled a Colt .45 automatic from his overalls and jabbed the barrel into Horner's stomach. His agents, guns drawn, covered the other men.

"You're under arrest," Gordon said. "Don't try anything stupid."

Horner glowered at him. "Who the hell are you?"

"U.S. Bureau of Investigation. We have a federal warrant charging you with sedition."

"Friend, you picked the wrong spot. All I gotta do is yell and a hundred armed men'll come runnin'. You done got your ass in a crack."

"Open your mouth and I'll shoot you for resisting arrest. Take my word on it."

A fragment in time slipped past. Horner saw something in Gordon's steady gaze that told him it wasn't a bluff. He shrugged with a lame smile.

"You'll never make it stick."

"Well, sir, that's for a court to decide. Let's go."

Gordon and the agents marched them around the side of the courthouse. At the rear of the building, Horner was loaded into a Chevrolet sedan, and the other Klan leaders were disarmed, then released. They were left to watch, cursing in impotent fury, as the car drove away.

Cullen Horner was placed in the federal lockup in Oklahoma City late that afternoon.

Special Agent in Charge David Turner was head of the Bureau for all of Oklahoma. The offices were located in a building at the corner of Fourth and Robinson, and Turner had sixteen agents under his command. Five of those agents, assigned to Gordon, were working the case on the Ku Klux Klan.

On April 20, Deputy Director J. Edgar Hoover arrived in Oklahoma City. Hoover was the number-two man in the organization, answerable only to the director, Forrest Holbrook. He was traveling by train, on a cross-country inspection of field offices, with a final destination of Los Angeles. His stop in Oklahoma City was routine, but nonetheless sensitive. He had special business to conduct.

Gordon was called to the SAC's private office that afternoon. He found Hoover ensconced in the chair behind Turner's desk, and Turner seated in one of the armchairs. Hoover was short and pudgy, with the face of a gargoyle and the fussy manner of a schoolmarm. He extended his hand across the desk.

"Congratulations, Frank," he said with a limp handshake. "You've done an excellent job with the Klan. Quite commendable indeed."

"Thanks, Edgar." Gordon was all too aware that Hoover preferred to be addressed by title. He accepted the handshake and dropped into one of the armchairs. "How's the old man doing?"

"Director Holbrook is very well, thank you. He asked me to convey his regards."

Gordon thought of Hoover as the quintessential bureaucrat. The U.S. Bureau of Investigation was created in 1908 as a division of the Justice Department, and agents had the power of arrest anywhere in America. The

Bureau was mandated to enforce federal laws, including those dealing with interstate fraud and acts of violence. Over the last fifteen years, Director Holbrook had increased the force to some five hundred agents and established offices in major cities across the country. In all that time, Hoover had never served in the field. He was an office man, and crafty as a politician.

"So," Gordon said, looking across the desk. "What brings you to Oklahoma?"

"A matter of the utmost importance," Hoover said in a piping voice. "Are you familiar with the Osage Indian tribe?"

"No more than the Cherokees or the Choctaws. Why do you ask?"

"In the last two years, thirty-one members of the tribe have died under suspicious circumstances. We have reason to believe they were murdered."

"Sorry to hear it, Edgar. But what's that got to do with me?"

"Director Holbrook wants you to undertake an investigation."

Gordon wasn't ready for a new assignment. He was tall, with ruddy features and chestnut hair, in his early thirties. He had a wife and four children in Dallas, and he wasn't suited to the monastic life. He wanted to go home.

"No disrespect intended"—Gordon spread his hands in dismissive gesture—"I still have to close out the Klan case, and I haven't been home in over a month. I'm not a eunuch, Edgar."

"Very funny," Hoover said testily. "SAC Turner will relieve you of this Klan matter. Isn't that correct, David?"

Turner clearly had his marching orders. He looked uncomfortable, but he nodded. "Just as you say, Deputy Director."

"As for you"—Hoover's gaze shifted back to Gordon—"Director Holbrook specifically requested that you be assigned to the Osage case. Consider it an order."

Gordon shrugged without enthusiasm. "When did the Bureau start investigating Indian murders?"

Hoover quickly explained the inner workings of government. Late in March, the Osage Tribal Council formally requested assistance from the Department of the Interior. The Commissioner of Indian Affairs then requested assistance from the Department of Justice. On April 10, the attorney general forwarded the matter to the Bureau of Investigation. Director Holbrook ordered a file opened on the case.

"President Harding has taken a personal interest," Hoover continued. "As you may imagine, Director Holbrook has assigned the case top priority."

Gordon accepted the inevitable. "Nobody says no to the president, right, Edgar? So tell me, why are all these Osages being murdered?"

"Oil."

"Oil?"

"Yes, rather a great deal of oil."

Hoover went on to elaborate. Oil, principally because of the automobile, was the lifeblood of the economy. The war in Europe had created a demand for gasoline and fuel oil such as the world had never known. When armistice was declared on the Western Front, the demand for oil increased rather than diminished. Throughout the war, automobile and truck manufacturers had become gigantic concerns; their expansion had a profound effect upon the oil business. By 1923 there were ten million passenger cars on the roads, and Henry Ford's fabled Tin Lizzie placed the automobile within the price range of even the lowliest families. The search for new oil fields accelerated at an ever quicker pace.

Competition among oil companies became increasingly fierce. The impact was never more apparent than in the last three years, when drilling rights to the Osage lands were auctioned off in Pawhuska, the largest town in Osage County. Giants such as Standard and Dutch Shell were challenged, and often outbid, by newcomers such as Phillips and Sinclair. Tracts of 160 acres were put on the block and routinely brought drilling bonuses exceeding a million dollars. One tract, considered the prime quarter-section of the lot, brought a whopping $1,990,000. Osage County was a vast reserve of black gold.

"Quite simply," Hoover noted, "the Osages are the richest people per capita in the world. This year, the average family will derive an income of over fifty thousand dollars."

Gordon was visibly impressed. He made less than three thousand a year, and considered himself more fortunate than most. "Wish I had an oil well," he said. "That's twenty years' wages for a lot of people."

"Not to mix my metaphors, but it's the tip of the iceberg. The Osages will ultimately realize tens of millions."

Hoover believed the devil was in the details. He'd thoroughly briefed himself on the case, and proceeded to make the point. Oil was discovered on the Osage reservation in 1897 and the first producing well yielded less than 5,000 barrels a year. There were currently 9,217 wells on Osage lands and the yield for 1923 was projected at 21,000,000 barrels. The Osages, in a manner of speaking, rivaled the Rockefellers.

"So what's happening?" Gordon asked. "Are they being murdered for their money?"

"Indeed they are," Hoover said. "The newspapers have labeled it 'The Reign of Terror,' and aptly so. Every headright will pay more than twelve thousand dollars by the end of the year."

"You lost me there, Edgar. What's a headright?"

"The communal share of oil royalties."

Hoover gave him a quick briefing. The federal government abolished the Osage reservation in 1906, and allotted

657 acres to every member of the tribe. At the time, there were 2,229 Osages on the tribal rolls, and the government decreed the number would remain constant forever. Unlike other tribes, however, the Osages negotiated a pact whereby the mineral rights, including oil, were reserved to the tribe as a whole. Every Osage was entitled to an equal share, known as a headright.

"What happens to these headrights?" Gordon said with a quizzical expression. "I mean, when an Osage dies, does his headright revert to the government? Or can it be inherited?"

"Very perceptive," Hoover allowed, nodding. "Headrights can be inherited, and therein lies the problem. People are quite willing to commit murder for an inheritance of such magnitude."

"Are you saying the Osages are killing each other?"

"Quite the contrary. The Osage Tribal Council believes the murders are being committed by white men. More specifically, white men who have married Osage women."

"You're kidding," Gordon said, one eyebrow arched. "Thirty-one Osage women have been killed?"

"To be precise, twenty-three," Hoover replied. "Eight men have been killed, some of whom were involved with white women."

"Have there been any arrests?"

"No arrests and rather dubious investigations. The politics of Osage County are controlled by whites, which includes the sheriff's department. The Tribal Council believes the Sheriff himself is involved in the killings."

Gordon frowned. "How could he cover up thirty-one murders?"

"I just imagine it's a conspiracy," Hoover said. "Most of the deaths have been attributed to accidental poisoning from tainted bootleg whiskey. Apparently, the death certificates were falsified by the coroner."

"Are there any honest law-enforcement officers in the county?"

"There's a deputy U.S. marshal by the name of Will Proctor. We are given to understand that he's aboveboard and trustworthy. He will be your local contact."

"When do you want me to start?"

Hoover smiled. "Yesterday."

"Why would I expect anything else?"

"How will you proceed?"

Gordon was thoughtful a moment. "Sounds like we need a little deception. I'll conduct an open investigation with the lawman you mentioned, Proctor." He paused, nodding to himself. "For the other part, we'll use an undercover agent. Someone they won't suspect."

"Do you have a particular agent in mind?"

"Yeah, I'd like to have Jack Spivey. He was the best of the bunch in the Klan investigation."

"Consider it done." Hoover rose from behind the desk, extending his hand. "On behalf of the Bureau, I wish you the very best of luck."

"Edgar, I just suspect I'm gonna need it."

Chapter Two

Pawhuska was located in the northeast corner of Oklahoma. The town was named after *Paw-Hui-Skah,* one of the great chiefs of the Osage tribe. Before statehood, and the elimination of reservations, it was the capital of the Osage Nation. Today, it was the county seat of the largest county in Oklahoma.

Gordon drove into town late in the afternoon. His Bureau car was a Chevrolet, and the road wound through steep hills studded with blackjack oaks and limestone boulders. Hundreds of oil derricks dotted the countryside amidst a rugged terrain vibrant with the first wildflowers of spring. Oil wells were situated everywhere, even in the yards of homes and brushy ravines. One, incongruously, pumped away beside a white-framed church.

The town was located in a small valley. Kihekah Avenue gradually descended into the business district, where it crossed Main Street. At the intersection, overlooking the old Osage Council House, were massive brick buildings erected following the oil boom. The most impressive structure was the Triangle Building, a five-story, three-sided monolith constructed in a distinctive wedge. The Osage County Courthouse, squared granite with Greek columns, was one block west, on Grandview Avenue. The Osage Agency, headquarters for the government agent overseeing tribal affairs, was at the crown of a hill north of the business district.

The Duncan Hotel, a three-story sandstone structure, occupied the northwest corner of Grandview and Main. Gordon parked on the street, removed his suitcase from the trunk, and went inside. The lobby was spacious, with a tiled floor and a grouping of leather chairs positioned before the front window. As he crossed to the registration desk, he noticed an older man, with a tall-crowned Stetson and dressed in a dark serge suit, seated in one of the chairs. The Bureau office in Oklahoma City had reserved his room for an indefinite stay, and he identified himself to the desk clerk. After signing the register ledger, he collected his bag and started toward the staircase. The older man rose from his chair and walked forward.

"Afternoon," he said with an amiable smile. "Guess you'd be Agent Gordon. I'm Will Proctor."

"Glad to meet you," Gordon said, exchanging a firm handshake. "How'd you know when I'd get in?"

"Your office called and told me. I live in Hominy, 'bout twenty miles south of here. So I just drove on over."

Gordon noted the badge of a Deputy U.S. Marshal on his vest. He noted as well the wide gun belt, with a single-action Colt six-gun riding high in a holster under the suit jacket. Dave Turner, the Bureau chief, had told him that the old lawman was in his early sixties, and something of a legend in Oklahoma. A frontier marshal who had made the transition into the twentieth century.

Proctor was appointed a federal marshal in 1893, four years after the land rush that opened Oklahoma Territory to settlement. In 1898, he was assigned to patrol the Osage Nation and, at the request of the Tribal Council, he also served as chief of the Osage Indian Police until the force was retired with the advent of statehood in 1907. According to Turner, he was reputed to have killed nine men in gunfights, the latest just three years ago. He was a horseback marshal who now patrolled the Osage in a Model T.

Gordon motioned Proctor to follow him upstairs, where he had been given a second-floor room that overlooked the street. There was a bed and dresser, with an armchair and two straight-backed chairs, and a private bathroom. He waved Proctor to the armchair, dropped his bag on the bed, and hooked his snap-brimmed fedora on the mirror frame behind the dresser. He seated himself in one of the straight-backed chairs.

"Marshal, I'm damned glad to be working with you," he said without pretense. "They've sent me here to solve these murders, and I don't have the first clue. I'll depend on you to steer me in the right direction."

"Call me Will, everybody does." Proctor pulled out the makings and began rolling a cigarette. "Hope you're a slicker detective than me, 'cause there's not a helluva lot to go on. The sheriff—that'd be Otis Crowley—he keeps the lid on pretty tight."

"Is he as crooked as I've heard?"

"Like a dog's hind leg." Proctor popped a match on his thumbnail, lit up in a haze of smoke. "You workin' the case all by your lonesome? Thought the Bureau would've sent a team in here."

Gordon wagged his head. "The two of us will work openly, divert everybody's attention. Another agent, Jack Spivey, will operate undercover. He'll be here day after tomorrow."

"Well, he's liable to sniff out more'n we do. Folks are mighty tight-lipped about this whole mess."

"Any chance some of these murders were committed by Osages?"

"Not likely," Proctor said in a gruff voice. "They've had the hell civilized out of them."

"What's that mean?"

"For the most part, white men look on Indians as

inferiors. So the government spruced 'em up with a dose of civilizing."

"How'd they do that?"

"Missionaries converted them to Christianity and gave 'em a half-assed education."

"You sound bitter."

"I've been among the Osages for twenty-five years. On their worst day, they're better'n most white men."

Proctor was a man of medium build, with iron-gray hair and a bristly mustache. His eyes were the color of carpenter's chalk, and as he spoke, his gaze turned cold. Gordon thought he'd touched a nerve, and decided not to press it further. He tried another tack.

"What's your best guess?" he asked. "Any idea who's killing these people?"

"Well, like you say, it's a guess," Proctor replied. "But I'd lay some powerful odds it's the guardians."

"I'm not following you, Will. Who are the guardians?"

"Sorriest sonsabitches on the face of the earth."

Proctor went on to relate a story of corruption and greed. Congress, in a misguided effort to protect the Osages, decreed that complete oil payments would be made only to those who were ruled "competent." Osages whose Indian blood was fifty percent or greater would have to prove their fiscal responsibility to be awarded a certificate of competency. Those unable to demonstrate competence would be judged "restricted," and the courts would appoint a guardian to manage their financial affairs. Osages whose Indian blood was less than one half were deemed capable of managing their own finances.

The upshot, Proctor observed with disgust, was a devilish form of graft. Judges were in collusion with the court-appointed guardians, and the law stipulated that "restricted" fullbloods could receive only $1,000 of their quarterly oil payments. The guardians, seizing on a loophole in the law, were not required to account for the surplus funds, either to the government or their wards. The end result was that the guardians, who legally charged 20 percent of the oil payments for their services, also stole a major share of the surplus funds. The fullbloods were being robbed blind.

"Pawhuska's a town of eight thousand," he concluded, "and by last count, there's eighty-four lawyers got offices here. Guess who the guardians are?"

Gordon rubbed his jaw. "So why are they killing their wards?"

"Let's say an Osage catches on he's being swindled, or maybe he just demands an accounting. Next thing you know, he dies dead drunk."

"Are you talking about this bad bootleg whiskey? What's listed on the death certificates?"

"All this stuff about rotten whiskey, that's just hogwash. I'd bet it's laced with arsenic or strychnine."

"Which explains why there are no autopsies. Question is, can you prove any of this?"

"Nope." Proctor stubbed out his cigarette in an ashtray. "Lawyers are never around when their clients kick the bucket. They hire somebody to slip the poor soul a batch of poisoned whiskey. Those are the ones we gotta catch."

"Okay," Gordon said. "Do you have any suspects?"

"Wish I did, but I don't. Whoever they are, they're damned tricky."

Gordon was silent a moment. "What about these Osage women who married white men? Aren't their husbands prime suspects?"

"No doubt about it," Proctor said. "Trouble is, none of them women was autopsied either. How we gonna prove it?"

"Today's the first I've heard of these guardians. I thought the investigation would center on the women with white husbands. Things have suddenly got a lot more complicated."

"Frank, I know exactly how you feel. I've scratched my head on this till I'm damn near bald. Any ideas how we get a fresh start?"

"Well, for openers, I want to make pals with the sheriff."

"What the hell for? Otis Crowley wouldn't give you the time of day."

"Hate to admit it, but I've got a devious nature. I want him to think he's part of the team."

"I'll be a sonovabitch!" Proctor woofed with a grin. "You're gonna run a con on him. Aren't you?"

Gordon smiled. "Some people say I'm a born grifter."

The next morning a mountainous range of clouds rolled in from the west. Scattered sunshine dappled the land and a breeze murmured softly across patches of tall grass. The forested hillsides blazed where shafts of light cavorted through the thickening sky.

Gordon and Proctor left Pawhuska in the Chevy after breakfast. A courtesy call on Fred Lookout, Principal Chief of the Osages, seemed to Gordon the first order of business. The night before, Proctor had explained that many tribal elders refused to live in towns, and instead dwelled in villages scattered about the county. Chief Lookout's village was two miles north of Pawhuska.

On the drive from town, Proctor related that the Osages used their Indian names only among themselves. On the old reservation, as part of the "civilizing" program conducted by agency officials, Osages were given Anglicized names to better prepare them for life on the white man's road. Chief Lookout's Osage name, Proctor noted, was *Wy-Tze-Kee-Tompa*. Translated, it meant Eagle That Dreams.

"Good name for a chief," Gordon said. "Having lived here so long, I take it you speak Osage."

Proctor chuckled. "Only enough to get myself in trouble."

The village wasn't what Gordon expected. The houses were two-story frame structures, all painted a striking shade of yellow, with modern conveniences and expensive furniture. Yet, despite the showplaces of their oil wealth, the Osages still followed many traditional customs. Everywhere, there were women tending pots and skillets by open campfires. Proctor commented that they rarely used the modern stoves in their homes.

Parked in every yard was a Pierce-Arrow, the most expensive automobile built in America. A massive vehicle, scarcely smaller than a hay wagon, the cars were appointed with brass fittings, mahogany paneling, and a tonneau lushly upholstered in Moroccan leather. When Gordon commented on the number of cars, Proctor remarked that there were more automobile dealers in Pawhuska than in Oklahoma City. Every Osage family owned at least one car, often three or four.

"Older ones use chauffeurs," Proctor said. "Never learned to operate a car, so they hire black chauffeurs to drive 'em around. Just like rich white folks."

"Well, why not?" Gordon observed. "Might as well enjoy their oil money."

"Cars are sort of like toys for most of the elders. They call 'em 'wagon-that-goes-by-itself.' "

The previous night, over supper, Proctor had talked at length about the Osages. Over the last century, the government had resettled them from their ancestral homelands in Missouri to southern Kansas, and finally, in 1872, to the reservation that was now Osage County. A fierce, warlike people, the Osages had terrorized other Plains Tribes until they were ultimately "civilized" by Quaker missionaries. In the old days, Osage warriors shaved their heads except for a roach of hair centered from the forehead to the neck in scalplock. The men were unusually tall for Indians, often over six feet, and conducted themselves in a dignified manner. Their culture, from ancient times, held that every man had the right to walk his own path, in his own way.

Chief Lookout greeted them beneath a shade tree outside his house. Tall and powerfully built, in his late forties, his features appeared adzed from dark hardwood. He wore the traditional garb of leather leggings and shirt, and suspended from his neck was a gorget made from freshwater mussel shells and a large, silver crucifix. He pumped Gordon's arm with an energetic handshake.

"By golly, good you're here," he said vigorously. "Wrote guv'mint and told 'em 'bout our bad times. Reckon you've come to fix."

"Chief, I'll do my best," Gordon assured him. "Deputy Proctor and I will investigate the murders of your people. We hope to bring the killers to justice."

"You gonna have to. Some Osages think Evil Spirit bring death to walk about our land. Wiser ones know buncha gawddamn white men do this thing. That's why Council write Washington."

The broken English threw Gordon at first. Then he caught the cadence and realized it was probably the rhythm of the Osage language. "Washington agrees with you and the Council," he said. "We know it's the work of white men and we intend to stop it. We won't quit until the job's done."

Lookout studied him a moment. The Osages considered most white men to be boastful, ill-mannered, and, worst of all, deceitful. But he found Gordon to be a man of respect, somehow genuine. A man who might be trusted.

"Don't let nobody fool you," he said, nodding wisely. "Sheriff and doctors say our people dyin' from bad whiskey. They die 'cause somebody feed 'em poison. Ask Proctor, he tell you."

"Already told him, Chief," Proctor said. "Nobody's gonna fool him on that score. Don't you worry."

"Not worried no more." Lookout turned the full force of his gaze on Gordon. "Think you're gonna fix 'em good. Huh?"

"Whatever it takes, we'll find them, Chief Lookout. You have my word on it."

Gordon thought it was a strange world he'd entered. Talking of murder with a man dressed in buckskins who was chauffeured around in a Pierce-Arrow. But there was no doubt in his mind about the man himself.

To an old Osage, the son of warriors, an oath had been extracted here today. Chief Fred Lookout would hold him to his word.

By midmorning, Gordon and Proctor were back in Pawhuska. The sky had cleared, and the courthouse looked like a granite fortress limned in bright sunlight. They left the car parked on Grandview Avenue.

The sheriff's department was on the ground floor, at the rear of a long corridor. Gordon identified himself to a deputy in the outer office, and they were asked to wait while the deputy crossed the room and rapped lightly on a door with frosted glass at the top. A moment later they were shown into the sheriff's private office.

Otis Crowley was a beefy man, on the sundown side of forty, with crafty eyes and heavy jowls. He wore a starchy white shirt and dress pants, with a badge pinned on his chest and a holstered revolver cinched around his bulging waistline. He rose from behind a walnut desk littered with paperwork and extended his hand. His expression was guarded.

"Agent Gordon," he said without inflection. "We been expectin' somebody from the Bureau to show up. Lookout and his Council sure enough raised a stink."

"Don't take it personally," Gordon said, exchanging a handshake. "Washington figured the Indians were about to go on the warpath. I'd sooner not be here myself."

"That a fact?" Crowley motioned them to chairs. "Will, how'd you get roped into this circus? Didn't know you worked with the Bureau."

Proctor waved it off. "Otis, when the head office barks, I sit up and listen. You might say I'm the official tour guide."

"Helluva note," Crowley groused, glancing at Gordon. "Nobody knows Osage County better'n me by a damnsight. Don't the Bureau trust me?"

"Sheriff, you've got it all wrong," Gordon said breezily. "The Bureau considers you an important part of any investigation. We're hoping you'll help us crack the case."

"Lookout and his bunch don't exactly think I'm Sherlock Holmes. How come the Bureau feels any different?"

"Director Holbrook himself ordered that you be included every step of the way. After all, it is your county."

No one could argue the point. There were twenty-eight oil boomtowns scattered across Osage County, and tens of thousands of oil field workers. Along with farmers, ranchers, and businessmen, and the several thousand people they employed, the white vote easily carried any election. The Osages were a minority in their own land, ruled by whites. Otis Crowley was serving his fourth term as sheriff.

"Director Holbrook, huh?" Crowley said, visibly impressed. "You wouldn't be shinin' me on, would you? He sent down the order himself?"

"Sheriff, you know how it works." Gordon mugged, hands outstretched. "When the Director says frog, everybody in the field squats. You're an integral part of the team. No doubt about."

"Well, now—" Crowley beamed like a trained bear. "Where do we go from here? How can I help?"

"Let me get the lay of the land and we'll go from there. I'll send along your regards to the Director."

"Yessir, you do that very thing. Tell him I'm proud to work with the Bureau."

"Never doubted it for a minute, Sheriff. Glad to have you aboard."

Outside the courthouse, Proctor rolled his eyes with amusement. "You a born liar, or they teach you that at the Bureau? Never heard the like."

Gordon laughed. "All I did was butter his ego. Maybe he'll be more cooperative."

"Yeah, maybe," Proctor said. " 'Course, you know he was lyin' to you too. Him and that courthouse crowd are in thick with the guardians. He's not gonna cough up any murderers."

"No, but from now on, he'll try to stay in our good graces. Somehow, someway, he might tip his hand."

"So you aim to trick him into an admission of some sort. That the idea?"

"Will, it's all about catching flies. Honey's better than vinegar."

Proctor grunted. "I'd sooner use a flyswatter."

"Tell you the truth, so would I."

"Then why are we spreadin' honey?"

"To bait the trap."

"What trap?"

"I'm thinking on it, Will. Thinking hard."

They walked off toward the car.

Chapter Three

"That's what they call the Million Dollar Elm."

Proctor pointed to an elm tree outside the Indian Agency headquarters. The buildings were at the top of a hill looking south onto the downtown business district. Gordon studied the tall elm a moment.

"How'd it get the name?"

"Oil auctions," Proctor said. "Indian agent always holds the auctions for drilling rights under that tree. Lots of tracts fetch a million or more."

"Have I got it straight?" Gordon asked. "The Osages divide the money from drilling rights and they also receive oil royalties. Right?"

"That's the way it works. They get a one-sixth royalty on every barrel of crude pumped. We're talkin' one helluva lot of money."

Gordon parked the car near the Million Dollar Elm. Yesterday, after their meeting with the sheriff, they had spent the afternoon reviewing old murder files. Today, while they were waiting for Jack Spivey to arrive, Proctor thought Gordon might like to see the annuity payments on oil royalties. They'd driven to the agency at the top of Kihekah Avenue.

When they got out of the car, Gordon still looked puzzled. "Meant to ask you earlier," he said. "The reservation's been split up and the Osages own their separate pieces of land. So why do they still have an Indian Agent?"

"Well, you know how it is, Frank. The government's got to keep its nose in people's business. 'Specially if they're Indians."

Proctor went on to note that oil had been discovered on Osage land before the reservation system was abolished. The Bureau of Indian Affairs was authorized to lease the mineral rights, and Congress had never acted to change the arrangement. The government collected revenues from oil companies, and distributed the proceeds to the tribe four times a year. Today, April 24, the Osages would receive their headright payments for the first quarter of 1923.

"Same old story," Proctor observed. "The government don't trust the Osages to manage their own affairs. 'Course, a cynic might say it justifies jobs for all those bureaucrats in Washington. Likely a little of both."

"I know what you mean," Gordon said. "We've got some deadwood in the Bureau. Politicians and patronage, that's the name of the game."

"Amen to that."

The Osages began arriving at the agency. Many of the older ones were in chauffeured cars, while the younger ones drove themselves. Proctor pointed out the elder full-bloods, who wore traditional garb, and the younger mix bloods, who were attired in expensive suits and silk dresses. By ten o'clock, the field beside the agency was packed with automobiles and well over two thousand Osages were mingling and socializing. There was an air of gaiety brought on by the prospect of a financial windfall.

Across the way, Gordon saw Chief Fred Lookout conversing with a group of older men dressed in buckskins with red-and-white striped blankets draped from their shoulders over their arms. Proctor explained that the men comprised the Tribal Council, elected to office every two years even though the position was now largely ceremonial. Only Osages with headrights were allowed to vote, and since headrights could be split among several heirs, the votes were fractionalized among many people. The purpose of the Council in modern times was to lead the tribe along the rocky path of the white man's road.

Isaac Gibson, the Indian Agent, opened a window at the side of the agency building. Inside was what amounted to a paymaster's office, with several assistants to check the tribal rolls. The Osages formed a long, serpentine line, and upon reaching the window, individuals presented their certificates. Those who were "restricted," judged by the courts to be incompetent, received checks for a thousand dollars, the balance being credited to their guardians. Those considered competent, readily identified by their broad smiles, received checks for more than three thousand dollars. With so many to be paid, the line edged forward at glacial speed.

"Amazing thing," Proctor said with a trace of irony. "Lot of those folks will be broke before the sun goes down. And I mean flat busted."

"With all that money?" Gordon said skeptically. "How could they go broke in one day?"

"Oil draws leeches faster'n fresh blood."

Proctor quickly related a tale of rampant greed. Oil wealth had brought an army of mercenary whites to the Osage Hills. Businesses and shops routinely doubled their prices for Indians, and allowed them unlimited credit at sky-high interest rates. Friendly bankers provided cash advances to illiterate fullbloods who unknowingly signed liens for repayment of ten times the amount of the loan. Unscrupulous salesmen slick-talked them into buying overpriced jewelry, showy tapestries, and grand pianos, which no one could play. The Osages were cheated in every way a quick-witted swindler could devise.

"Osages are honest to a fault," Proctor concluded,

"They'll pay down their debts by this afternoon, and if it doesn't settle the account, nobody complains. The merchants just extend them more credit."

"Quite a racket," Gordon said thoughtfully. "They get in deeper and deeper, and no way to get out. Why doesn't someone audit the merchants?"

"Same reason nobody's solved these murders. Who cares what happens to a bunch of Indians?"

"You've got a point. If the Tribal Council hadn't filed a protest, I wouldn't be standing here today. The Bureau never knew there was a problem."

"Frank, the people in Washington are like ostriches. Nobody *wants* to know."

A large, four-door Cadillac pulled into the agency compound and halted nearby. When the engine was shut off, Sheriff Otis Crowley crawled out of the passenger-side door. The driver was a man of medium stature, with salt-and-pepper hair and thick glasses, somewhere in his late forties. He wore a somber three-piece suit, with a bowtie and a homburg fixed squarely on his head. His eyes swept the crowd as he stepped from the car.

"You ready to be glad-handed?" Proctor said out of the corner of his mouth. "Here comes the King of the Osage Hills."

"King?" Gordon repeated. "Who is he?"

"William Hale," Proctor said dryly. "Around these parts, he's known as 'Big Bill' Hale."

Crowley approached with Hale at his side and performed the introductions. After a round of handshakes, Crowley grinned like a horse eating briars. "Thought you'd like to meet Mr. Hale," he said, nodding to Gordon. "Couple of months ago he offered a ten-thousand-dollar reward for whoever solves these so-called murders. He's a mighty good friend to the Osages."

"Otis makes too much of it," Hale said modestly. "So far, no one's demonstrated that these unfortunate deaths are actually murder. I just felt a reward would put a spotlight on the situation."

"Well, it's certainly commendable," Gordon said. "Ten thousand's a lot of money, gets people's attention. Somebody might come forward."

"Nothing would please me more. There's no question the Tribal Council believes it's murder. Otis tells me you're convinced as well."

"I go where the Bureau sends me, Mr. Hale. With so many suspicious deaths, I'd say it has the look of murder."

Hale's glasses were as thick as bottles, and magnified the intensity of his eyes. "Whatever the case," he said pleasantly, "I wish you luck with your investigation. Don't hesitate to call on me if I can be of assistance."

"I appreciate the offer, Mr. Hale. I'll keep it in mind."

Hale and Crowley walked off into the crowd. Several Osages greeted Hale with diffident smiles and cordial handshakes. But Gordon noticed that Chief Lookout and the Tribal Council kept their distance, aloof if not antagonistic. He glanced at Proctor.

"What's the story on Hale?"

"For openers, he's the richest man in the county. Owns a ranch, a bank, a mercantile store, and a funeral parlor. Got his finger in lots of pies."

"Sounds like it." Gordon nodded across the way. "Chief Lookout and the Council look a little frosty. What's their problem with Hale?"

"Politics," Proctor said simply. "Hale pretty much controls who gets elected to county office. Chief Lookout thinks the Osages get the short end of the stick."

"Do they?"

"Well, there's no Osages in the courthouse. White men run the county."

"And Hale jumps them through hoops."

Proctor smiled stiffly. "That's why they call him Big Bill."

. . .

Jack Spivey drove into town late that afternoon. His car
was a sporty Ford Roadster, provided courtesy of the
Bureau, and he wore a fawn-colored suit with a flashy
necktie. He looked every inch the traveling salesman.

The sun dropped steadily westward as he parked in
front of the Duncan Hotel. He took a valise and a briefcase
from the backseat, locking the car, and went inside. The
desk clerk, who also manned the switchboard, finished putting a call through and moved forward. Spivey set his bags
on the floor.

"Howdy there," he said with a loopy smile. "I'll be
needing a room for a while."

"How long will you be staying with us?"

"Week, two weeks, maybe longer. Depends on the
welcome I get."

The clerk knew a salesman when he saw one. "What
line are you in?"

"The lifeline!" Spivey flashed a toothy grin. "Name's
Jack Sprivey, with the Centennial Life Insurance Company. How you fixed for insurance, brother?"

"Got all I need, thank you just the same. You want a
single room?"

"Only if there's no pretty girls looking for a room-
mate. How about something on the second floor, back
toward the rear? I don't like street noise."

"Not much of that." The clerk reached for a key as
Spivey signed the register. "We generally roll up the side-
walks after dark."

"Sounds like my kinda town."

"You're in room two-oh-nine, Mr. Spivey."

"Thanks a load, cousin."

Spivey carried his bags upstairs. He got settled into
the room, hanging his extra suit in the closet, and went
back down to the lobby. He asked for a place with good

food and the clerk directed him to the Osage Grill, across
the street beside the Constantine Theater. On the marquee,
he noted there was a Western silent film playing, starring
Buck Jones. He thought he might catch it another night.

Dark had fallen when Spivey came out of the café. The
Bureau had informed him that Gordon was in Room 202; a
meeting had been prearranged for seven o'clock tonight. In
the hotel, he waved to the desk clerk, took the stairs to the
second floor, and checked both ways to make sure the corridor was empty. There was every imperative, working
undercover, that no one establish a connection between him
and Gordon.

The door opened when he knocked. Gordon waved
him inside, then quickly closed and locked the door. Will
Proctor was seated in one of the chairs and Gordon made
the introductions. Spivey was surprised by Proctor's age,
but since working with Gordon on the Ku Klux Klan, he'd
learned to trust the senior agent's judgment. Gordon
waited till Spivey was seated and looked at Proctor, wagging his head with a wry smile.

"Jack should have been in the movies," he said. "Got
the looks and he's a natural-born actor. Best undercover
man I've ever seen."

"Fooled me," Proctor admitted. "I wouldn't've
pegged him as a lawman."

Spivey was unusually handsome, a very youthful
twenty-five. His dark hair and striking green eyes were set
off by high cheekbones and chiseled features. He was slim,
with the lithe build of an athlete, and tougher than he
looked. He carried a snub-nosed revolver holstered at the
small of his back.

Gordon motioned to him. "Tell Will about your
cover."

"I'm an insurance salesman," Spivey said with cheery
confidence. "Work for Centennial Life, headquartered in
Oklahoma City. They've sent me here to check out the

market in Osage County. We might open a branch office."

David Turner, the Bureau's SAC in Oklahoma, had made the arrangements. Spivey was duly licensed by the state as an insurance agent, and Centennial Life was indeed headquartered in Oklahoma City. The president of the company had agreed to assist the Bureau, and Spivey was officially carried on the rolls as a sales manager. Anyone who inquired would be told Spivey's assignment was to evaluate the sales prospects of Osage County.

"Sounds good to me," Proctor said. "Are you actually gonna sell insurance?"

"Sure am," Spivey replied. "Lets me go anywhere in the county and call on anybody, white or Indian. It's the perfect cover."

"Let's move on," Gordon interjected. "We've got a lot of ground to cover, and Jack's missing some of the pieces. Will, tell him about the guardians."

Proctor reviewed the system of guardians being appointed by the courts for certain Osages. He explained that an Osage who could not read and write English well enough to conduct business would be denied a certificate of competency. The courts were empowered to act under a 1906 law granting such discretion to the Bureau of Indian Affairs.

"There's all kinds of tricks," Proctor went on. "One of the dirtiest revolves around an alimony racket. A guardian will get a white woman—usually a whore—to marry his Osage ward. Then, after a quick honeymoon, she sues for divorce."

"Which the courts grant," Spivey said, quickly visualizing the scheme. "And award her a generous alimony."

"Generally half the Osage man's oil rights," Proctor said. "So there's plenty to pay off the court and the woman, and still leave a chunk for the guardian. Often as not, the biggest chunk."

"Or they get it all," Gordon added, "by murdering the

Osage husband. Then the white wife inherits everything."

"Yeah, that happens," Proctor acknowledged. "But mostly it's Osage women who get goo-goo eyed that a white man wants to marry 'em. Women are easier to kill."

"Lots easier," Gordon said gravely. "Twenty-three women and eight men. Almost three to one."

Spivey looked serious. "These guardians add a whole new wrinkle to the case. Where do we start?"

"We'll hold off on the guardians," Gordon said. "They probably get someone to do the killing for them. That means we'd have to catch the killer before we've got a shot at the guardian."

"Conspiracy's hard to prove," Spivey agreed. "Especially when it depends on the killer turning stoolie on the guardian."

"Might never happen," Gordon said. "We'll concentrate instead on the white men with dead Osage wives. There's a greater likelihood the men did their own killing."

"That raises a question," Spivey said. "Are they still in Osage County? Or for that matter, Oklahoma?"

"Most are," Proctor remarked. "Even after a court probates the estate, the oil payments come through the Indian agent. A man likes to stay close to his money."

Gordon brought out the files on the murder cases. Those that were considered cold, two years or older, he set aside. Several cases that had occurred within the last year were assigned to Spivey. In his guise as an insurance agent, Spivey was to call on relatives of the murdered women, as well as the white husbands. His goal was to uncover proof that would ultimately lead to a murder conviction.

At the same time, Gordon cautioned, he would have to call on white merchants and tradesmen, and try to sell them insurance. The tactic was meant to dampen the suspicion of anyone, white or Osage, that he was interested only in those involved with the murders. Proctor and

Gordon, meanwhile, would work a case only a month old, an Osage woman who had died under strange circumstances. Their purpose, aside from solving a murder, was to focus attention on themselves and further divert attention from Spivey. There was every likelihood that people would talk more openly, inadvertently reveal their secrets, to an insurance salesman.

"We'll meet every night," Gordon finally said to Spivey. "After supper here in my room, when things have quieted down. Just make sure no one spots you in the hall."

"I'll watch myself." Spivey was silent a moment. "You know, it never really hit me till you pulled out all those files. What we're dealing with here is a murder industry."

Proctor laughed sourly. "They're damn sure industrious about it, awright. Killin' Osages for profit."

Gordon was reminded of a report in the papers when Warren Harding assumed the presidency. Upon taking office, Harding commented with perfect sincerity that "the business of America is business." The thought, with a slight exception, was no less true in the Osage Hills.

The business here was the business of murder.

Chapter Four

The band was playing "Margie." Couples dipped and swayed around the dance floor as a fat man on the clarinet took the lead. The tune was just lively enough for a fast fox trot.

Anna Brown was drunk. She clung to Bryan Burkhart, her head on his shoulder, lost in the music. The dance floor was crowded with a mix of Osages and whites, some better dressed than others. There was a certain democracy among those who frequented roadhouses.

The Tip Top was outside the town of Fairfax, some twenty miles west of Pawhuska. The establishment was large, with booths around the walls and tables and chairs closer to the dance floor. The five-piece band played seven nights a week, and every form of liquor, from rotgut bourbon to bonded scotch, was served. The price of admission was a drink.

Burkhart led Anna off the dance floor when the song ended. He was white, short but stoutly built, an inch or so taller by virtue of his cowboy boots. Anna was a fullblood Osage, attractive if a little plump, her hair dark as a raven's wing. They were lovers for the night, perhaps longer depending on Anna's mood. She changed boyfriends with whimsical vagary.

Their friends were seated in a booth off to the side of

the dance floor. Katherine Cole was also a fullblood Osage, slim and lissome, her dusky features somehow exotic. Kelsey Morrison was white, a tall, saturnine man who always seemed to be amused by some private joke. A waiter appeared as Anna and Burkhart slid into the booth.

Morrison ordered another round. The women were drinking gin rickeys and the men ditchwater highballs, bourbon with a splash of water. Burkhart and Morrison, both in their late twenties, worked on a ranch north of Pawhuska. Anna was twenty-five and Katherine barely twenty, and neither of them worked. Deemed competent by the courts, they collected their oil royalties in full. Yesterday, they had each banked more than three thousand dollars.

"Here's mud in your eye," Burkhart said, lifting his highball. "Whiskey and wild, wild women, that's my motto. Let the good times roll."

"Who you calling wild?" Anna said, her speech slurred "Watch what you're saying, buster. You might be sleeping alone tonight."

"Hey, we're havin' fun here. Don't take it wrong."

"Yeah, Bryan's right," Morrison said with a sly wink. "What the hell, we're celebrating."

Anna laughed. "Celebrating on my money. And yours too, Kathy. Isn't that so?"

"Why not?" Katherine said with a lighthearted smile. "You have to spend it somewhere. Who wants to die rich?"

"Now there's a motto!" Anna whooped drunkenly. "Spend it like there's no tomorrow. I love it!"

Anna and Katherine were casual friends. Like many Osage girls, they preferred to date white men rather than men from the tribe. Katherine had been dating Morrison almost a year, and she had introduced Anna to Burkhart. Their attraction to white men was but one of many things they shared. They were, as much as young white girls, a product of their generation

The climate of the Roaring Twenties was one of bally-hoo and whoopee. A time when all traditional codes of behavior were under assault and an entire generation practiced cynicism. The girls drank as much as the boys, patterning their lives on some distorted image of the flapper ideal; sexual promiscuity was as rampant in the Osage Hills as it was in New York City. Convention was now old hat, sloughed off by the younger set as a snake sheds its skin. "Let the good times roll" was the credo for those who lived for the moment.

The band broke out in an earsplitting Charleston. Morrison exchanged a glance with Burkhart, and pulled a face. "Let's take this party somewhere else," he said, looking around the table. "I've had enough of this joint for one night."

"Suits me," Burkhart said. "I'm tired of dancin' anyway."

Anna shrugged. "Just so there's something to drink. I'm a thirsty girl."

"What about your place?" Morrison said, glancing at Katherine. "No reason Anna and Bryan couldn't sleep over."

"Okay by me," Katherine said agreeably. "But I'm not cooking breakfast. You're on your own."

"Hell, I'll cook," Burkhart said, tossing money on the table. "Let's get out of here."

Katherine and Morrison slid out of the booth. The last gin rickey had apparently been one too many for Anna. She wobbled unsteadily when she got to her feet, and Burkhart supported her with an arm around her waist. In the parking lot, he waited until Katherine and Morrison climbed into the backseat of his Studebaker sedan. He helped Anna into the passenger seat.

On the road, Burkhart turned southeast. Katherine's house was in Pawhuska, and after a moment, she realized they were headed in the wrong direction. She didn't think

Burkhart was that drunk, and she couldn't imagine he would take the long way around. She finally looked across at Morrison.

"Kelsey, we're going the wrong way."

"Don't worry about it," Morrison said. "We're gonna pick up another bottle from a bootlegger."

"But it's out of the way," Katherine persisted. "There are plenty of bootleggers in Pawhuska."

"Just sit back and enjoy the ride."

A few miles out of Fairfax, Burkhart took the turnoff to Gray Horse, a small Osage village. He drove a short distance and then veered onto an old wagon trail that bordered a creek. He slowed, braking to a halt, and doused the headlights as he switched off the engine. The burbling sound of the stream abruptly filled the silence.

"What are you doing?" Katherine said, suddenly frightened by the odd turn of events. "Why are we stopped here?"

"Katie, listen to me." Morrison's tone was impassive, somehow cold. "You trust me to do the right thing by you?"

"Yes . . ."

"Then pretend you were never here and don't ask questions."

"But—"

"Just stay in the goddamned car!"

Anna was asleep, passed out in the passenger seat. Burkhart stepped from the car, and Morrison, with a last warning look at Katherine, crawled from the backseat. When they opened the passenger-side door and took hold of Anna, she awakened in a drunken stupor. Her head lolled as she tried to bring them into focus.

"Wha's matter?"

"Nothin' at all," Burkhart said calmly. "We're just gonna take a little walk."

"Where?"

"You'll see."

Burkhart got hold of one arm and Morrison the other, and they half-carried her as she tottered along between them. They walked her down into a ravine where the creek tumbled noisily over a rocky streambed. Some thirty yards deeper into the ravine, they stopped and lowered her to the ground. She sat down heavily, her dress hiked up over her knees, on the verge of falling over. Her glazed eyes fixed blankly on the creek.

The men stood there a moment, looking down at her. Burkhart finally darted a sideways glance at Morrison. "You know what's gotta be done."

"Yeah."

"Then do it."

Morrison pulled a compact .32 automatic pistol from his pocket. He clicked off the safety, placed the pistol to the back of Anna's head, and fired. The small-caliber report was hardly more than a loud *pop,* like a firecracker. Anna's head snapped forward and her body went slack, slumping facedown on the creekbank. Her left leg jerked in an afterspasm of death.

"Jesus," Morrison said, almost to himself. "Don't take much, does it?"

"No, it don't," Burkhart said. "And I still say we oughta do Katherine. You're thinkin' with your pecker instead of your brain."

"Bryan, don't start up again. I told you I'd keep her in line."

"You'd goddamn sure better. For an Injun gal, she must be some piece of ass."

"I just like her, that's all."

They walked back to the car. Katherine was scrunched up in the corner of the backseat, her eyes round with terror. She'd heard the report of the pistol shot and she knew what it meant. Anna Brown, her sometimes friend, was dead.

Burkhart leaned through the car door. "You pay close attention," he said in a rough voice. "There's others in this

with me and Kelsey. You try squealin' on us and somebody'll stop your clock. Got me?"

"Yes." Her eyes were glassy with fear. "I'll never say
anything. I promise."

"Tellin' you for real, your promise better be good as
gold. One peep and you're dead."

Katherine silently made a promise to herself. One to
keep as if her life depended on it. She would forget tonight.

Forever.

A bright morning sun crested the knobby hills. Somewhere in the distance a mockingbird trilled and then took
wing against the muslin blue of the sky. Goldenrod, in
springtime bloom, lined the roadside.

Gordon brought the Chevy to a stop behind two sheriff's vehicles. He and Proctor stepped from the car and
walked toward the old wagon trail that cut north through
the woods. A heavyset deputy sheriff stood smoking a cigarette a few yards down the trail.

"Mornin', Noah," Proctor said as they approached.
"We got a call from somebody in the sheriff's department.
Said you'd found a dead woman out here."

"Deader'n hell," Deputy Noah Perkins said. "Sheriff
and Doc Tuttle are down at the creek. Not a pretty sight."

"Who found her?"

"One of the elders over at Gray Horse. Came to do a
little fishin' and got more'n he bargained for. He called it
in to the sheriff."

"Well, I reckon we'd better have a look."

Proctor started forward, then abruptly stopped. He
motioned Gordon aside and turned back to the deputy.
"You boys had a car in here?"

"Nope," Perkins told him. "You saw we're parked on
the road."

"What is it?" Gordon asked. "What do you see?"

"Tire tracks, maybe something more."

Proctor had spent half a lifetime trailing outlaws through the wilderness. One of the first lessons he'd learned was that a seasoned tracker always awaited sunrise before trying to cut sign. On hard ground the correct sun angle often made the difference between seeing a print or missing it entirely. In early morning, with the sun at a low angle, the tracker worked westward of the trail. The easterly sunlight cast shadows across the faint imprints of man or horse. Or in this case, an automobile.

"Stay behind me," he said to Gordon. "Walk where I walk."

A tracker seldom saw an entire footprint unless the ground was soft. What he looked for instead were flat spots, scuff marks, and disturbed vegetation. Only hooves or footprints, or tire tracks, something related to man, would leave flat spots. Small creatures might leave scuff marks or disturbed pebbles. But a flat spot, unnatural to nature, was always made by a hooved animal or a man.

Proctor kept the sun between himself and the prints. He slowly worked his way into the ravine, observing the change of color caused by the dry surface of the earth being disturbed to expose a moister surface. Heat increased the rate at which tracks age, and on hard terrain the sun dried the ground at an even faster rate. The undersurface of the prints he followed was restored to the normal color of the earth. All the signs indicated the tracks were at least a day old.

"Two men," he said, pausing to study the sign. "They took a woman out of a car and practically dragged her off toward the creek. She was hardly able to walk."

"Unconscious?" Gordon ventured. "Or maybe already dead?"

"No, she was alive," Proctor said with certainty. "Crowley and the others that've been through here messed it up with their tracks. But the sign's there to read."

"Anything else?"

"See them pointy little spots in the ground?"

"Yeah?"

"The men was wearin' cowboy boots."

Sheriff Otis Crowley and Dr. Orville Tuttle, the Osage County coroner, were farther along in the ravine. As Gordon and Proctor approached, they saw the body of a woman near the creek bank. Crowley waved them closer.

"Got a cold one," he said. "Told you I'd call if anything popped up that wasn't ordinary. Figured you'd want to see it for yourselves."

Crowley introduced Gordon to Dr. Tuttle. The coroner was a reedy man with thinning hair and a pencil-thin mustache. His handshake was surprisingly firm and there was the impression of intelligence beyond that expected of a country doctor. He moved aside to give them a better view of the body.

The woman's eyes were open, her mouth parted in death. An animal of some sort had chewed off her nose, and ragged bits of bone and cartilage protruded from the hole. Blowflies buzzed around the grisly cavity, as well as the top of her tongue, their wriggling maggot droppings like tiny filaments of parchment. Her features were bloated and a putrid stench hung in the air.

"You'll note the absence of rigor mortis," Tuttle said in a pedantic tone. "Usually occurs twenty-four hours or so after death, and that's in keeping with the onset of decomposition we see here. I would estimate she died somewhere between yesterday morning and the night before."

Gordon had seen many bodies, but none more pathetic than the woman on the ground. He glanced at the coroner. "How did she die?"

"I'm not certain, but I suspect she was shot. Have a look at this."

Tuttle parted the thick black hair at the crown of her

head. He spread the hair with his fingers and revealed a small hole encrusted with dried blood. He turned back to Gordon.

"You'll notice there's no exit wound. That would indicate the bullet is lodged in her brain. I'll find out when I do an autopsy."

Gordon nodded, his expression thoughtful. As he moved away from the body, he caught a coppery glint out of the corner of his eye. He looked closer and saw the sun reflecting off something in a patch of grass by the creek bank. He stooped down, gently parting tufts of grass, then stood. He held up a brass shell casing.

"No question she was shot," he said. "That's a casing from a .32 caliber automatic, probably a Colt. All we have to do is find the man with the gun."

"Two men," Proctor said, his gaze on the sheriff. "I tracked 'em from where they dragged her down here. You know anybody with a little popgun that wears cowboy boots?"

Crowley snorted. "Hell, Will, half the men in Osage County wear cowboy boots. That's not much to go on."

"Yeah, but it's something," Gordon said, pocketing the shell casing. "Have you identified the woman?"

"Her name's Anna Brown," Crowley said. "Or leastways it was."

"A fullblood?"

"Yessir, and I know what you're thinkin'. But I got a hunch this here's no headright murder."

"Why not?"

"Anna was divorced. She married a white man, but after the divorce, he moved to California. He wouldn't get no part of her oil money."

"Who would?"

"Why, her kinfolks," Crowley said. "Her mother and one of her sisters live in Pawhuska. Her other sister lives outside Gray Horse."

"What about her father?" Gordon asked. "Where does he live?"

"Off in the great beyond, or whatever the Osages call it. He died four, maybe five years ago."

"How about other men?" Gordon said. "Did she date anyone in particular?"

"Hate to speak ill of the dead." Crowley ruefully shook his head. "Anna dated anything in pants, and the more the merrier. Some folks called her the county punchboard."

"I'll want to speak with her mother and her sisters. They might have some idea who killed her."

"The mother's name's Lizzie Kile, and this being a Friday, you'll find her at Chief Lookout's village. She always attends the weekly Stomp Dance."

"What's a Stomp Dance?"

Crowley grinned. "Why, it's sort of a half-assed religious shindig for heathens." He looked at Proctor. "Am I right, Will, or am I right?"

"Otis, you don't know beans from buckwheat about the Osages. You never did."

"What would you call it, then?"

"What the Osages call it."

"And what might that be?"

"A talk with God."

Chapter Five

Stars were sprinkled like diamond dust through a pitch-black sky. The road was faintly visible in the starlight, a narrow ribbon winding through stands of blackjack and elm. The only sound was the muted throb of drums.

The church was located on the outskirts of the village. The building was octagonal, some thirty feet in diameter, with a conical roof. Atop the roof was a large white cross, and the rest of the structure was painted a shade of red almost ochre in color. A glow of light filled the open door.

Gordon parked the Chevy off to the side of the church. The sound of drums became louder as he and Proctor stepped from the car. White men were normally unwelcome at a Stomp Dance ceremony, but Proctor had assured him that their presence would be tolerated. Chief Lookout could be counted on to act as their patron.

On the drive north from Pawhuska, Proctor had explained that the tribal elders practiced a curious form of religion. The practice originated in the 1890s, when all Indians were at the mercy of whites, and combined ancient Osage beliefs with Christianity. The Osages worshiped *Wah' Kon-Tah*, their Creator, and *Wah' Kon-Tah E Shinkah*, the Christ, the white man's Son of God. The strange admixture brought the blessings of the two most powerful forces in the universe.

"We're outsiders here," Proctor said as they walked toward the church. "Stay back close to the wall and don't speak unless you're spoken to. What we're attendin' here is a religious service."

"What about Lizzie Kile?" Gordon asked. "How do we talk to her?"

"We don't till they're finished talkin' to God."

The inside of the church was constructed in the ancient form, with a hard-packed earthen floor. A fire of scented logs burned in the center of the room, willowy tendrils of smoke drawn through a smoke hole at the top of the roof. Opposite the door, four men sat cross-legged before tom-toms covered with taut deerskin scraped white as a bone. The steady throb of the drums was all but hypnotic.

The dance floor was oval, the earth tramped solid from thousands of ceremonies. The women were dressed in shrouds of doeskin and sat ringed around the walls of the room. The men wore leggings, their faces painted a vivid array of colors, tinkling bells attached to their ankles with rawhide. Some carried eagle-wing fans, while others held braided quirts, mussel-shell gorgets and bear-claw necklaces suspended from their necks. Their hair was clamped tightly into the warrior's roach of olden times.

The women chanted to the melodic beat of the drums. Framed in the orange glow of the fire, the men danced with religious gravity and around the circle. One would wave his eagle-wing fan in a sweeping motion, while another touched the ground with his quirt, as though tracing the tracks of some ancient foe. Their songs honored the deeds of their ancestors, and, even more, offered prayer to *Wah' Kon-Tah* and Christ, the twin deities. Their bodies shone with a fine sheen of perspiration in the glare of the fire.

Gordon noticed two women across the room rhythmically pounding a substance in wooden pestles. He recalled Proctor telling him earlier in the evening that the Osages practiced peyoteism as part of their religion. Dried pods of the mescal plant were imported from Mexico, and the buttons were ground to the consistency of flour, then mixed with water and rolled into little balls. The peyote balls, when eaten, produced a hallucinatory effect that was quick and strong, and gave the worshiper a sense of dreamy content. The Osages believed they talked to the gods through the visions induced by the peyote balls.

The root of their religion, according to Proctor, was *Wah' Kon-Tah.* From ancient times, they were taught that the Creator had separated earth and sky, land and water, to form the universe. Later, when the god of the whites proved to be invincible, the Osages adopted *Wah' Kon-Tah E Shinkah,* the Christ, into their spiritual world. Still later, yearning for deliverance from their white oppressors, they adopted peyote as their sacred sacrament, much as bread and wine were the sacrament of Christians. Their prayer songs, heightened by peyote, allowed them to confess their misdeeds and absolve themselves of evil. They were cleansed of their sins, their spirits worthy of the afterworld.

Chief Lookout, who was standing by the drummers, circled around the room. He joined Gordon and Proctor by the door and solemnly shook their hands. He directed Gordon's attention to the dancers. "We talk to the Great Spirit here," he said with a sage look. "You a believer, good Christian?"

"I try," Gordon said diplomatically. "I doubt I'm as faithful as the Osages."

"Nobody that good," Lookout said with a jokester's smile. "Osages know what Great Spirit wants to hear. Talk to Him better'n anybody."

"Maybe I can learn something while I'm among the Osages."

"Catch the killers and that put you right with everybody's God. Sheriff sent deputy tell us what happened poor Anna Brown. You here to talk with mother?"

"I don't want to intrude," Gordon said. "I'll wait until your services are finished."

"You wait long time, 'cause Osages dance all night. Little talk won't hurt nothin' much. I get her for you."

Lookout walked along the wall and stopped behind one of the women. Her voice was raised in prayer song, but she went silent when he bent down and whispered in her ear. She nodded, looking at the door, her gaze touching first on Gordon and then Proctor. She rose stiffly, smoothing her doeskin shroud, and moved around the room.

By the gray in her hair, Gordon judged she was in her early fifties. She was overly plump, her features rounded, but he thought she'd been an attractive woman in her day. As she approached, he saw that her eyes were glazed from the hallucinogenic effects of peyote, and he wondered how many of the little balls she'd eaten tonight. He saw as well the sorrow in her eyes, a dulled grief. She stopped in front of them.

"I'm Lizzie Kile, Anna's mother."

"Mrs. Kile," Gordon said softly. "Let me say how sorry I am for your loss. I'm Special Agent—"

"I know who you are, and Will Proctor too. All Osages know."

"Mrs. Kile, I wonder if we could step outside? I'd like to talk to you in private."

"Sure."

Lizzie Kile led the way through the door. They walked a ways in the darkness, far enough that the chanting and the throb of the drums was not so insistent. She suddenly stopped and turned, facing them. Her eyes were fierce with hate.

"You fixin' to catch the man that killed Anna? You do, you shoot him for me."

"We're looking into it," Gordon said, avoiding a direct answer. "Do you have any idea who Anna was out with Wednesday night?"

"Don't know." She hesitated, her eyes downcast, somehow embarrassed. "Anna had her own house and her own life. She never talked about her men . . . and I never asked."

"We've been told her former husband moved to California. Do you know if that's so?"

"Not him you lookin' for. He's been gone long time now."

Gordon nodded. "You'll have to excuse some of the questions I ask. Some things are personal, but it might bear on our investigation into Anna's death. Could you tell me how her headright will be divided?"

"Regular way," she said with a weary shrug. "I get half and her sisters—Rita, Mollie—they get other half."

"Can you think of anyone who might have wanted to do her harm? Did she have any enemies?"

"Nobody had any reason to hurt Anna. Maybe she wasn't what everybody calls good girl. But she wasn't bad . . . not that bad."

"Well, we're going to do everything we can to find the man responsible. You can depend on it, Mrs. Kile."

"You find him, don't arrest him or nothin' else. Kill him like he killed Anna."

Lizzie Kile walked back into the church with all the dignity she could muster. Gordon watched after her a moment, then glanced at Proctor. "What do you think, Will?"

Proctor shook his head. "Not a helluva lot to go on."

"No, there's not."

"But when we find him—"

"Yeah?"

"Turn the bastard over to Lizzie. She'd fry his gizzard."

Gordon thought it was the least she would do, and justice of sorts. Osage justice.

Late that night Gordon was seated in the armchair in his room. He was in shirtsleeves, scrunched low in the chair, his eyes fixed on the ceiling. He was mentally reviewing a long and uncertain day.

Until this morning, he and Proctor had spent three days investigating a guardian whose female client had died under suspicious circumstances. Her death certificate, like so many other Osage women, was signed by Dr. Orville Tuttle and attributed her death to tainted moonshine. The guardian, as were so many guardians, was a lawyer with offices in the Triangle Building. The investigation, thus far, revealed that the woman had died after a drunken binge lasting four days. No direct link had been established between her death and her guardian.

Nor had an autopsy been performed. In Osage County, when the judges were in league with the guardians, hard evidence would be needed to obtain a court order and have the body exhumed. Further complicating the case was that an independent examiner would have to be brought in to perform a postmortem, specifically looking for traces of arsenic or strychnine. The county coroner, or any other doctor in Osage County, could not be trusted to render an impartial opinion. The conspiracy appeared so widespread that anyone in an official capacity was automatically suspect. Anna Brown's murder merely compounded an already murky situation.

There was a light knock at the door. Gordon rose from his chair, crossed the room, and turned the key. When he opened the door, Jack Spivey took a last look along the hallway and quickly moved into the room. His mouth creased in a slow smile.

"Hard work being a spy," he said. "Waited till everyone was bedded down for the night."

Gordon locked the door and motioned him to a chair. "For an insurance salesman, you do pretty good. How's it going?"

"Sold my first policy today. Ten thousand dollars term life on an Osage man. Think my sales pitch is getting better."

"Maybe you've found a second career."

"Thanks, but no thanks," Spivey said lightly. "Not my cup of tea."

Gordon nodded. "Anything new?"

"Not a whole lot. The Osage man's the father of one of the murdered girls. Got him to talking while I was writing up the policy, and it's pretty much the same story. He's convinced her husband killed her."

"Let me guess," Gordon said. "All supposition and no proof."

"Kee-recto," Spivey affirmed. "But I called on her husband day before yesterday, and used her death to salestalk him about insurance on himself. Guy was nervous as a whore in church."

"Guilty nerves, or just upset about losing his wife?"

"I'd say it was guilt. Couldn't even look me in the eye when I mentioned her name."

"So you have a candidate," Gordon said. "What are the chances of developing a case?"

"I'll keep poking around. Who knows, maybe he was dumb enough to buy poison locally. Somebody might remember him."

Arsenic and strychnine were routinely sold at feed stores. Farmers and ranchers used the deadly poisons to protect their livestock from coyotes and wolves. But the chances of anyone remembering the husband, or implicating him, were marginal at best. Or he might have used common rat poison, stocked on the shelves of hardware and grocery stores. The variables in making a case were too many to calculate.

To maintain his cover, Spivey was pitching insurance to Osages, the husbands of dead women, and the town's merchants. He alternated his calls among the various groups, to defuse any thought that he was something other than an insurance agent. But any inquiry about arsenic and strychnine would have to be done with subtlety and great cleverness. Otherwise, suspicions would be aroused.

"Heard about the killing," Spivey said. "Word on it spread real fast."

"No question this one's murder," Gordon said deliberately. "Two men walked her into a ravine and shot her in the head. Just as cold as it gets."

"Any leads?"

"Proctor and I talked to her mother tonight. According to the mother, she didn't have an enemy in the world."

Gordon related details from the day's investigation. As an aside, he covered all he'd learned about the Osages' unusual form of religion. His thought was that the younger agent might be able to somehow use the information in questioning the relatives of the dead women. He finished by wagging his head.

"So far, we haven't got a clue."

"Peyote and Christ," Spivey said with an amused laugh. "That's some combination."

"Don't knock it. Works for the Osages and that's all that counts. Hope it worked for Anna Brown."

"Are you sure it's a headright murder?"

"She has two sisters I plan to question tomorrow. We'll see where it goes from there. Why do you ask?"

"Maybe she was killed by a jealous boyfriend. I hear she played around."

"Yeah, everyone says she was a loose woman. But from the sound of it, she didn't have a regular boyfriend. Where do you hear this talk?"

"Osages, mainly," Spivey said. "The one I called on today brought her up when I mentioned his daughter. Practically everybody knew about it."

"Murder gets people's attention," Gordon said stolidly. "Do you hear anything else?"

"Well, there's lots of talk about your investigation. To hear the Osages tell it, there are people who have knowledge about these murders. But they're afraid to come forward until you make an arrest."

"I'd say that's a good angle to follow. Get people to gossip and they could spill something to you that they wouldn't say to me. You might just turn up the break we need."

"I'll do my best," Spivey said. "Thought I'd be reporting to you and your chief scout. Where's Proctor?"

"Gone home," Gordon replied. "Someone in our little gang deserves a good night's sleep."

"Old as he is, I wouldn't doubt it. Bet he was a rough customer in his day."

"Don't let his age fool you. I wouldn't want to get crosswise of Will."

"You think he's still got it?"

"Three years ago, he killed a bank robber in a pretty hairy shootout. You judge for yourself."

Spivey was young and single, and sometimes overly confident of his skills. But he, like a whole generation of new agents, looked upon Gordon as an icon. Though only a few years older, Gordon was something of a legend in the Bureau, particularly for his exploits in the field. His reputation got its start on the Rio Grande.

Eight years ago, in 1915, Gordon had been assigned a case in southern Texas. War was raging in Europe, and Germany was desperate to prevent America from joining the Allied Forces. German provocateurs organized and funded a band of Mexican insurgents who raided across the river and killed hundreds of Texans. The Germans' goal was to incite a border war with Mexico, and keep America out of Europe. They almost succeeded.

Gordon, working with the Texas Rangers and the U.S. Army, organized an undercover operation in Mexico. The intelligence gathered by his operatives enabled Gordon to kill the Mexican rebel leaders and capture the German military officers behind the revolt. Within the Bureau, he was known as the man who had brought peace to the Rio Grande. He was also known to have killed five men in quelling the rebellion.

Jack Spivey was sometimes overconfident, but he respected the man seated across from him. If Gordon thought Proctor could still cut the mustard, he wasn't about to argue the point. He spread his hands in a bland gesture.

"I could use some sleep myself," he said, rising from his chair. "Like the old philosophers say, tomorrow's another day."

"Keep digging, Jack. I've got a feeling you'll turn over the right rock."

"Just call me the badger. I'm on it, boss."

Spivey unlocked the door and peeked into the hallway. He slipped out, closing the door behind him with a gentle click. A stillness again settled over the room.

Gordon went back to thinking about Anna Brown.

Chapter Six

Early the next morning Proctor met Gordon at the hotel. They took Gordon's car and Proctor directed him up the hill north of the business district. The day was bright and clear, a wad of puffy clouds drifting westward on a light breeze.

Their immediate task was to interview Mollie Burkhart, one of the older sisters of Anna Brown. Mollie was married to Ernest Burkhart, a white man, and last night they'd discovered that Lizzie Kile lived with her daughter and son-in-law. That afternoon they planned to interview the other sister, Rita Smith.

On the way up the hill, Proctor pointed out the Immaculate Conception Catholic Church. A showplace of Pawhuska, the stone church was two stories with an arched façade and a tall bell tower. One of the stained-glass windows, depicting a Jesuit priest baptizing Osages, had been crafted by artisans in Bavaria, Germany. The window was a gift from a wealthy Osage benefactor.

"Funny thing about religion," Proctor noted dryly. "Some folks figure if a little's good, then more's better. Lots of Osages belong to the Catholic church."

Gordon looked at him. "Are you saying they practice the peyote ceremony we saw last night and also belong to a regular church? Both at the same time?"

"You stop and think about it, there's not a whole lot of difference between what we saw last night and a Catholic mass. There's folks that are great believers in hedgin' their bet."

"The happy hunting ground or heaven, whichever comes first. That the idea?"

"I'd tend to say they're one and the same. Gettin' there's the problem for most folks—white or red."

The Burkharts lived on East Twelfth Street. The house was a modern stucco structure, two stories under a peaked roof, with a covered porch and broad columns. A shiny Pierce-Arrow was parked in the driveway; the neighborhood was an enclave for those grown wealthy from the oil boom. Most of the homes in the area were owned by Osages.

Gordon had called ahead to arrange the appointment. A black maid met them at the door and ushered them into a lavishly furnished living room. Ernest Burkhart walked forward to greet them with a cordial handshake and an expression of restrained sorrow. He was a man of medium height, with dark hair, lively green eyes, and ruddy features. He was dressed like a banker.

Mollie Burkhart was a surprise. She wore a short skirt, her stockings rolled below the knee, and her ebony hair was bobbed in a shingle cut. As was the fashion with thoroughly modern girls, she wore a bandeau to flatten her breasts, affecting a boyishly slender figure, and painted her face with a rosy blend of cosmetics. She looked like a sultry Osage flapper.

"Mrs. Burkhart," Gordon said with somber respect. "Please accept our condolences for your loss. We're very sorry."

"Thank you." Her eyes brimmed with tears. "I just can't imagine anyone would do that to Anna. She was such a sweet girl . . . a good sister."

"I apologize for coming at such a bad time. But we need to ask you a few questions."

"Oh, of course, I understand. We're burying Anna tomorrow . . . so today's really better."

Through the front windows, they saw a tan and burgundy Pierce-Arrow pull into the driveway. A black chauffeur in a beige uniform and a leather-billed cap jumped out and rushed to open the rear door. Lizzie Kile, still dressed in her doeskin shroud from the all-night church service, stepped from the car. Her balance was off and she seemed to list as her feet touched the ground. The chauffeur took her arm and walked her to the house.

A moment later she wobbled into the living room. Gordon caught the smell of liquor, and he wondered that she could navigate on a combination of peyote and whiskey. She lurched to a halt, ignoring her daughter and son-in-law, her red-rimmed eyes fixed on Gordon and Proctor. Her gaze was thick with malice.

"Well, well," she said, slurring the words. "You two get around some whichaway, don't you? Have you killed the bastard yet?"

"Not yet, Miz Kile," Proctor said in a conciliatory tone. "We're still tryin' to track him down."

Lizzie Kile smirked at her daughter. "I told 'em not to bother arrestin' the sonofabitch. Just kill him like he killed my baby." She burped, then glowered at Proctor. "Get off your ass, old man, and get it done."

"Mama!" Mollie protested. "You're being rude."

"Who the hell cares! Somebody hurt my baby and I want an eye for an eye. Just like it says in the Good Book."

"Dorothy," Mollie called out, and the maid appeared as if expecting the summons. "Help Mama to her bedroom, will you, please? She needs to rest."

Lizzie Kile allowed herself to be led off. She looked back over her shoulder with a malevolent, ugly grin. "You just remember what I told you. Kill the rotten sonofabitch!

"I apologize," Mollie said, glancing shyly at Gordon. "Anna really was her baby, and she's not herself. She's just upset."

"Understandable," Gordon said, waving it aside. "Was Anna the youngest?"

"Yes, she was twenty-five last October. I'm two years older, and Rita—my other sister—she's thirty."

"I take it everyone in your family is very close."

"Oh, my goodness, yes! There's nothing more important than family."

Gordon was a master of understated interrogation. His years in the Bureau had taught him that leading questions, mixed with a friendly manner, put people off guard and relaxed their inhibitions. He easily got Mollie and Ernest Burkhart to talk about themselves.

Burkhart was a local boy who had enlisted when America joined the war in Europe. He'd fought at Chateau-Thierry and the Argonne Forest, and been awarded the Distinguished Service Cross and the French *Croix de Guerre.* Upon returning home in 1919, he felt the War to End All Wars had been a sham and a delusion. Like many dough-boys, the naïve patriotism was gone, replaced by massive cynicism and a retreat into apathy. The postwar millennium failed to deliver a brave, new world.

Mollie, meanwhile, had attended the Chevy Chase School for girls in Maryland. Wealthy Osages sent their children East for an education, and unlike her sisters, she'd taken advantage of the opportunity. But like her husband, and an entire younger generation, she found the war had destroyed her belief in a Pollyanna world of rosy ideals. At the Chevy Chase School, she joined white girls and Osages in rejecting the starchy, outdated customs of an older generation. She retuned home a flapper.

"Nothing's the way it should be," Mollie said in a soft voice. "We live in this grand house with more money than we can spend, and what does it mean? What does anything mean when someone murders your sister?"

Gordon nodded sympathetically. "On the phone, I mentioned we spoke with your mother last night. She told us Anna had no enemies, no one with reason to hurt her." He paused, held her gaze a long moment. "Do you think that's true?"

"Why, yes, of course I do. Anna was a fun-loving girl, the life of the party. Everybody loved her."

"Apparently someone didn't. I know it's painful for you, but we need you to be open and frank about your sister. Who might have wanted to harm her?"

"No one," Mollie insisted. "Nothing about it makes any sense. I talked to her the day she was killed and she was happy as a lark. She was going partying that night."

Gordon was suddenly alert. "Who was she going partying with? Did she mention any names?"

"Anna was very private. Mama never approved of her . . . well . . . her ways with men. She became very secretive."

"Even with you? I always thought sisters told their sisters everything."

"We did, when we were younger. But after she was divorced, she changed somehow. She started partying every night, and drinking too much, and Mama wouldn't stand for it. So she kept everything to herself."

"Think hard now," Gordon said intently. "She must have told you something. A special boyfriend. A name."

"No." Mollie swiped at a tear rolling down her check. "Not for a long time."

Gordon ended the interview. He thanked her for her time, asking her to call him if she thought of anything more. She nodded, her eyes wet with tears, and he motioned to Proctor. Burkhart walked them to the door.

"She's really broken up," he said, almost apologetic.

"Anna and Mollie were awful close, more so than Rita. She's taken it real hard."

"I can see that." Gordon hesitated at the door. "By the way, I forgot to ask. What business are you in, Mr. Burkhart?"

"Finances," Burkhart said with an easy smile. "I manage all of Mollie's oil properties. It's a full-time job."

"Yes, I imagine it would be. Thanks again for your time."

"Like Lizzie said, just catch the bastard. Least he deserves is the electric chair."

"We'll do our best to put him there."

Proctor was silent as they drove back down the hill. Gordon finally looked across at him. "Why so quiet?"

"Just thinkin' we're getting nowhere fast. Nobody wants to admit the truth."

"About what?"

"Anna Brown," Proctor said. "A woman don't get killed for no reason."

"Well, the day's still young. Maybe we'll get lucky."

"Pardner, I think we're gonna need it. I surely do."

Gray Horse was some five miles southeast of Fairfax. The village was little more than a crossroads, with one general store and a scattering of houses. The homes were occupied mainly by Osage elders.

On the drive to Gray Horse, Gordon and Proctor passed Boar Creek, where Anna Brown had been killed. The stream was lined with sycamores and walnuts, and then the land gave way to rolling prairie broken by stunted hills. The clear call of a meadowlark rose on a vagrant breeze from the roadside.

"Too bad it's not sunrise," Proctor said as they drove through Gray Horse. "You'd see something not many white men ever laid eyes on."

Gordon glanced at the store and houses. "What happens at sunrise?"

"The elders turn out to greet *Tzi-Sho*—Grandfather Sun."

Proctor recounted how the Osage men went to the hillsides when the morning star appeared in the sky. There, they chanted their prayers, while the women stood facing east to welcome Grandfather Sun to another day. They believed that *Wah' Kon-Tah*, the Great Spirit, spoke to them through the wind on the prairie and the formations of clouds. Sunrise was a special time.

"Times change," Gordon said. "I got the feeling Mollie Burkhart doesn't share her mother's religious convictions. Probably thinks it's all superstition."

"Lots of young Osages do," Proctor observed. "They worship oil and see sunrise through the end of a whiskey bottle. Likely part of what got Anna Brown killed."

Outside Gray Horse, the countryside was dotted with small herds of grazing cattle. Proctor noted that the Osages had originally chosen the hilly landscape for their reservation because they thought it was land no white man would ever want. The fullbloods tended to live in the southern part of the county, and over time, many Osages had sold off their surplus lands in the northern district. There, where the terrain was mostly tallgrass prairie, white ranchers who'd bought the land ran thousands of head of cattle. Ultimately, in a perverse twist, the oil boom brought the Osages wealth at the loss of isolation. White men, in the end, coveted all they had.

The Smith ranch was a few miles east of Gray Horse. The land was owned by Rita, a fullblood Osage, and her white husband, Ray Smith. The house, unlike the home of Mollie Burkhart, was plain and utilitarian, a sprawling one-story structure badly in need of a paint job. The barn and equipment shed were constructed of ripsawed lumber that looked weathered with age. A Ford flatbed truck and a Reo sedan were parked in the front yard.

Proctor grunted. "Rita don't live as good as her sister. Bet she don't wear short skirts, neither."

"From the look of it," Gordon said, "they travel in different circles. No high society here."

A white servant girl met them at the door. Rita Smith came through the hallway and the contrast with her sister was immediately apparent. She was short and plump, with broad features and no makeup, her dark hair pulled back in a long braid. Ray Smith, following behind her, was thin as a rail, with close-set eyes and a lantern jaw. He looked to be in his early thirties.

After a round of introductions, the servant girl disappeared into the kitchen and Rita led them into the living room. There were overstuffed chairs and a worn sofa before a stone fireplace, and she took a moment to get everyone seated. Gordon expressed sympathy on behalf of himself and Proctor for her loss, and she merely nodded, her features stoic. He quickly briefed her on the conversations he'd had with her mother, Lizzie Kile, and her sister, Mollie Burkhart. He noticed that Ray Smith was watching him with an enigmatic, guarded expression.

"Frankly, we're at a loss," he said. "According to your mother and your sister, no one had any reason to harm Anna. We're hoping you'll be able to shed some light on the situation."

Rita stared back at him with round, guileless eyes. "Anna and I didn't see much of each other. She lived her own life her own way. She knew I thought it was pretty trashy."

"You're talking about the men?"

"The men and the drinking, and out partying every night. Anna was my sister and I loved her, everybody did. But she had no sense of shame."

"These men?" Gordon asked. "Does a name stand out? Anyone in particular?"

"No," Rita said woodenly. "Any man would do, and there were too many of them. Who could keep track?"

Ray Smith cleared his throat. Until now he'd said hardly a word, but he shifted forward in his chair. "Lemme ask you," he muttered. "You fellas working with the sheriff?"

"Yes, we are," Gordon said. "We're trying to determine if Anna's death has anything to do with these so-called headright murders. Why do you ask?"

"Nothin' special," Smith said with a veiled look. "Heard you was a federal agent of some sort. Just curious."

Gordon sensed the interview was going nowhere. He tried another tack. "Mrs. Smith," he said, turning back to Rita. "Anna didn't have any children, and Mollie doesn't either. How about you and Mr. Smith?"

"No," Rita said quietly. "Not yet."

"Any other relatives?"

"Well, I had another sister, Minnie. But she died."

"Oh?" Gordon tried to hide his surprise. "How did she die?"

"Tuberculosis."

"Was she married?"

"Yes." Rita darted a glance at her husband. "She was married to Ray. We got married afterward."

"I see." Gordon kept a poker face. "If you don't mind my asking, how did that come about?"

"Mama wouldn't have it any other way . . . the Osage way."

"I don't understand."

Rita went into a rambling explanation. Ancient Osage tribal custom held that if an older sister died, the next youngest sister would marry the widowed husband. Upon Minnie Smith's death in 1919, Lizzie Kile insisted that Rita uphold the Osage tradition. She and Ray were married three months after Minnie died.

"Four years ago," Gordon said in a speculative tone. "How was your sister's headright divided?"

"The way Minnie had it in her will. Mama got half and Ray got half."

There was a moment of uncomfortable silence. The situation Rita had just described bore a remarkable similarity to the deaths of twenty-three Osage women over the past three years. On the surface, the single difference was that Minnie Smith had died a year before the multiple murders began. None of which obviated the fact that Ray Smith had inherited a half-headright worth tens of thousands in his lifetime.

"Leave well enough alone," Smith bridled, his fists clenched. "And don't go playin' hotshot detective, neither. I didn't kill Minnie."

"No one said you did," Gordon told him. "Why would you jump to that conclusion?"

"'Cause it's written all over your face. I know what you're thinkin'."

"Then you're way ahead of me, Mr. Smith. I'm after the man who killed Anna."

Gordon saw nothing to be gained with the situation suddenly turned adversarial. He decided to let it drop and perhaps catch Rita another day, when she was by herself. Smith remained seated, refusing to meet his or Proctor's gaze, as Rita walked them to the door. She looked embarrassed, and nervous.

When they were back on the road, Proctor let out a gruff laugh. "Never know what you're gonna stumble across. Think he killed her?"

"Water under the bridge," Gordon said. "The question is, did he kill Anna Brown?"

"Well, if he did, he's a cool customer. Kill two sisters and marry another one? That'd take real balls."

"Even so, how does it tie together? He didn't get any part of Anna's headright."

"Maybe not," Proctor allowed. "But that creek where Anna was shot deader'n hell? It's not five miles from Ray Smith's place. Think on that a minute."

"Something else," Gordon said, his eyes narrowed. "You probably noticed it back there. Smith wears cowboy boots."

"Sonovabitch, you're right! Just like the tracks we found by the creek."

"I think Mr. Ray Smith bears watching."

They drove off through the stunted hills and bluestem prairies. Neither of them said anything more, but their thoughts were along the same lines. Something more than a hunch, if not yet a hard fact.

Ray Smith was a prime candidate for murder.

Chapter Seven

The Proctor home was on a hill overlooking the town of Hominy. The house was a two-story frame structure with lots of windows, brick columns, and a shady veranda. A low stone wall fronted the road.

Gordon drove over from Pawhuska late the next morning. Yesterday, after leaving the Smith ranch, Proctor had invited him to dinner, which was the term country folk used for the noon meal. Sunday dinner was considered a special occasion.

Proctor was waiting for him on the veranda. "See you found your way all right."

"Straight as an arrow," Gordon said. "You give good directions."

"Come on inside and meet the family."

The interior of the house was sparkling clean and appointed with comfortable, lived-in furniture. Gordon knew it was more than a regular Sunday dinner when he saw the people gathered in the parlor. Martha Proctor, the old lawman's wife, was a dumpling of a woman with a sunny smile and a warm disposition. Proctor's son, Bob, was there with his wife and their two children, a boy and a girl. The presence of the whole family indicated that Gordon was more than a casual guest.

After a round of introductions, Proctor shooed everyone into the dining room. The table was laden with dishes customary to a traditional Sunday dinner. Martha served fried chicken, mashed potatoes and cream gravy, green beans cooked with sow belly, and buttermilk biscuits. The dishes were passed around family-style, and Martha insisted that Gordon load his plate. He noticed she'd used her best china and silverware, and suspected it was for his benefit. Crystal glasses were filled with sweetened iced tea from a large amber pitcher.

Proctor clearly doted on his grandchildren. The boy was fourteen and the girl twelve, and he bragged with open pride on their grades in school. In between Proctor's bragging, Martha peppered Gordon with questions about his life in the Bureau. She knew something of federal agencies, as her husband had been a Deputy U.S. Marshal for thirty years. But the Bureau was new to her experience, and her inquisitive nature kept him talking throughout dinner. In the course of the conversation, he mentioned that his last assignment had been an investigation of the Ku Klux Klan. Her eyes crackled with fire.

"Those terrible people," she said, pursing her lips. "Riding around in white sheets and spouting their bigotry in the name of God. It's a blasphemy!"

"Yes, ma'am, they're mostly a bunch of thugs."

Bob Proctor looked interested. "Couple weeks ago, I read about a fracas down in Okmulgee. The paper said some Klan grand wizard was taken into custody. Was that you?"

"One of my better days," Gordon admitted. "His name's Cullen Horner and he's in the federal lockup in Oklahoma City. I think we'll send him away for a long time."

"How did you take him in that crowd? I read there was three or four hundred Klansmen there."

"Well, I'd have to say we got lucky. Grabbed him while the others weren't looking."

Bob Proctor nodded as though he'd heard only half the story. He was about Gordon's age, a history teacher and basketball coach at the high school in Hominy. All his life, from a toddler to a man, he'd watched his father hunt down, and sometimes kill, the most dangerous outlaws in Oklahoma. He secretly longed to be a lawman.

"You talk about luck," he said with a slow smile. "I remember reading what Abraham Lincoln had to say about luck."

"Oh?" Gordon paused, his fork loaded with mashed potatoes. "What was that?"

"Honest Abe said 'I'm a great believer in luck, and the harder I work, the more luck I seem to have.'"

"Frank, he got you there!" Proctor cackled gleefully. "You took that Klan fella because you set it up with hard work and a good plan. Luck was just an itty-bitty part of it."

"Maybe so," Gordon said with a straight face. "But I wouldn't write off luck altogether. That's why I carry a rabbit's foot."

"You're joshin' me," Proctor said with an incredulous look. "You carry a rabbit's foot?"

Gordon grinned. "Only when I work with U.S. Marshals."

Everyone broke out laughing. Proctor wagged his head with a sly smile. "Gonna have to keep my eye on you. You're quicker'n you look."

Martha served blackberry cobbler for dessert. She insisted Gordon take a second helping, and fussed over the children when they got the juice smeared on their faces. After dinner, the women shanghaied the children into helping clear the table and wash the dishes. The men retired to the shade of the veranda.

Proctor pulled out his tobacco and papers and began fashioning a roll-your-own. Bob smoked tailor-made cigarettes and lit up with a pack of the new book matches. There were cane-bottomed rockers on the veranda, and the men got themselves seated as the noonday sun tilted a degree westward. Gordon loosened his belt a notch.

"I'm plumb stuffed," he said, patting his stomach. "Haven't had a meal like that since I don't know when."

Proctor popped a kitchen match on his thumbnail. "Martha's always been a mighty fine cook. Wonder I'm not fat as a hog."

"Dad, you're too onery," Bob said, exhaling a thin streamer of smoke. "Mom says you could start a fight in an empty room."

"Your mother's a wise woman." Proctor set his rocker in motion, glanced over at Gordon. "Never asked before, but I see you wear a weddin' ring. Got family down in Dallas?"

"Wife and four kids," Gordon said. "Three girls and a boy."

"I reckon you do have family! Your wife a Texan?"

"Texan by way of being Mexican. Her name's Guadalupe."

"Fine name." Proctor hesitated, somewhat taken aback and wary of offending. "How'd you meet her?"

"On the Rio Grande."

Gordon was proud of his wife. In 1915, when he'd exposed the German conspiracy on the border, Guadalupe had been one of his most valued undercover operatives. Her Mexican heritage, along with that of the other operatives, produced intelligence that would have been unattainable with Anglo agents. Through their efforts, he'd broken the conspiracy and destroyed the rebellion by Mexican insurgents. He told the story with a certain gusto, pride in his voice.

"So I married her," he said. "Figured I'd never find another one like her."

"Smart move," Proctor observed, exhaling a wad of smoke. "Sounds like a mighty brave woman."

"Will, she makes most men look like wallflowers."

Proctor was silent for a time. He finally brought his rocker to a halt, knuckled his mustache. "Sometimes a man's mouth gets ahead of his brain. I expect I owe you an apology."

"You lost me," Gordon said, clearly baffled. "Apology for what?"

"Last week or so I've been lecturin' you on how white people look down on the Osages. And all the time you knew more about prejudice than I'll ever learn. You're quite a feller, Mr. Frank Gordon."

"I'll tell Guadalupe you said so. She needs reminding now and then that I'm such a sterling character."

Bob laughed. "Know what this reminds me of?"

"I'm afraid to ask," Proctor said. "But I reckon you're gonna tell us anyway. Go ahead."

"Back in the days of ancient Rome, some Roman senator dropped a pearl of wisdom I've never forgot. He said, 'I have often regretted my speech but never my silence.' Tell you, Dad, you ought to take that as your new motto."

"Helluva note," Proctor grumped. "Frank, don't ever treat your children to a good education. Always comes back to haunt you."

"I'll keep it in mind," Gordon said with a humorous grin. "Must hurt to have a son smarter than you."

"Damned if it don't!"

"Well, forget that," Bob said, scooting forward in his rocker. "I came over here to hear about the Osage murders. What's the latest dope?"

"Have to keep it quiet," Proctor said in a mysterious voice. "We think we've got ourselves a suspect."

"No kiddin'!" Bob said, suddenly all ears. "What's his name?"

"Can't tell you."

"What do you mean, you can't tell me?"

"You're a scholar and we're lawmen. You can read about it in those history books of yours."

"For cryin' out loud! It'll be in the papers before it's in books."

Proctor smiled. "Son, you're getting smarter all the time."

Barsdall was some twenty miles east of Pawhuska. Despite oil rigs scattered about the countryside, the small community remained much as it had since the reservation days. The main street ran straight as a carpenter's plumb through the center of town.

On Monday morning Jack Spivey stopped at a gas station. He bought an orange soda pop and told the attendant to fill the tank of his Ford Roadster. He asked directions to the home of Thomas Standeven, and the attendant drew a map in the thick coat of dust on the trunk of the car. The general route, with a turn here and there, was south of town.

Thomas Standeven was a fullblood Osage. His daughter, a month shy of her twenty-second birthday, had died not quite a year ago. At the time, she was married to a white man, and her death had occurred four days after their first wedding anniversary. The husband had produced a will, drafted by a lawyer and properly witnessed, which made him the sole heir to her headright. The death certificate, signed by a local doctor, attributed the girl's death to contaminated moonshine whiskey.

Around ten o'clock Spivey pulled into the yard of a modest home on a backcountry dirt road. A man who looked to be in his early forties was splitting chunks of fire wood with a double-bladed axe. Off to the side of the house, a woman was tending steamy pots over the embers of an open fire. Spivey was struck again by the fact that Osages with a fortune in oil money rarely used the stoves in their modern kitchens. A Model T Ford and a shiny Maxwell Roadster were parked in the yard.

"Mornin'," Spivey called out as he crossed the yard.

"I'm Jack Spivey with the Centennial Life Insurance Company. Would you be Mr. Standeven?"

"Yep, that's me." The man deftly stuck his axe in a knotty chunk of wood. "What you want?"

"Well, sir, we're offerin' a special annuity plan available only to those of the Osage tribe. Safer than a bank and earns interest till you're ready to retire."

"Nothin' safer'n a bank. What's this annuity?"

"The latest thing," Spivey said with cheery vigor. "You put some money in for ten or twenty years on a monthly installment. God forbid you die, but if you do, your wife gets a bundle of cash. Or if you live, you earn back half again what you put in." He paused, gestured extravagantly. "Nothing like it since sliced bread!"

"Huh." Standeven looked at him like a stuffed owl. "Sound like 'nother white man's get-rich game."

"Well, sir, there's no doubt life's a roll of the dice. But what I'm talkin' about—you can't lose!"

A young man in his early twenties came out of the house. He was dressed in a sky blue silk shirt, creamy linen pants, and cordovan oxfords polished to a luster. His black hair was slicked back with pomade and he reeked of cologne. He looked like an Osage in the guise of a white playboy.

"I'm off, Pop," he said, waving jauntily to Standeven. "See you when I see you."

"You all time gone," Standeven grouched sternly. "Don't never stay home no more."

"Gotta see a girl about you know what, Pop. I was born to party."

The youngster climbed into the Maxwell Roadster and fired the engine. He backed into the road, smoothly shifting gears, and sped off in a whirlwind of dust. Standeven stared after him with a glum expression.

"Don't even say g'bye," he mumbled, as if thinking out loud. "You got children, insurance man?"

"No, sir, I don't," Spivey said. "I'm single and plan to stay that way."

"You got good horse sense. Young people don't hold to old ways no more. All time runnin' off."

Spivey casually asked if Standeven had other children. An even sadder look came over the Osage's face, and he launched into a tirade about his daughter's murder and the sheriff's refusal to investigate her death. Occasionally, Spivey would nod sympathetically and ask a question, but Standeven needed little prompting. He told a tale of a young girl beguiled by a fast-talking white man, and killed for her headright. His sadness deepened all the more when he admitted there was no proof.

Some while later, Spivey drove away with a beep of his horn. He'd managed to sell Thomas Standeven a twenty-year annuity, but he thought it more a matter of a sympathetic ear than salesmanship. The thing that bothered him most was that it was again a case of conjecture mixed with grief, and no hard evidence. Over the past week he'd talked with the parents of four murdered girls, and it was always a story long on allegations and short on facts. He felt like he was spinning his wheels.

Early that afternoon Spivey drove into Wynona. The town was eight miles south of Pawhuska, with a skyline spiked here and there by oil derricks. His target was Paul Russell, a white man whose Osage bride had died scarcely seven months after the honeymoon. Although the girl's family was from Fairfax, the couple had built a modern stucco home on the outskirts of Wynona. The Bureau case file indicated that Russell was originally from Tulsa, a small-time grifter with champagne tastes. He'd come to Osage County to make his fortune.

Spivey found the house on a hill overlooking Wynona. Trees had been cut back from the road, and the property offered a sweeping view of the town. A large four-door Buick was parked in the driveway, and a hedgerow of neatly trimmed shrubs fronted the house. Briefcase in hand, Spivey went up the stone walkway and rang the doorbell. The man who opened the door was hardly taller than a midget, dressed in expensive slacks and shirt, with a diamond pinky ring. His eyes flicked from the briefcase to Spivey.

"Whatever you're selling, I don't want any."

Spivey gave him a waggish grin. "How do you know till you've heard my pitch? I'll even throw in a joke or two."

Russell hesitated, then shrugged. "What the hell, I could use some entertainment. But I'm warning you, it better be good. I used to be in the sales game myself."

The living room was a monument to bad taste. The furniture was overstuffed, done in garish colors, and the walls were painted a dizzying shade of mauve. Russell got him seated on the couch and sank down to his armpits in one of the chairs. A bottle-blonde walked in from the kitchen wearing a flimsy housecoat that did little to hide her curves. She carried a coffee cup, daintily crossing the room on high-heeled slippers, her mouth a bee-stung artwork in red. She batted her eyes at Russell.

"Paulie, you didn't tell me we were having company."

"Get lost, Vera," Russell said in a weary voice. "Go paint your toenails."

"Well, I never!"

Vera indignantly wig-wagged her hips as she disappeared down a hallway. Russell shook his head. "Never yet saw a woman that knew when to butt out."

"Yessireebob." Spivey slapped his knee and laughed. "Can't live with 'em and can't live without 'em."

"You can say that again." Russell dismissed it with a flashy wave of his pinky ring. "So what are you selling?"

"Latest thing in life insurance. I'm with Centennial, and we've come up with an annuity plan that'll knock your socks off. Almost like printing money."

"Sport, you're talking to the wrong man. I've got more money than God."

"I know."

"What do you mean, you know?"

"Somebody in town told me your wife died and left you a bundle. Figured you'd know the value of life insurance."

Russell regarded him with an odd, steadfast look "You've got a funny way of coming at it, friend. I'm not impressed."

"Hold on." Spivey raised a floppy hand. "You told me you were in sales once, so bear with me. I'm just trying to make a point."

"What's your point?"

"Well, for starters, how'd your wife die?"

"The hard way," Russell said truculently. "She got hold of some bad moonshine."

"I'll be switched!" Spivey feigned amazement. "Heard it'd turn you blind. Didn't know it'd kill you."

"Took her before the doctor got to the house. One minute she was there, next minute she was gone."

"How much did she drink?"

"What's that got to do with anything?"

"Well, I've got a taste for 'shine myself, so it'd pay to be careful. Where'd you buy it?"

"I didn't," Russell said too quickly. "She brought it home herself. Osage women like their liquor."

"Godalmightybingo!" Spivey made a face. "Lucky you didn't drink any yourself. Did you sic the sheriff on the moonshiner?"

Russell squinted querulously. "Told you, I don't know where she bought it. What's this got to do with insurance?"

"Life's a flighty thing. Like you said, here one minute and next minute you meet your Maker. Little insurance makes it easier on your loved ones."

"Tell you, sport, you ought to work on your sales pitch. Besides, I already told you, I'm not in the market."

Spivey quickly found himself ushered out the door. As he drove down the hill, his gut told him everything he'd heard was lies. Paul Russell was trying to whitewash his future by fabricating the past. Treachery and death wore a thousand guises.

The man with the pinky ring rode a pale horse.

Chapter Eight

Mollie Burkhart sat before the mirror of her dressing table. She artfully applied rouge to her cheeks and kohl to her eyelids, and touched up her mascara. Her lips were a crimsoned bee-stung pucker.

One of the new table radios played on a stand near the bed. Of all the modern conveniences, the radio was Mollie's favorite. In a way, it was as if she was eavesdropping on the sometimes bizarre secrets of faraway neighbors. Better, in fact, for the news was pithy and fresh, and generally phrased in such a way as to make it highly repeatable. There was an immediacy to the broadcasts that gave them a certain verve and excitement.

Saturday night was the night for Al Jolson's weekly radio show. Jolson, once the preeminent star of the vaudeville stage, had catapulted to fame at the fabled Winter Garden Theater in New York. He was acknowledged as the musical comedy star of the century and billed as "The World's Greatest Entertainer." Millions listened to his radio show every week, and as Mollie finished her makeup, he began singing "April Showers." Her toes tapped the floor in tune to the music.

The isolation of rural America had been shattered forever by the magic of radio. A flick of the switch brought instant access to the outside world, but it hadn't yet expanded to the local scene. Word of mouth was still the quickest, if not the most accurate, source of information in a small town. Although Pawhuska had mushroomed in growth, it remained, at heart, a small town, and hadn't lost its obsession with the affairs of others. The telephone had replaced back-fence gossip but little else had changed.

Tonight, Ernest was taking Mollie to the country club. Located on the western edge of town, the club was the playground of affluent whites and rich, young Osages. Mollie hadn't been anywhere socially since the burial of her sister two weeks ago, and she was excited by the prospects for the evening. She knew the usual busybodies would be whispering about Anna's murder, and someone would inevitably question her about the whole sordid affair, but she didn't care. She just wanted to dance and have fun.

Mollie seldom thought of herself as an Osage. Perhaps because of her eastern education, she felt a greater kinship with the sophisticated people pictured in slick magazines at play in New York and on the beaches of the Riviera. She realized her oil money placed her in the category of nouveau riche, but she had nonetheless adopted the manners and look of fashionable, liberated women. Her hair was freshly bobbed from a trip to the beauty shop, and her outfit tonight was a creamy crepe de chine dress with pleated flounces, her silk stockings rolled below her knees. She thought she would look smashing on the dance floor.

Ernest came in from the bathroom. He wore a tux shirt with onyx studs and his bow tie was squared neatly on his collar. Mollie glanced at him in the mirror, and as so often happened, she felt a little flutter that she'd captured such a handsome husband. They had met shortly after his return from the war, and the attraction was both mutual and instant. Their honeymoon six months later had taken them to San Francisco, and after nearly four years of marriage, she still got goose bumps when he touched her. He was gentle and considerate, and something of a tender stallion in bed. She considered herself the luckiest girl in Pawhuska.

"Too bad about dinner," he said, removing his tux jacket from the closet. "Everybody will wonder why we got there so late."

"I'm sorry, sweetheart." She gave her hair a last little fluff. "You know I would have preferred to have dinner at the club. I'm just thinking of Mama."

"Honey, she was out at the Stomp Dance all last night. What's the difference?"

"She thinks of that as religious, not social. She probably spent the night praying for Anna."

"Yeah, I suppose you're right. She's still pretty broken up."

"She loves Rita and me—and she always will . . . but Anna was her baby."

Ernest understood perhaps better than his wife. Lizzie Kile was already widowed when they'd been married, and shortly afterward, he had agreed to let her move in with them. His brother-in-law, Ray Smith, didn't want the old woman in his house, and there was never any question of her living with Anna. She was openly critical of Anna's life, but the county tramp was nonetheless her last born, her baby. She'd never lost hope of redeeming her daughter's lost and wayward soul.

More so than most, Ernest could relate to lost souls. Like many American boys, he had marched off to war in 1918 in the belief that he was off to fight the war to end all wars. Yet he quickly discovered that there was nothing chivalrous about the mustard gas and machine guns found in the trenches of France. There was instead a war waged by generals pitilessly committed to the tactic of *attaque a outrance*. A brutal pitting of massed strength against massed strength, in which victory fell to those who demonstrated a superior ability to bleed. To the doughboys their crusade became nothing short of an apocalypse.

A war hero, unmarred by visible wounds, Ernest had returned to Pawhuska a confirmed cynic at the age of twenty-six. At times, when his dreams were darkened by the war, it was as if his vision was haunted by the memory. He joined a generation who transformed America into a paradise of hedonists, and adopted materialism as their credo. One writer hit the bestseller list by stating that Jesus was a hardheaded go-getter who had put together the greatest little sales organization on earth. Everyone laughed, while they poured themselves another slug of gin, and Ernest wondered if he'd survived France only to fall in an age that made truth of lies. He often thought marrying Mollie had been his salvation.

After they were finished dressing, they walked through the house to the dining room. Dorothy, their housekeeper and cook, was carrying steaming dishes from the kitchen. Ernest saw that she'd prepared his favorite, an eye-of-the-round roast beef, along with thinly sliced fried potatoes, boiled okra, and a heaping bowl of squash. He took his seat at the head of the table, ready to carve the roast, but Mollie appeared distracted. She looked at Dorothy.

"Where's Mama?"

"I done told her supper's fixed. She be here directly."

"We can't wait," Ernest said. "Come on, honey, let's eat."

Mollie seated herself. "I hate to start without her."

Lizzie came through the door. She was still hungover from the Stomp Dance last night, and she carried a quart bottle of moonshine. She looked drawn and haggard, her eyes bloodshot and her hair tangled in frizzy knots. She flopped down in her chair.

"Mama!" Mollie scolded. "You shouldn't be drinking before dinner. And especially that terrible stuff."

"Don't start on me." Lizzie filled her water glass to the brim and set the bottle on the table. "Hair of the dog that bit me's the only cure for what I got."

Ernest smiled indulgently. "Solid food's what you need." He passed her a plate piled high with roast beef and vegetables. "Have some of that and you'll feel better."

Lizzie drained half her glass. "Little 'shine's what I need."

Older Osages, who were largely a product of the reservation system, favored moonshine over modern bonded whiskey. Moonshine was as clear as water, and supplied in bottles often disguised with bourbon or Scotch labels. The alcohol content was usually one hundred per-cent pure, and for good reason, it was known by the collo-quial term "white lightning." A generation of Osages remembered a time when it was the only form of spirits to be found on the reservation.

"What's this?" Lizzie looked up from her glass. "What're you all dressed up for?"

"We're going to the club," Mollie said, cutting a dainty bite of beef. "There's a dance tonight and everyone will be there. I can't wait."

"And I won't have it! Your sister's not in the ground two weeks and you're gonna go off partyin'? Don't you have any shame?"

"Mama, please don't be like that. I've grieved over Anna till I haven't any tears left. I just want to have a little fun."

Lizzie emptied her glass. She poured it full again and gulped down a long swallow. Her eyes simmered with anger. "You gotta dance, why don't you go dance on your sister's grave? Wouldn't be no worse!"

"Mother Kile," Ernest said in a quiet voice. "Time to put the grieving in the past and get on with living. Mollie deserves a night out."

"You shut your mouth," Lizzie snapped. "This here's between me and—"

"Mama!" Mollie cut in sharply. "Don't you dare talk to Ernie like that!"

"I'll talk to him any damn way—"

Lizzie suddenly stiffened. Her features contorted and she made a gagging sound deep in her throat. She jerked to her feet, knocking her chair to the floor, and clutched desperately at her chest. Her legs collapsed and she keeled over, a strangled sigh escaping her mouth. Her eyes rolled back in her head.

Ernest knelt beside her as Mollie rushed around the table. He'd seen enough dead men on the battlefield to know he was looking at a dead woman. He put a finger to her throat, searching for a pulse, and found none. Mollie dropped to her knees.

"Mama!" she screamed. "Mama!"

"Honey—"

"Mama!"

"Honey, she's gone." He wrapped Mollie in his arms. "God save us all, she's gone."

"Noooo! *Noooo!*"

Dorothy ran in from the kitchen. She stopped, her hand to her mouth and her eyes wide with fright, staring down at the old woman. Ernest glanced up at her.

"Dorothy."

She didn't move.

"Dorothy!"

"Sir!"

"Go call the doctor."

Ernest almost told her to hurry, but he caught himself. He knew it was too late.

"You look a little down in the mouth."

"You're no prize yourself, Will."

"Guess nobody's gonna accuse us of being ace detectives."

"Any day now, I expect to hear something along those lines from the Bureau."

Gordon and Proctor were seated at a table in the Osage Grill. Proctor had stayed for supper and planned to drive on to Hominy afterward. He'd extended another invitation to Sunday dinner, but Gordon had begged off. There was little to celebrate.

The murder of Anna Brown had occurred more than two weeks ago. So far, they had no leads, no viable suspects; as a practical matter, they were at an impasse. Their investigation into guardians suspected of murder had effectively hit a stone wall. No judge would issue an order to exhume the bodies of Osage victims.

Proctor pushed the remains of a T-bone steak aside. He rolled a cigarette and glanced up as he popped a match. "How long since you've been home?"

Gordon grimaced. "Almost two months."

"Must be tough on your wife."

"I call her every couple of nights. Four kids keep her busy, and she has lots of friends in Dallas. But it's not the same."

"No, not by a long shot."

Deputy Sheriff Noah Perkins entered the café. He spotted them and walked to their table. "Gordon. Proctor," he said, hitching at his gun belt. "Desk clerk told me you was over here. The sheriff wants to see you."

Gordon frowned. "Something wrong?"

"Yep, I reckon you could say that. Lizzie Kile's dead."

"How'd she die?"

"Don't rightly know. Sheriff's up at the Burkhart place now. He sent me to find you."

"We're on our way."

Ten minutes later they stepped out of the car on Twelfth Street. Perkins was waiting on the porch and nodded as they entered the house. Ernest and Mollie Burkhart were seated on the couch in the living room, her sobs audible as she kept her face pressed to his shoulder. Sheriff Crowley and Dr. Orville Tuttle were in the dining room.

Crowley turned as Gordon and Proctor came through the door.

"'Evenin',", he said with a closed expression. "Like we agreed, I'm keepin' you advised on things. Figured you'd want to have a look."

Lizzie Kile lay sprawled on the floor. Her eyes were open and dried spittle was gummed around her mouth. Her features were twisted in a mask of pain, and her bladder had voided, soaking her dress. She appeared somehow smaller in death.

"Helluva sight," Proctor said, shaking his head. "Looks like she died hard."

Crowley grunted. "Nobody ever said dyin' was easy."

"You're right," Gordon remarked, studying the body. "What happened here?"

"They were havin' supper. Her and her daughter got in an argument, and all of a sudden she jumps up and keels over. Just dropped dead."

"What were they arguing about?"

"Family squabble," Crowley said. "Ernest and Mollie was gonna attend the dance at the country club. Lizzie'd been drinkin' and she lit into Mollie. Didn't think it was proper."

"Proper?" Gordon repeated quizzically. "Are you talking about attending the dance?"

"Yeah, that's about the size of it. Some of these old Osages think you oughta mourn a loved one forever and a day. She got hot 'cause Mollie aimed to go off partyin'."

"By mourning, I assume you mean Anna Brown. That's what brought it on?"

"For a fact," Crowley replied. "Their darkie maid said Lizzie was screamin' to beat the band. Then she sorta gagged and her lights went out."

Proctor moved around the body. The quart bottle was upended on the edge of the table, the contents having emptied in a dark splatter on the wooden floor. He picked up the bottle and took a sniff. He wrinkled his nose.

"Moonshine," he said, glancing at Gordon. "Wonder how it got spilt on the floor."

"No mystery there," Crowley observed. "She must've knocked it over when she jumped up from the table."

"Maybe so," Proctor said, placing the bottle on the table. "'Course, it might be some of this bad moonshine we've been hearin' about."

"Nonsense," Dr. Tuttle said, as though delighted by the opening. "She died of a massive coronary thrombosis. It's quite obvious."

"A heart attack?" Gordon asked. "How can you be so sure?"

"Nothing could be more apparent, Mr. Gordon. A heated argument and an old woman in a fit of temper. Classic pattern for heart failure."

"Well, I suppose the autopsy will bear you out, Doctor. You can test her for moonshine poisoning at the same time."

"Why waste the county's money?" Tuttle said curtly. "Don't you think I know a heart attack when I see one? I have no intention of performing an autopsy."

Gordon stared at him. "I'm formally requesting an autopsy."

"Request denied," Tuttle retorted. "Do not presume to question my medical judgment. I've made my ruling."

"Doc's right," Crowley broke in quickly. "We're not talkin' murder here, for chrissake. Her heart just gave out."

"Sheriff, I expected more cooperation." Gordon fixed him with a look. "I'll have to inform the Bureau you're interfering with my investigation."

"Inform the Bureau of any damn thing you please. While you're at it, tell 'em I could've left you sittin' down at your hotel. You're here 'cause I asked you here."

"I'll note your courtesy in my report. But I still want an autopsy."

"You've had your answer," Crowley said testily. "Doc's the coroner and he calls the shots on medical matters. We're done talkin' about that."

"Well, like you say, it's your county."

"Bet your boots it is!"

"I'll see you around, Sheriff."

Gordon turned toward the door, followed by Proctor. As they moved through the hallway, Ernest Burkhart came out of the living room. His features were ashen.

"What's happening?" he asked distractedly. "Aren't they through yet?"

"Won't be long," Gordon said. "How's your wife?"

"I had to put her to bed. I was thinking maybe Dr. Tuttle could give her a shot or some sleeping pills. She's in bad shape."

"Under the circumstances, I'd think so. Tell me, Mr. Burkhart, did your mother-in-law have heart trouble? Who's the family doctor?"

"Mother Kile didn't have much to do with doctors. Lots of the old Osages are that way. Why do you ask?"

"According to Dr. Tuttle, she had a heart attack."

"Aww, Jesus," Burkhart muttered. "Mollie's going to believe she killed her mother. I can hear it now."

"Her mother was really that upset?"

"She went off like a skyrocket. Told Mollie she ought to be ashamed of herself."

"How much had Mrs. Kile been drinking?"

"Too much," Burkhart said absently. "She brought her bottle to the table. She was already drunk."

"Do you know where she bought the moonshine?"

"Probably from a bootlegger at Chief Lookout's village. She went to the Stomp Dance last night."

"Well, give your wife our condolences. I know it must be hard on her."

"You don't have any idea. Losing Anna and now her mother . . . it's brutal."

On the drive back to the hotel, Proctor let out a long sigh. "You think Tuttle was right about a heart attack?"

"We'll never know," Gordon said. "Just like we'll never know about the moonshine."

"We could ask around at Chief Lookout's village."

"Do you think anyone would admit selling it to her? Or put the finger on a bootlegger?"

"No, likely not."

"So where does that leave us?"

"Pretty much between a rock and a hard spot."

Gordon thought that summed it up all too neatly. A rock and a hard spot. Nowhere.

Chapter Nine

The burial ground was on a bald, windswept hill north of the village. In the distance, a range of tall wooden derricks pumped black gold from deep in the earth. Elders often remarked that the Osages could never escape the white man's road. Not even in death.

The burial service was being held on Monday, two days after Lizzie Kile's death. Older Osages, those who had known Lizzie in life, traveled from Gray Horse and other villages for the service. Chief Lookout and the elders from his village had made all the arrangements and prepared the burial ground. Lizzie was one of their own.

Mollie Burkhart and Rita Smith, demurely dressed in black, were there with their husbands. William "Big Bill" Hale, with his wife and daughter, was on hand to pay his respects. Gordon and Proctor joined the throng at the bottom of the hill, where an array of Pierce-Arrow limousines were parked, the chauffeurs standing by their cars. The mourners trooped up the hill in solemn procession.

Earlier, Proctor had explained the rite of passage into the Spirit World. The Osages believed that death was merely a transition from one life to the next, a journey to a faraway place. There was no dread; they looked upon the end as though one simply went to sleep, the beginning of a new life. They never referred to it as death, but rather spoke of it as if one went away, to join ancestors who had passed on before. The passage was but a part of life.

Gordon and Proctor were there not so much as mourners than as observers. Over the years, Proctor had cultivated a few friends at the county courthouse. That morning, he'd discreetly put out inquiries and a clerk in the probate court, just as discreetly, had provided confidential information. Lizzie Kile had left a will, duly witnessed and notarized, which revoked all previous wills. The will was dated April 30, 1923, five days after Anna Brown's murder.

In the will, Lizzie bequeathed all her worldly possessions to her surviving daughters, Mollie and Rita. With the half-headrights inherited from her dead daughters, Anna and Minnie, and the headright of her deceased husband, Lizzie had controlled three headrights, including her own. Her estate, according to the county clerk, was conservatively estimated at more than $200,000. Mollie Burkhart and Rita Smith were now wealthy beyond imagining.

After obtaining the information that morning, Proctor had met with Gordon at the hotel. "Mighty peculiar," he'd commented. "Daughter murdered and mother dies all in a matter of two weeks. Seems a little too coincidental."

"More than a little," Gordon said. "I've never been a great believer in coincidence."

"Heck Thomas was about the savviest lawman I ever knew. He used to say, 'Wherever there's a pile of horseshit, sooner or later you're gonna find a pony.' All this smells like a pile to me."

"Trouble is, we haven't found the pony. A couple weeks ago we halfway pegged Ray Smith for Anna's murder. But trying to prove it got us nowhere fast."

"Not to mention Lizzie Kile," Proctor observed. "Nobody said boo about him being anywheres around when she kicked the bucket. No connection there."

"Except that his wife gets half of Lizzie's estate."

"So what?" Proctor said. "He was twenty miles away when it happened. Not to mention, there's nothin' to indicate she was murdered. Could've been a heart attack, just like Doc Tuttle says."

"Our chances of proving it either way are somewhere between slim and none. We might as well be standing on a street corner with a tin cup and a monkey. We'd probably get more leads."

Gordon was far from sanguine as the procession wound its way up the hill. Toward the front, he saw the bereaved sisters, and thought again how different they were. Mollie wore a fashionable dress, somewhat longer than usual, with a pillbox hat and a veil over her face. Rita was dressed simply, her black outfit almost a shroud, with no hat, no veil, and no care for fashion. The family similarity was striking, but it stopped with their oval features. They were two very different women.

The procession halted on the crest of the hill. The sun was directly overhead, and a warm noontime breeze wafted in from the south. A cairn of large rocks, oval in shape, had been constructed in the center of the hill, one end still open and facing west. Lizzie Kile was seated inside the cairn, dressed in a white doeskin smock with colorful quillwork on the breast, her legs bare and her feet encased in moccasins. Her hands were folded in her lap, and her hair, neatly braided, shone in the bright sunlight. She looked at peace, somehow beatific.

Osage elders were buried in the ancient manner. While women dressed the one who had went away in regal finery, the men built a cairn of rocks some five feet in height on the crown of a hill. The older Osages believed that the dead should start their journey to the Spirit World only when *Tzi-Sho*, Grandfather Sun, was directly above them at the noon hour. Tradition held that the "door was open" then, and the soul of the dead one could then travel westward with *Tzi-Sho* into the spiritland. The one who went away was always positioned facing west, to follow *Tzi-Sho* into the sunset.

The mourners gathered before the mound of rocks. The village holy man, sometimes called the shaman, moved to the westward opening in the burial cairn. He was dressed in fringed buckskins, an eagle-wing fan in one hand and a mussel-shell gorget and a silver crucifix suspended from his neck. He began chanting a death song, gracefully waving his eagle-wing fan westward, alternately turning his face overhead to *Tzi-Sho* and back again to look upon Lizzie Kile. His final benediction, as he lifted his voice in a keening wail, was to toss tufts of scented grass to the four winds.

A group of older men stepped forward and began sealing the cairn with rocks that were piled nearby. Mollie broke out in wrenching sobs while Rita looked on with a stoic expression, tears puddled at the corners of her eyes. They watched as the men, working in respectful silence, placed stone upon stone to cover the top of the cairn and close off the westward door. In a matter of minutes, the mound was conical and solid, stones carefully joined to form the roof. The onlookers caught a final glimpse of Lizzie Kile's face, limned in a streamer of sunlight, as the last rock was fitted into place.

Chief Lookout and elders from the farflung villages filed by to express their sorrow to Mollie and Rita. Big Bill Hale stood off to the side, waiting his turn, and Gordon saw again that Chief Lookout ignored the wealthy rancher. When Hale and his family finally reached the sisters, Gordon noticed that Ray Smith moved away from Rita, avoiding eye contact and all but turning his back on Hale. The rancher shook hands with Ernest Burkhart and gave Mollie a fatherly kiss. Rita turned her cheek away.

"What's all that about?" Gordon said. "Ray Smith and Rita just gave Hale the bum's rush."

"Don't know," Proctor said curiously. "Looks like there's some bad blood there. Odd way to act at a funeral."

"Have you ever heard of a falling out between them?"

"Nope, not till just now."

Hale spotted them and left his family by the edge of the hill. He walked over, his thick glasses glinting in the sunlight, and shook hands with a rueful smile. "Sad day," he said. "Lizzie Kile was a fine woman. A credit to the Osages."

"Yes, I believe she was," Gordon agreed. "By the turnout today, I'd say she was well respected."

"I'm surprised to see you here. Was Lizzie part of your investigation?"

"Only by way of her daughter being murdered. We'd talked with her a couple times."

"Terrible thing," Hale said. "God knows that family has had enough tragedy for a lifetime. Any leads on Anna's murder?"

"Nothing for publication," Gordon said evasively. "We're still working the case."

"Well, like I told you before, let me know if there's anything I can do to help. We need to make the Osage Hills safe again."

"I'll keep it in mind, Mr. Hale. Thanks for the offer."

"Good luck and good hunting."

Hale rejoined his family. As they made their way down the hill, Gordon shook his head. "Maybe I should've asked him who runs moonshine in the county."

"Wouldn't tell you on a bet," Proctor said tartly. "He put Crowley in the sheriff's office and Crowley's likely gettin' a payoff from the bootleggers." He paused, one eye cocked. "Don't know why, but it reminds me of what the Osages say about moonshine."

"What's that?"

"Well, in their language, they call it *Pet-sah-ne*. They say the white man puts the evil spirit in their heads so's he can cheat 'em easier. Lizzie Kile would likely agree with them."

"Assuming it was moonshine that killed her."

"I reckon she's tellin' *Wah' Kon-Tah* all about it right now. The whole story."

Gordon dearly wanted to know the story himself, even half the story. He silently wished Lizzie Kile Godspeed on her journey to the spiritland.

Harry Grammer was seated at his desk. He listened through the earpiece of the phone, occasionally offering a comment, his face screwed up in a frown. The voice on the other end was commanding, and when the conversation concluded, he hooked the earpiece on the phone stand. He had his marching orders.

Only three days had passed since Lizzie Kile's funeral. Grammer's personal opinion was that further action so soon was both ill-timed and dangerous. The Bureau man was nosing around, working with the old lawdog, Will Proctor, and another killing was certain to raise a red flag. But orders were orders, and no argument was allowed. He would do as he was told.

Grammer's office was in his house. He owned a ranch ten miles west of Pawhuska, and through his wife of seventeen years, a fullblood Osage, he controlled an oil headright. But his principal business was distilling moonshine and distributing bonded whiskey to roadhouses and bootleggers throughout Osage County. By virtue of political connections, and the judicial use of violence, he had a monopoly on the liquor business. He often thought of Prohibition as a gift from the gods.

The Volstead Act, enacted by Congress in late 1919, had ushered in the era of Prohibition. A decade of campaigning by temperance leaders, who decried the evil of strong drink, was the moving force behind a law that took effect in 1920. Tens of thousands of speakeasies sprang up across the land, and the ubiquitous hip flask became a mainstay in American culture. Oklahoma had gone dry on the day of statehood, some sixteen years past, and the bootlegger had become an institution. In a very real sense, Oklahomans had a head start on the rest of the country.

Prohibition shifted a market worth tens of millions to a trade controlled exclusively by the underworld. American mobsters were homegrown capitalists, and their ideology was a remarkable marriage of free enterprise and brass knuckles. The rackets grew and diversified, proliferating amid a climate of tommy-gun rubouts, cheered on by Americans who simply wanted a drink. Bootlegging and speakeasies operated openly, and for the most part, law enforcement officials turned a blind eye. The accommodation, buttressed by graft, was made easier by the fact that lawmen were merely mirroring public opinion.

Backcountry gangsters such as Harry Grammer generally conducted their affairs without the tommy-gun sensationalism of big cities, but there were exceptions. The strife came about when the oil boom generated vast amounts of money and rival gangs attempted to claim a share of the market. The revenue from illicit liquor in Osage County exceeded $1 million a year, a sum tempting enough to make murder commonplace. At least nine men had been killed on Grammer's order, and the bodies were left as object lessons for outsiders with big ideas. No one any longer disputed who controlled Osage County.

After the phone call, Grammer left the house by the back door. A short distance away was a barn and a large slat-sided corral, and off to the north a broad expanse of woods. To the west were grasslands fenced with barbed wire, and a herd of some three hundred cows grazing under a clear sky. He walked past the barn and continued along a rutted trail cut deep by truck tires through the trees. The trail ended in a clearing perhaps a hundred yards beyond the barn.

The still was in a weathered frame building forty by forty square. Several trucks, a mix of Fords and Reos, were parked haphazardly in the clearing. Grammer produced his own moonshine, favored by the Osages, and imported bonded whiskey that was then distributed to nightspots throughout the county. Men were loading cases of whiskey and quart bottles of moonshine packed in cartons for the daily truck runs to bootleggers and scattered oil towns. He waved to them as he entered the wide double doors at the front of the building.

The inside of the still sweltered with heat. There were huge copper vats with boilers and pipes, and steam and smoke vented through blackened funnels rising into the roof. A crew of men were mixing corn mash, which was then combined with yeast and sugar, and water from a creek behind the building. The concoction was brewed and strained, and ultimately distilled into a clear, potent liquid very close to pure alcohol. Bonded whiskey, imported by truck from the Gulf Coast and Kansas City, was usually eighty proof, while a good batch of moonshine teetered on a hundred proof. Osage County consumed all the 'shine Grammer could produce.

Bryan Burkhart was foreman of the ranch as well as the liquor operation. His crew chiefs, responsible for distribution and payment collections, were Kelsey Morrison, Asa Kirby, John Ramsey, and Joe Johnson. With the exception of Burkhart, the men were all ex-convicts, having served time on charges ranging from armed robbery to manslaughter. They were the enforcers, hard, brutal men who kept the crews in line and occasionally employed strong-arm tactics on bootleggers and roadhouse owners. Their business was swift, memorable violence.

Burkhart and his crew chiefs were standing by the door when Grammer walked into the still. Grammer was forty-three, with a paunch and thinning hair, and the mild manner of an accountant. Yet the men snapped to attention, all smiles and polite nods, as if a gladiator had entered their midst. They had worked for him for years, busting heads and breaking legs and sometimes committing murder, but they treated him with the deferential respect reserved for those destitute of moral restraint. He was the coldest killer they'd ever known.

"Boys," he said in a genial tone. "How's things going?"

"Just fine, boss," Burkhart spoke up. "Trucks oughta be rollin' any minute now. We've got it covered."

"Well, that's good, real good. Latest batch of 'shine got a sharp taste, does it?"

"Goddurn, it'd scald the hide off a hog. Them Osages must have a gullet like cast iron."

Grammer stared at the vats and boilers like an alchemist inspecting the blend of some rare elixir. He watched the operation a moment, a faint smile at the corner of his mouth, apparently pleased with what he saw. Then, hands clasped behind his back, his gaze swung around to the men. His eyes were like dark agates.

The men knew the look. They went stock-still, forcing themselves not to fidget or blink, as he slowly inspected them one by one. His assessment was impersonal, a long moment of weighing and deliberation, as though the future of the planet rested on his decision. He finally nodded to John Ramsey.

"John, why don't we step outside? I'd like to talk to you about something."

"Sure thing, Mr. Grammer."

The other men moved aside as Grammer led the way out the door. Ramsey obediently fell in behind and followed him to the corner of the building, near the treeline. A bluejay squalled, flitting through the canopy of leafy branches, and winged off in a blur. Grammer stared after the bird with an absent expression.

"I have a job for you," he said. "The usual thousand, and you don't say anything to the boys or anyone else. Are we straight?"

Ramsey bobbed his head. "You don't have to worry about me, Mr. Grammer. I know how to keep my lip buttoned."

"There's a man who lives in Fairfax, an Osage. His name is Henry Roan."

"Yessir."

"I want you to kill him."

"Be glad to, Mr. Grammer. How you want it done?"

"Nothing fancy, but quietly, John. Take him out somewhere and shoot him."

"How soon you want it done?"

"Within a couple days, three at the most. And, John?"

"Yessir."

"Be sure nobody can tie you to it. Play it quick and slick."

"Don't give it a thought, Mr. Grammer." Ramsey let go a woofing laugh. "I'll handle it fine and dandy."

"I like your spirit, John. Let me know how it goes."

"Yessir, I shore will."

Grammer walked off along the rutted trail toward the house. His wasn't to reason why, but he still thought it was a mistake. Too much, too fast.

Too many dead Osages.

Chapter Ten

Gordon drove through the night. Bugs splattered on the windshield, and he kept the windows down so the cool air would keep him awake. He arrived in Oklahoma City shortly before nine in the morning.

The call had come in yesterday evening. Gordon had just returned to his room from supper when the phone rang. Dave Turner, Special Agent in Charge for Oklahoma, informed him that J. Edgar Hoover wanted to see him posthaste. No later than the next morning.

Deputy Director Hoover was passing through Oklahoma City. He'd completed his inspection of field offices on the West Coast and was returning by train to Bureau headquarters in Washington. His layover in Oklahoma City was less than a day, and his train departed at four that afternoon. His priority was the Osage murders.

Gordon realized it was all but a royal summons. Hoover conducted himself with the imperious attitude of a bureaucrat who held field agents in thinly disguised contempt. By the same token, Gordon found it impossible to muster respect for a man who had never operated in the field, never heard a shot fired in anger. He thought of Hoover as a political toad.

There were times when Gordon wondered at the vicissitudes of life. He'd begun his career in law enforcement in the Virginia State Patrol, and his natural skills as an investigator led to headlines in several sensational cases. Then he'd been recruited into the Bureau and three years later assigned to break the conspiracy on the Rio Grande. There, he'd fallen in love with one of his undercover operatives.

The Rio Grande assignment made his reputation. Forrest Holbrook, Director of the Bureau, anointed him for great things and offered him any post in Washington. Guadalupe, though proud of her Mexican heritage, feared she wouldn't be accepted in Washington, where prejudice was all but socially acceptable. The decision for Gordon was between the woman and advancement into the upper echelons of the Bureau. He chose the woman.

Holbrook arranged for him to be posted to the Bureau office in Dallas. Gordon and Guadalupe were married shortly afterward, and began raising their family in a household filled with love and happiness. Over the next eight years Gordon's reputation as an investigator, particularly on undercover operations, set a new standard in the Bureau. He was routinely offered promotion to Washington, and he routinely refused. He'd found all he needed in Texas.

On the night of Lizzie Kile's funeral four days ago, he'd spoken with Guadalupe by phone. She missed him terribly, and the children were starting to wonder if they'd lost their father. He promised he would try to break away, at least for a weekend, and make a flying trip to Dallas. Guadalupe knew him too well, and she'd heard the frustration in his voice, the simmering anger over a stalled investigation. She told him to come home when he could, and not to worry. She understood his conflict, his determination to halt the murders.

Gordon's mood was irritable when he walked into the Bureau office. His jaws were covered with stubble and his eyes were bleary from having driven all night. He hadn't slept in twenty-four hours, and he resented being summoned on a moment's notice by some popinjay bureaucrat. He knew Hoover planned to call him onto the carpet, to find fault and criticize, and the temptation would be to tell the little turd to go to hell. He promised himself he'd play it for laughs.

A secretary showed him into Turner's private office. The SAC greeted him with a firm handshake and a quick roll of the eyes in warning. Hoover, as befitted his exalted sense of himself, was seated in Turner's chair behind the desk. The Deputy Director was dressed in a three-piece suit and a crisp white shirt with a dark charcoal tie snugged tight beneath his jowls. His gargoyle features were set in a scowl and his prim manner indicated levity was not the order of the day. He looked Gordon over with an expression of fussy disapproval.

"I'd think you would take more pride in your appearance. You set a poor example for younger agents."

Gordon's suit was rumpled, his shirt collar wilted. He rubbed a hand across his bearded jaw and smiled. "Good to see you too, Edgar. How was Los Angeles?"

Hoover winced at the use of his given name. "In Los Angeles," he said querulously, "the agents understand the meaning of respect. They address me as Deputy Director."

"Yeah, but they haven't known you as long as I have, Edgar. Why stand on ceremony?"

"I don't care to bandy words, Agent Gordon. Have a seat."

Turner took one of the armchairs and Gordon seated himself in the other. Hoover opened a file folder on the desk. "I've read your reports," he said. "To term them superficial does them far too much credit."

"Thought they were pretty good myself," Gordon said matter-of-factly. "You have to remember they're field reports, Edgar. Not the chapter and verse you boys write in Washington."

Hoover flushed. "I suggest you save your witty

remarks for another time. I am not pleased with your progress—or the lack thereof."

"Well, like you say, you're the Deputy Director. What is it that displeases you, exactly?"

"You were assigned the case three weeks ago. In that time, one Osage has been murdered, and another"—he paused, consulted the file—"this Lizzie Kile, might well have been poisoned. According to your reports, you haven't the faintest notion as to who's responsible."

"Not altogether accurate," Gordon corrected him. "We think her son-in-law, Ray Smith, might have murdered her daughter. But as yet, we can't prove it."

"Precisely my point," Hoover said, again consulting the file. "Now we come to the matter of these guardians, and your supposition that many of them may have murdered their wards. Your reports indicate you've made no headway whatever."

"The courts have refused to issue an order for exhumation of the bodies. I guess I could put a gun to a judge's head and obtain a writ, but that wouldn't reflect too well on the Bureau. Of course, I'm always open to ideas, Edgar."

"The very reason for my asking you here. I want you to obtain a federal court order and convene a special grand jury in Pawhuska. We will smoke the culprits out of their holes."

Turner looked startled and Gordon groaned. "Total waste of time," Gordon said without hesitation. "The sheriff will lie to protect the coroner, and they'll both lie to protect the guardians. We'd have ourselves a convocation of perjurers."

"Deputy Director, I'm afraid he's right," Turner added. "Osage County is a pesthole of crooked politicians, graft, and corruption. If one talked, they'd all fall like a row of dominoes. They'll close ranks to save themselves."

Hoover pursed his lips with a frown. "Are you telling me there's nothing to be done?" he demanded. "I remind you that President Harding has a personal interest in this case. Are we to have him believe the Bureau is incompetent?"

"Three years of murders," Gordon said evenly, "and I've been on the case three weeks. I doubt the president will think we've fumbled the ball."

"Be that as it may, we still appear very unprofessional. How do you propose to turn the situation around?"

"Edgar, the first tenet for an investigator is roughly the same as for a bloodhound. Keep your nose to the ground, don't become distracted, and stay alert. The bad guys always get careless."

"How very glib," Hoover said. "Your manner borders on impertinence, perhaps insubordination. Substance was never your strong suit, agent."

Gordon shrugged. "I love you too, Edgar."

Hoover gave him a withering look. "Have you heard Director Holbrook plans to retire the first of the year? Would you care to hazard a guess as to his replacement? Someone you know, perhaps."

The news caught Gordon off guard, and made his stomach churn. Forrest Holbrook had been his mentor, and the rock upon which the Bureau was built. He felt faintly nauseated by the thought that Hoover, ever the voracious bureaucrat, would become the next director. He covered his repugnance with an idle wave.

"Sorry to hear about the old man," he said. "The Bureau will never be the same without him."

"Indeed." Hoover's eyes narrowed in a hard stare. "You might very well be concerned about your own future. I want a quick resolution to the Osage murders. Do we understand one another?"

Gordon smiled indulgently. "Are you threatening me, Edgar?"

"Nothing so crass," Hoover said with a bogus chuckle. "I merely point out that fame is fleeting, and an investigator's reputation rests solely on his latest case. Solve the murders."

"And if I don't?"

"Why ask rhetorical questions."

Gordon took it as an ultimatum. Solve the murders or say good-bye to eleven years in the Bureau. He wondered if Pinkerton's needed a good man.

"You a betting man, Edgar?"

"No," Hoover said archly. "Why do you ask?"

"Well, it's like the tipster's sheet at the racetrack. Some people bet the favorite and other people bet the long shot. You want my tip for the day?"

"I can hardly wait."

"Get it down on me to win, Edgar. You can't lose."

"I'll hold you to it."

"Oh, one other thing."

"Yes?"

"Tell Director Holbrook I said they broke the mold. There'll never be another one like him."

Hoover flinched, stung by the insult, and SAC Turner smothered a laugh in his fist. Gordon walked out of the office.

The Hilltop was a mile or so south of Fairfax. The roadhouse was on the crest of a hill, with a large parking lot just off the highway. Saturday night was the busiest night of the week, and the parking lot was full.

The front door of the roadhouse opened onto a hallway. Off to one side was a room with a bar, where the house girls mingled with customers, and for a reasonable tariff took them upstairs to a warren of cheaply furnished bedrooms. On the opposite side was a larger room with a dance floor and a five-piece band. There were tables around the dance floor and cozy booths along the walls. The place was crowded, waiters scurrying back and forth serving drinks. The music, with a trumpeter blasting away, was all but deafening.

John Ramsey sat on a stool at the bar. He was drinking a ditchwater highball, and had a clear view into the nightclub across the hallway. For the past two nights, he'd been trailing Henry Roan, and it quickly became apparent that the Hilltop was the Osage's favorite hangout. He'd discovered as well that Roan was a good dancer, laughing and personable, but not a ladies' man. He always came alone and went home alone.

From his barstool, Ramsey could see Roan gyrating around the dance floor. The music was a frenetic Charleston, and the Osage was high-stepping it with a young Osage woman in her twenties. Roan was an amiable sort, and because he never made a move on the women, men didn't mind if he danced with their girlfriends. At first, Ramsey thought he might be a queer, one who liked to dance and kept a boyfriend stashed somewhere in secret. But then he noticed that Roan wasn't just the charmer he appeared on the dance floor. He always finished the night by going upstairs with a whore.

The band segued into "St. Louis Blues." Ramsey turned back to the bar, reminded that he didn't much care for what he called "nigger" tunes. In large part, the music of the twenties was lacking in nostalgia, the ballad replaced by blues and jazz. Drifting upriver from New Orleans, the stuttered wailing of black music became popular with whites in an era desperate for the need of escape. Songs were abbreviated, a series of vocal ejaculations, evoking a mood of primitive revelry, or spiritual misery. Jazz in particular was brazenly defiant, music in the nude, rapid and feverish and erratic. The outré syncopation seemed an aberrant rhythm of the mad.

Henry Roan came into the bar. He was tall, handsome

in the way of many Osage men, his hair parted in the middle and slicked down with pomade. A slim man in his early thirties, he was sweating lightly from his exertions on the dance floor. Last night, seated at the bar, Ramsey had engaged him in casual conversation, complimenting him on his natural ability as a dancer. They had bought one another a couple of drinks, and tonight, he took the stool beside Ramsey, nodding pleasantly. He signaled the bartender.

"This one's on me," Ramsey said with a humorous smile. "Anybody that hotfoots it the way you do deserves a drink."

Roan grinned, "Tell you, I think I could dance all night. They got the best band of any joint around."

"Yeah, like 'em myself." The bartender wandered over and Ramsey tossed a five spot on the bar. "Give my friend here a bourbon and—what was it?—a splash of water."

"Little water goes a long way," Roan said, lighting a cigarette. "Too much and you just spoil good booze."

"You took the words right out of my mouth."

Ramsey wasn't worried about being seen with Roan. The bartender, the owner of the roadhouse—everyone in Osage County involved in the liquor business knew he worked for Harry Grammer. Even more, they knew what would happen if they later talked to the authorities, or tried to bear witness against one of Grammer's enforcers. The punishment would be swift and brutal, and if necessary, permanent. See no evil, hear no evil, speak no evil was the motto of the sporting crowd. Anything else would get you killed.

"Next one's on me," Roan said as the bartender placed a drink in front of him. "I got money to burn."

Ramsey shrugged. "Don't think nothin' of it. What's a drink between friends?"

"I always say the same thing myself. What's your name again? I was so loaded last night I forgot."

"John Willard, over from Wynona way. You're Henry, right?"

"That's me, ol' hotfoot Henry."

One of the bar girls drifted over. Her dress was short at the bottom and skimpy on top, allowing customers a peek at her cleavage. She put an arm around Roan's shoulders.

"Hi there, Henry," she said in a sultry voice. "Wanna take a little trip upstairs? I'll show you a good time."

"Maybe later," Roan said, staring down her dress. "I'm havin' a drink with a friend."

"Well, you just whistle when you're ready, sweetie. I'll be around."

"Why pay for it?" Ramsey said as she moved away. "You want some poontang, I'll cut you in free."

"You talkin' about tonight?"

"Sure am. I'm meetin' a couple married gals from Pawnee. Their hubbies are workin' the graveyard shift on an oil rig."

Roan looked amazed. "You take two on at once?"

"Don't like to brag," Ramsey said with a leer. "But hey, what are friends for? We'll make it a foursome."

"You're not pullin' my leg?"

"C'mon, we'll go call 'em."

Ramsey led the way to a pay phone by the rest rooms in the hall. He took the receiver off the hook and turned sideways to Roan. He leaned into the phone, blocking Roan's view, and depressed the hook with his shoulder.

"Operator," he said, nodding confidently to Roan. "Get me 4184 in Pawnee." Listening, he nodded again and fed a dime and a nickel into the pay slots. A moment passed, then he smiled. "Hi there, Ruthie. Guess who?"

Ramsey panned a face and silently mouthed *yackata, yackata, yackata* to Roan. "Listen, Ruthie," he finally said. "I got a pal with me. A real good-lookin' devil too. I think Gracie's gonna like him."

He listened, pulled another face. "Yeah, would I lie to

you? Put Gracie on and she can talk to him herself."

"No kiddin'," he said after a moment. "That's a riot! We're outside the pisser ourselves." He glanced at Roan. "Gracie's on the can."

Henry Roan got a mental picture of a woman, her panties around her ankles, squatted on the toilet. The image, since he'd never seen a white woman relieve herself, was somehow all the more erotic. He felt himself harden.

"Okay, kiddo," Ramsey said. "We'll see you at the usual place. Half an hour."

He hung up the phone. "All set," he said with a conspiratorial smile. "You're gonna like Gracie."

"Bet I will," Roan said. "Where do we meet them?"

"A place I know between here and Pawnee. Nice and quiet, regular lover's lane."

"Maybe we oughta buy a bottle at the bar."

"Nah, I got a jug of moonshine in the car. Whyn't you follow me and stick close. We don't wanna be late."

The band was playing "There'll Be a Hot Time in the Old Town Tonight" as they went out the door. Ramsey crawled into his Studebaker coupe, and Roan swung around the parking lot in his Duesenberg. The car was long and sleek, somehow phallic in appearance, a showboat for a wealthy playboy. Roan wondered if Gracie would be impressed.

Ramsey led the way south from the Hilltop. Four or five miles along, he turned west onto a dirt road that meandered off into the countryside. A mile or so farther on, he pulled into a clearing off the shoulder, wide enough for a car to be turned around. He cut the engine and doused the lights as Roan braked to a halt beside him. He got out and walked to the driver's side of the Duesenberg.

A full moon floated in the sky like a great oval lantern. "What'd I tell you?" he said jovially. "Lover's lane right out of the story books."

Roan was still seated behind the wheel. "Real good spot," he said, looking across the moonlit landscape. "How long you think it'll take Ruthie and Gracie?"

"Not long."

Ramsey took a bulldog revolver from his pocket and shot the Osage in the back of the head. Roan pitched forward, the front of his skull exploded, blood and brain matter splattered across the windshield. His ears still ringing from the report, Ramsey inspected his handiwork and decided a second shot wasn't needed. Henry Roan was off to the happy hunting ground.

He got in his car and drove away.

Chapter Eleven

A bank of puffy clouds scudded past beneath the mid-morning sun. High overhead turkey vultures wheeled in lazy circles, floating on a warm updraft. Below the road a farmer plowed a field of dark, loamy earth.

Deputy Sheriff Noah Perkins stood by a patrol car on the road. Gordon brought his Chevy to a halt a few feet away, and stepped out with Proctor. The call from the sheriff had come into the hotel an hour earlier, just after they'd returned from the café. Proctor had driven over for Sunday breakfast, and they took Gordon's car from Pawhuska. The message left by the sheriff was cryptic, but nonetheless plain to read. There was another dead Osage.

"'Mornin'," Perkins said, leaning against the patrol car. "Got ourselves a cold one."

Gordon nodded. "Man or woman?"

"Why I'd have to say it's a man. Somebody shot him."

"Who found him?"

"Feller out there." Perkins jerked a thumb at the farmer on his tractor. "Come to start plowin' and saw the car parked up here. Thought it was a little strange, so he took a look inside. Called us straightaway."

"Who's the dead man?"

"You'll have to ask the sheriff about the particulars. I'm just directin' traffic."

"Lots of it," Proctor said, motioning along the empty dirt road. "Watch out you don't get run over."

Perkins sniffed. "You always was one for the wisecrack. Anybody'd think you was a comedian."

"Noah, you've got me beat hands down in that department."

Gordon and Proctor walked off the road into the clearing. There were scattered blackjacks to either side, and in the distance, the farmer plowed neat furrows across the field. The Duesenberg was parked on the west side of the clearing, the driver's door hanging open. Sheriff Crowley and Dr. Orville Tuttle stood by the car.

"Gordon. Proctor," Crowley said without ceremony. "See you got my call."

"We came right along," Gordon said. "Have you identified the dead man?"

"Osage by the name of Henry Roan. Sporty fellow and always drove a sporty car. Wouldn't mind havin' a Duesenberg myself."

Gordon and Proctor approached the car. Henry Roan was slumped over the steering wheel, his left arm dangling on the floorboard. The windshield and dashboard were splattered with congealed blood and gray smears of brain matter. A bullet hole was visible behind his left ear and part of his forehead was torn away in a gory exit wound. Blowflies swarmed around his face.

"One shot," Tuttle said in an erudite manner. "Appears he was facing forward when someone shot him behind the ear. Powder burns indicate the gun was only a few inches from his head."

Gordon stepped back. "How long has he been dead?"

"Well, as you see, we still have some vestiges of rigor mortis. In my opinion, he was killed sometime in the last twelve hours. An educated guess would be somewhere around midnight."

"Looked for shell casings," Crowley added, "and didn't find any. Likely shot with a revolver."

Proctor moved to the rear of the Duesenberg. He squatted down, facing east, shielding his eyes with one hand. The angle of the sun allowed him to discern tracks and disturbed vegetation across the width of the clearing. He rose, walking to the opposite side, and then, carefully studying the ground, moved back to the Duesenberg. His face was solemn.

"Killer parked over there," he said, gesturing to the east side of the clearing. "Got out of his car and walked over here and shot Roan. Then he walked back, backed into the road, and drove off. Roan never got out of his car."

"Sounds like they met here," Gordon said. "Was the shooter wearing cowboy boots?"

"Tracks say he was wearin' street shoes."

Proctor went to the opposite side of the Duesenberg and opened the passenger door. Gordon turned to Crowley. "Tell me about Roan."

"Henry was a single man," Crowley said. "Fullblood Osage, only child of Timothy and Selma Roan. They passed away a year apart, three or four years ago."

"So he inherited their headrights."

"Just suppose he did."

"Who's his next of kin?"

"Likely his cousins." Crowley hesitated, his features unreadable. "That'd be Mollie Burkhart and Rita Smith."

Gordon stared at him. "Which means they've inherited another three headrights. Lot of death in that family, all of it sudden."

"I know what you're thinkin'," Crowley said defensively. "I'll talk with the girls and their husbands, but you're barkin' up the wrong tree. No way they killed Henry."

"Well, Sheriff, somebody did."

Proctor returned from inspecting the Duesenberg. Gordon talked with Crowley and Tuttle a while longer, then asked to be kept informed. He led the way to the Chevy, and got the car turned around. They drove back toward the highway.

Gordon related what he'd learned about Henry Roan. Proctor was silent a moment, then grunted softly. "We're about three miles from where Anna Brown was shot, and maybe eight or nine miles from Ray Smith's place. I'm likin' him better all the time."

"What do you want to bet he has an ironclad alibi?"

"Well, pardner, alibis was made to be broken. Look what I found on the front seat of Roan's car."

Proctor pulled a pack of book matches from his shirt pocket. He held them out, displaying the front, which was green with red letters reading THE HILLTOP. He grinned.

"That's a honky-tonk roadhouse we passed on the way out here. Pack of cigarettes and matches on the seat, and only a couple of matches used. I'll lay you odds Henry Roan was at the Hilltop last night."

"Will, you're a sneaky man," Gordon said with a laugh. "Did you on-purpose forget to tell Crowley?"

"Wouldn't tell that peckerwood nothin'. He's not exactly tryin' to solve these murders."

"I'd say the Hilltop's our next stop. Who's the owner?"

"Feller name of Owen McSpadden. Toughnut from way back when who runs whores and sells cheap hooch. Known him since he come to Osage County."

"Maybe he'll tell us Ray Smith was in there last night."

"Frank, you're readin' my mind."

Ten minutes later they pulled into the parking lot of the Hilltop. The day was still early, going on eleven o'clock, and there were only three cars outside. They parked and went through the front door into a vestibule that opened onto the nightclub and the bar. The place was silent and dim, and smelled faintly of stale liquor.

A bartender was stocking the shelves of a mirrored backbar. He looked around as they came through the door. "Sorry, gents, we don't open till noon."

Proctor flipped his jacket aside, flashed his badge. "We're here on official business. Where's McSpadden?"

A man came through the door of a storeroom at the end of the bar. He was stout, wide in the shoulders, with a broad, flat forehead and the flattened nose of a pugilist. His eyes narrowed in a wary look.

"Well, haven't seen you in a spell, Marshal. What brings you around?"

"McSpadden," Proctor said shortly. "We're checkin' into a man that was murdered. Got reason to believe he was in here last night."

"Your man got a name?"

"Henry Roan."

"Henry the alky," McSpadden said without expression. "Drinks like a fish and drives a fancy car. Yeah, he was here last night."

"Thought so," Proctor said. "We've got it on good information he was drinkin' with another man. Who might that be?"

"Saturday nights there's probably a couple hundred men through here. How'd you expect me to remember one face?"

"You remembered Roan."

"Yeah, but I don't remember who he was drinking with. Could've been anybody."

"How about you?" Proctor turned to the bartender. "You put a name to a face?"

The bartender exchanged a nervous look with McSpadden. He shook his head. "Don't recollect that he was drinking with anybody in particular. We was pretty busy."

"You boys got short memories," Proctor fixed a hard

stare on McSpadden. "There's such a thing as accessory to murder, and it'll get you the electric chair same as you pulled the trigger. Do yourself a favor and give me a name."

McSpadden's eyes veiled with caution. "I've told you all I know, Marshal. That's the straight of it."

"Well, you change your mind, you get in touch. Hate to see you ride Old Sparky for somebody else's killin'. You think about it."

"Why, sure, I'll think about it, Marshal. Just don't know anything, that's all."

"So you say."

Gordon had let Proctor do all the talking. He was impressed by the old lawman's style, even though it had uncovered nothing of value. In the car, they turned on to the highway and headed back to Pawhuska. Neither of them said anything for a while, and Gordon finally looked around. He raised an eyebrow.

"I got the feeling we didn't hear anything close to the truth."

"Truth!" Proctor snorted. "The sonsabitches were lyin' through their teeth. Coverin' for somebody."

"Trouble is, who's the somebody?"

"Dollar to a doughnut says it's Ray Smith."

They drove off in a funk of silence.

Jack Spivey stepped out of his car in front of the hotel. The town was dark except for streetlights, and as he entered the lobby, he noted it was quarter after nine by the wall clock. He waved to the sleepy desk clerk and took the stairs.

On the second floor, he walked to his room and unlocked the door. Inside, he flipped the light switch and tossed his hat on the dresser. He sat down on the bed and forced himself to slowly count to three hundred. Anyone who'd heard him come in would be asleep again before he went out.

A few minutes later he stood and crossed the room. All Bureau agents carried a weapon, and he unconsciously checked the revolver in a hideout holster beneath his suit jacket. He pressed his ear to the door and listened to a count of twenty, then moved into the hallway. No one was about, but he was aware of creaky floorboards as he went past the staircase. He rapped lightly on the door.

Gordon admitted him, quickly closing and locking the door. A single lamp burned in the room, and Proctor was seated on one of the straight-backed chairs. He was surprised to see the marshal on a Sunday, and all the more so late on a Sunday night. Proctor grinned.

"You're a regular night owl," he said. "Don't tell me you was off sellin' insurance on a Sunday."

Gordon took the armchair and Spivey seated himself in the other wooden chair. He smiled back at the old lawman. "I got invited to Sunday dinner and stayed late. What's your excuse?"

"Beatin' the bushes," Proctor said, suddenly sober. "There's been another murder."

"I know," Spivey said. "The moccasin telegraph's faster than a phone. Heard about it early this afternoon."

"Where were you?" Gordon asked.

"You remember I told you about Paul Russell. The guy in Wynona whose wife died of bad moonshine?"

"Sure, the one who moved in with his girlfriend."

"A real blonde bombshell," Spivey said, trying to recall her name. "Anyway, I'd already talked to the wife's parents, and they didn't have anything solid. So I decided to try her brother. He lives outside Pearsonia."

Pearsonia was a small Osage town northwest of Pawhuska. "Wait a minute," Gordon said, confused. "You were trying to sell him insurance on a Sunday?"

"Sold him an annuity plan yesterday. He invited me to Sunday dinner with him and his family. Got to talking and I stayed over for supper."

"Learn anything useful?"

"Think I got a lead," Spivey said. "The brother's name is Albert Hollis. His sister was partial to moonshine, but she'd always been shy about dealing with bootleggers. He said her husband—Russell—always bought it for her."

"Presto," Gordon said quietly. "All you've got to do is find the bootlegger."

"And tie him to Russell on August sixth of last year. That's the day his wife died."

"Lots of bootleggers," Proctor commented. "You're liable to have a long search."

"Well, it's a start," Spivey said confidently. "So what's the story on this latest murder? I heard his name was Henry Roan."

Gordon related the discovery of the body on the dirt road outside Fairfax. He went on to explain that Henry Roan was shot in the head, and how Proctor had found the matchbook in the Duesenberg. Then he recounted their interrogation of Owen McSpadden, at the Hilltop roadhouse.

"McSpadden's a poor liar," he concluded. "We're both convinced he saw the killer with Roan last night. Not much chance he'll admit it, though."

"Just another weasel," Proctor added. "Him and people like him know enough to solve a dozen murders. 'Fraid they'll get shot if they talk."

Gordon rubbed his jaw. "Will thinks Ray Smith probably killed Anna Brown and Roan. I'm leaning that way myself."

"Stop and think about it," Proctor said. "First there was Anna, then her mother, and now Henry Roan. Between 'em they held *six and a half* headrights. All that's been passed along in one family in less'n a month."

"We figured it out," Gordan remarked. "Their estates were worth four hundred thousand, maybe more. The whole works went to Rita Smith and Mollie Burkhart."

"And Ray Smith gets half," Proctor said with a wise smile. "Maybe Rita was the heir, but that don't matter a hill of beans. He's got his fingers on the money."

Gordon looked thoughtful. "Just occurred to me, you could say the same thing about Ernest Burkhart. You'll remember he told us he manages Mollie's financial affairs."

"Anything's possible," Proctor said. " 'Course, I tend to doubt we'd ever prove it, much less convict him. His uncle's cronies at the courthouse would bury it faster 'n scat."

"Who's his uncle?"

"Why, Big Bill Hale, who else?"

Gordon was stunned. "Why haven't you ever said anything about Hale and Burkhart?"

"Never occurred to me," Proctor admitted. "Not till just now, when you put Burkhart in the same boat with Smith. I've had my sights set on Smith all this time."

"Wish you'd told me," Gordon said. "That might explain a whole lot about Lizzie Kile's death. Crowley and Tuttle were double-damn determined there wouldn't be an autopsy."

"Yeah, you're right," Proctor said in a musing tone. "You think Burkhart fed her poisoned moonshine?"

"She died in his house, at his dinner table. Who's to say he didn't dose her bottle with arsenic?"

"Yessir, could've happened just that way. Fact is, him and Ray Smith might be in it together. Smith kills Anna and Henry Roan, and Burkhart slips Lizzie a little hemlock. What could be neater?"

"Partners in crime," Gordon ageed. "Weed out the family and deliver the headrights to Mollie and Rita. Burkhart and Smith control it from there."

"Hell's bells!" Proctor barked. "What if they're plannin' to kill off Mollie and Rita? Then they'd have the whole shebang to themselves."

"Will, you might be on to something. They're certainly

not shy about who they murder. Question is, will they quit while they're ahead?"

"I wouldn't put anything past 'em. Burkhart's likely not worried one way or another. He knows Big Bill'd bail him out come hell or high water."

"You know, that's funny," Spivey broke in. "This afternoon, when Albert Hollis finished talking about his sister, he got started on Hale and how crooked things are in Osage County. He blames Hale for the sheriff not investigating his sister's murder."

"Wouldn't surprise me," Proctor observed. "What else did he say?"

"Told me one of the jokes among the Osage is how Burkhart fetches and carries for his uncle. Everybody calls him Big Bill's errand boy."

"Huh!" Proctor grunted. "Might be more'n that."

Gordon nodded. "You're thinking what I'm thinking?"

"I just suspect so. No tellin' where things like this might end. Maybe Hale's got his finger in the pie."

"Somebody once said there's nobody greedier than a rich man. Enough's never enough."

"So what'd we do now?"

"We investigate Big Bill Hale."

"What about me?" Spivey said. "You want me on Hale too?"

"Yeah, but quietly," Gordon said with a note of caution. "Nose around with the Osages, but don't push so hard you make people suspicious. You're still our ace in the hole."

Spivey laughed. "Discreet's my middle name."

Gordon stared off into the middle distance, He thought it was a twisting trail that led from Anna Brown to Lizzie Kile to Henry Roan. One final step might lead to Ray Smith and Ernest Burkhart.

And Big Bill Hale.

Chapter Twelve

Early the next morning Gordon and Proctor drove to the village north of Pawhuska. On the outskirts they passed the octagonal church, where they'd first met Lizzie Kile. As they entered the village, Gordon noted again that all the houses were painted a bright yellow. He wondered why.

"Never thought to ask," he said. "Why do they paint their houses yellow?"

"All part of their tradition," Proctor said, looking out the window. "Their way of honoring *Tzi-Sho*, Grandfather Sun. Yellow sun, yellow houses."

"Too bad the younger Osages are into fast cars and aping white people. I think the old ways are probably a lot better."

"Yeah, the elders have got their heads on straight. Oil money didn't cause 'em to lose sight of what counts."

"Like murdering people for their headrights."

"Pardner, that's strictly for white folks who worship the almighty dollar. These older Osages know it won't buy you nothin' in the spiritland."

They found Chief Lookout seated beneath the shade tree beside his house. His Pierce-Arrow, parked in the yard, looked as though it was seldom driven, and not far. His wife was tending a battery of pots and skillets over an open fire ringed by rocks. He watched them approach with a somber countenance.

"Mornin'," he said, motioning them to take a seat on the grass beneath the shade tree. "Guess you're here to talk about Henry Roan. Heard he got shot."

"Over by Fairfax," Proctor said. "Somebody left him dead in his car."

"Somebody," Lookout repeated. "Your somebody got a name?"

"Not yet," Gordon told him. "We've come across something that has us puzzled. We thought you might be able to help."

"Old man like me don't know whole lot. What's this puzzle?"

"Chief, I'll have to ask you that it goes no further. Anything we say here stays here."

"You askin' for my word, you got it. Always good at keepin' secrets."

Gordon quickly briefed him on their new theory. He traced the links that led them from Anna Brown, Lizzie Kile, and Henry Roan to Ernest Burkhart and Ray Smith. The coincidence, he said, of so many murders in one family seemed no coincidence at all. There was the appearance instead of wholesale conspiracy.

"Never figgered that," Lookout said when he finished. "You think Burkhart fella killed Lizzie Kile?"

"We don't know," Gordon said honestly. "What we do know is that he's William Hale's nephew. We're wondering if Hale could be involved."

"Don't know 'bout Lizzie and her girl and the Roan boy. But everybody know he's part of it."

"Part of what?"

"All this killin'," Lookout said. "Who you think put sheriff and judges in courthouse? Who you think tells 'em what to do?"

"You're talking about the guardians," Gordon said. "Are you saying Hale ordered the sheriff *not* to conduct investigations into the deaths?"

Lookout chuckled derisively. "'Course I'm sayin' that. How else nothin' got done?"

"Do you have any proof? Anything that would hold up in court?"

"Courts belong to white man. Osage County belong to Big Bill."

"You mean his control of the elections?"

"Politics bad medicine," Lookout said dourly. "Big Bill hands over Osage County vote ever' time there's state elections. Governor kiss his ass."

"That's hard to believe," Gordon said. "I know Governor Trapp from other work I've done."

"Just sayin' somebody big protectin' Big Bill. How else we got thirty-one killin's before you come here? Now we got three more."

Proctor cleared his throat. "Chief, what we're lookin' for is a link between these new murders and Hale. Or at the least, a tie to Ernest Burkhart and Ray Smith." He paused to underscore the thought. "Do you know anybody that hasn't spoke out for fear of gettin' killed? Anybody you could convince to talk?"

"Won't talk to me, won't talk to you," Lookout said in a weary voice. "Thought things change when Council write letter to Washington. Looks like all the same."

Gordon couldn't argue the point. "These latest murders," he said, "are the ones most easily solved. Could you quietly put out the word that any information will be treated confidential? We'll never reveal the name of anyone who comes forward."

"Osages not dumb," Lookout said. "Why you think nobody ever claim Big Bill's reward for killers?"

"I hadn't really thought about it."

"'Cause they never live to spend ten thousand. Big Bill's reward nothin' but trap, bait on hook. Anybody talks get killed plenty fast."

"So we're not likely to get any help from the Osages."

"I ask around, but nothin' gonna happen. You gotta find killers yourself."

The conversation ended on that note. In the car, on the way back to Pawhuska, there was a prolonged silence. Before the day was out, they planned to interrogate Ernest Burkhart and Ray Smith as to their whereabouts Saturday night. But they held little hope that either man could be tied to the death of Henry Roan. And none at all that they would implicate Big Bill Hale.

"Lookout's a wise old bird," Proctor finally said. "He was right too, about solvin' the murders. We do it or it don't get done."

"You know what they say about the Royal Mounties?"

"How they always get their man?"

Gordon smiled. "That's our new motto."

Jack Spivey drove into Pearsonia late that morning. The town was some fifteen miles northwest of Pawhuska, hardly more than a crossroads. There was a store with a gas pump and three houses.

Last night, after meeting with Gordon and Proctor, Spivey had put his mind to gathering new intelligence on the murders. Lying in his bed, with the lights out, staring at the ceiling, he had decided that Albert Hollis was the most forthcoming Osage he'd yet come across. He thought Hollis might be persuaded to talk about Big Bill Hale.

Albert Hollis lived a mile or so outside town. He was tall, in his late twenties, with prominent checkbones and his hair worn in a long braid. He had a wife, three children, and a younger sister who had been murdered by a white man. Unlike most Osages, he cared nothing about fancy cars or the sporty life so many bought with their oil money. He cared, instead, about his murdered sister.

A Ford truck, the only car in the family, was parked in the yard. The house was a one-story frame structure with peeling paint and a two-holer privy out back. Hollis was seated on the front steps, skinning a brace of rabbits he'd shot that morning, when Spivey braked to a halt behind the truck. He was surprised to see the insurance man again, particularly since they'd spent most of yesterday together. He promised himself he wouldn't buy any more insurance.

"Good morning," Spivey called out as he crossed the yard. "See you've been hunting."

"Deer take hunting," Hollis said, a wry smile at the corner of his mouth. "Rabbits just sit around and wait to be shot. You're back soon."

"Well, Albert, I enjoyed our talk yesterday. Appreciate that fine dinner your wife fixed too."

"Gonna fry these rabbits for dinner pretty quick. You're welcome to stay."

"No, thank you anyway," Spivey said. "Insurance man has to keep moving, and I've got business down the road. Just happened to think of something you mentioned yesterday. Thought I'd stop by."

"What'd I say?" Hollis asked. "We covered lots of ground."

"You'll recall you were talking about your sister. You said her husband bought all the moonshine."

"Yeah, that's right, he did."

"Well, you know, I keep hearing how so many Osages have died from poisoned liquor. Got me to wondering."

"What about?"

"Big Bill Hale," Spivey said with a look of innocent curiosity. "A man with all his money, the political kingfish of the county. Why would he cover up murder?"

Albert Hollis normally didn't like white men, and went

out of his way to avoid them. But there was something different about Spivey, a sense that he thought himself no better, or smarter, than an Osage. Or at least, that's how he'd felt about Spivey yesterday. He wasn't so sure now.

"You ask funny questions for an insurance man."

"Like I told you yesterday, I'm planning on opening an office in Pawhuska. Figured I ought to know who's who and what's what in Osage County."

"Sounds right." Hollis flicked a piece of bloody rabbit fur off his skinning knife. "Or maybe you got some other reason for askin'."

"I'd like to think we're friends," Spivey said genuinely. "Maybe I'm just interested in helping you nail Paul Russell for what he did to your sister. Part of that would be in understanding why Hale would cover up murder."

Hollis hesitated a moment. There was more to this than met the eye, more than he was being told. But some men you trusted and some you didn't, that was the way of things. He decided Spivey was on the square.

"Hale covers up lots of things," he said. "You know the moonshine that killed my sister?"

"Yeah, what Russell bought from a bootlegger."

"Well, it's made by a fella name of Harry Grammer. White man with a ranch out west of Pawhuska. Got a still off in the woods behind his house."

"So he sells the moonshine to bootleggers?"

"Not just 'shine," Hollis said. "Him and his men smuggle regular whiskey in by the truckload. He supplies every speakeasy and honky-tonk in the county."

"Okay," Spivey said, wondering where this was headed. "What's that got to do with Hale?"

"Grammer and Big Bill are real thick. Maybe they're partners, maybe they're not, but one thing's for sure. Grammer couldn't operate without protection from Hale."

"Any rumors around about that? Does Grammer pay him off?"

"Everybody knows he pays off the sheriff. So why not Hale?"

Spivey thought it made sense. Political bosses all over America took payoffs for protection. "This Harry Grammer," he asked, "does he have connections with mobsters in Kansas City and other places? You know, big-city gangsters?"

"Don't need 'em," Hollis said. "Got his own gangsters, buncha hoodlums, served time in prison. Killed eight or nine men and run other gangsters out of the county."

"Sounds like a pretty rough crowd."

"Yeah, and nobody rougher'n Bryan Burkhart. He runs everything, still and whiskey smugglin', for Grammer. He's Big Bill's nephew."

"His nephew?"

Hollis nodded. "Told you things was thick. Big Bill probably put Burkhart in there to watch Grammer. Protect his share of the rackets."

"This Bryan Burkhart, he any relation to Ernest Burkhart?"

"Bryan and Ernest are brothers. Their mother was Hale's sister, and her and her husband got killed in a car crash. Orphaned the boys and Big Bill raised 'em on his ranch."

Spivey was hardly able to hide his amazement. He tried for a casual tone. "Well, Albert, you've given me something to think about. There's more to Osage County than I thought."

"Like you said, we're friends." Hollis dropped the skinned carcass of a rabbit into a pail of water. "You want the friendliest advice you'll ever get?"

"Why sure, you bet I do."

"Don't go askin' questions about Harry Grammer."

"Why not?"

"'Cause he'll kill you deader'n hell."

• • •

Grodon and Proctor were waiting in the room. Spivey rapped on the door about nine that night, taking a last look along the hallway. The door opened and Gordon motioned him inside.

Proctor was leaned back against the wall in a chair. He deftly creased a paper, poured tobacco and rolled the paper tight, then sealed it with a lick. He struck a kitchen match on his thumbnail and lit up in a puff of smoke. He glanced at Spivey as he snuffed the match.

"Don't even ask," he said, exhaling smoke. "We talked to Ray Smith and Ernest Burkhart, and guess what? They was home with their wives Saturday night. The little women alibied 'em."

"Talked to Chief Lookout too," Gordon said as he dropped into the armchair. "His considered opinion was that there would be snowballs in hell before any Osages come forward with information about anything. How'd your day go?"

"Not too bad." Spivey was scarcely able to contain his excitement. "I think I hit the jackpot."

"Did you now?" Proctor looked at him through a haze of smoke. "What do you call a jackpot, just exactly?"

"I went back and called on Albert Hollis. When you ask the right questions, he's got some interesting answers. Talked a blue streak."

"So?" Proctor tucked away his tobacco sack. "What'd he tell you?"

"For starters, a man named Harry Grammer controls the liquor business in the county. His protector is none other than Big Bill Hale."

"Nothin' new there, Jack. That gossip's been around for years."

"How about this, then? A fellow named Bryan Burkhart is Grammer's chief henchman."

"No, have to say, I hadn't heard that."

"And Bryan Burkhart is the nephew of Big Bill Hale. And he's the brother of Ernest Burkhart."

Proctor dropped the legs of his chair to the floor. Gordon sat up in the armchair with a startled expression. Spivey looked at them with a jackanapes grin.

"It gets better," he said with vigor. "Grammer has a pack of ex-convicts on his payroll. They killed eight or nine men to gain control of the rackets in Osage County."

"Yeah, that's the rumor," Proctor acknowledged. "'Course, there wasn't no way to prove it. Nobody ever found anything but corpses."

"Maybe not," Gordon said, his eyes intent. "But we're way past coincidence here. Grammer controls the rackets and Hale controls the county. Ernest and Bryan Burkhart just happen to be Hale's nephews." He paused, on the edge of his chair. "And Bryan Burkhart bosses a crew of killers."

Proctor knuckled his mustache. "Which explains why McSpadden wouldn't say nothin' about who was with Henry Roan. He buys all his liquor from Grammer and knows a loose lip could get him killed. Gave him a case of lockjaw."

"Don't forget Ernest," Gordon said. "Three members of the family are killed and his wife inherits three and a quarter headrights. And his brother's a hired gun."

"Add Ray Smith to the mix," Proctor reminded him. "He's rollin' in headrights, the same as Ernest. Wouldn't surprise me he's tied up with Grammer somehow."

"Looks like they're all involved," Spivey speculated. "Hale and the sheriff provide protection. Burkhart and his brother, with a little help from Smith, kill off Mollie's family. Grammer's thugs are probably hired killers for the guardians." He laughed, shook his head. "We're knee-deep in suspects."

"Maybe so," Proctor said. "But these boys stick together tighter'n a mustard plaster. How we gonna prove it?"

Gordon got to his feet. He paced to the window and stood looking down at a street shrouded in lamplight. For weeks they'd been running in circles, and now there were so many suspects he hardly knew where to start. The one thing that seemed clear was that it all revolved around a single man. He turned back to Proctor and Spivey.

"Everything centers on Grammer," he said. "If we're right, then his men were involved in most of the murders. He's the key to the case."

"You're on the mark," Proctor said. "Get him and the whole house of cards falls down. Big Bill Hale included."

"Sounds good to me," Spivey said. "So where do we start?"

"Harry Grammer," Gordon said firmly. "We have to investigate him up, down, and sideways. We need to find his weak spot."

"How about his liquor operation?" Spivey suggested. "We break that and we might just break him."

Gordon nodded. "Good idea, Jack."

"Hell, boss, I'm full of them."

They began discussing strategy.

Chapter Thirteen

Burbank was illuminated by the coppery blaze of hundreds of flares. A forest of timbered derricks dotted the town and countryside; the volatile casinghead gas at each well was piped high in the air and set afire. From far away it was if an army of towering giants stood shoulder to shoulder, torches in hand, bathing the earth in an ethereal glow.

Derricks were everywhere, seemingly scattered at random, some even wedged between buildings. All across town there was a rhythmic pounding thud, like mechanical heartbeats, as hungry pumps sucked up the black blood of the earth. Hauled to the surface, thick with the viscera of extinct and ancient beasts, the oil gave off the primeval stench of something old and dead.

Yet if the air was saturated with the cloying smell of death, there was something vital, almost galvanic, about the town itself. Burbank was twenty miles west of Pawhuska, the largest oil field in Osage County, wells drilled helter-skelter across a 20,000-acre pool of black gold. Roughnecks and roustabouts, over forty thousand men, lived in company barracks spread across the landscape. The field was one of the richest in all of Oklahoma.

Gordon and Proctor crested a low hill shortly before noon the next day. Spread out before them was the oil field, stretching north and south on what was once isolated farm-land at the western edge of the county. A broad central road traversed the terrain, jammed with trucks and cars, and everyone seemed in a hurry to get somewhere else. Burbank was laid out on a grid, stretched east to west not quite a mile, with Osage Avenue the main thoroughfare.

The street was clogged with flatbed trucks hauling equipment and trucks mounted with huge oil drums bound for distant refineries. Buildings were wedged side by side, slapped together with ripsawed lumber, many of them three and four stories high. Up ahead, at an intersection, Gordon saw a hotel, a bank, saloons with bat-wing doors, and several dance halls painted in garish colors. The boardwalks were crowded with men in work clothes; automobiles, parked on an angle, lined the street. The rank smell of raw crude permeated the town.

"Stinks, don't it?" Proctor commented, wrinkling his nose. "Next to this, a barnyard's a bed of roses."

Gordon laughed. "I suppose a man could get used to anything. Maybe they just lose their sense of smell."

"Wouldn't surprise me you're right. This the first time you've been in a real, live oil town?"

"Will, hopefully it's my first and my last."

"I been watchin' the boom for thirty years. Doubt there was anything like it in all the world."

The pace of oil development seemed to Proctor a sym-bol of the Roaring Twenties. As they drove along Osage Avenue, he was reminded that oil men were hardly new to Oklahoma. The first well drilled in Indian Territory was outside Muskogee, in the Creek Nation, late in 1884. At eighteen hundred feet it came in a duster and was aban-doned, dampening exploration for a few years. Then, in 1889, a producing well was completed on Spencer Creek in the Cherokee Nation, drilled a mere thirty-six feet deep. Wildcatters continued to sink wells, and after the World War and the advent of the automobile, a whirlwind of exploration roared across the country. The race was still on to feed the gas tanks of a nation on wheels.

The boardwalks swarmed with men. For the most part, they were roughnecks, who worked the derricks, and roustabouts, who performed manual labor. Their clothes were grimy, their hands blackened with oil, and many stood picking their teeth after dinner in one of the greasy spoons along the street. Their workday began at sunrise and ended at sundown, with only a short break at noontime. They were hard men, made harder by work on the rigs, and few of them escaped without injury. A missing finger or a crushed foot was not unusual in the oil fields.

Gordon nosed the Chevy into a vacant spot at the curb. He and Proctor sat for a moment watching the throngs of men milling along the boardwalk. Their purpose today was to put Harry Grammer on notice that the law was investigating his illicit trade in booze. Jack Spivey was working closer to Grammer's ranch, trying to uncover information related to the murders. To divert attention from Spivey, they planned to make inquiries in Burbank, the crown jewel in Grammer's liquor empire. Their intent was to distract him with a threat to the largest market in Osage County.

"Where do you want to start?" Proctor asked. "Throw a rock in any direction and you'll hit a saloon."

"One's as good as another," Gordon said. "We'll work our way along the street."

A hardware store was directly in front of the car and a saloon was next door. They collared the owner of the saloon, flashing their badges, and grilled him on the source of his liquor. He was uncooperative, deflecting their questions, and denied any knowledge of Grammer's liquor operation. They next hit a dance hall, where a doughy woman with chubby features manned the ticket booth. The interior was decorated with bunting and Japanese lanterns, and a balustrade separated the oil workers from the twenty or so young women who waited on the dance floor. The charge was a quarter a dance, and the men purchased tickets that allowed them to go through an opening at the end of the railing. One ticket entitled them to ten minutes on the dance floor.

The oil field operated around the clock, and men who worked the late shift found their nightlife during the day. On a platform at the rear four musicians wailed away at "Margie," a popular tune of the day. The girls were dressed in cheap peek-a-boo gowns, and the roughnecks and roustabouts shoved them around the floor with more enthusiasm than style. There was a bar outside the balustrade, and the men waiting in line fueled themselves for a whirl with the girls. A drink, like a dance, was two bits a shot.

"You boys are a riot," the woman behind the ticket counter said pleasantly. "Even if I knew somebody named Grammer, I wouldn't admit it. Nobody else in town will either."

"Well, ma'am, you've got a bar," Proctor pointed out. "Who supplies you with whiskey?"

"You'll have to ask my husband. He handles the business end of things."

"Is he around?"

"No, he works the night shift. I tend the place during the day. He comes in at six."

"Then I reckon we'll be back at six."

The woman smiled slyly. "He don't know nothin' neither."

Outside, Proctor rolled a cigarette. "We're gettin' the runaround," he said, popping a match. "Mention Grammer's name and people go stone deaf."

"Not surprising," Gordon remarked. "Anyone who talks likely gets a busted head."

"Maybe we ought to be talkin' to the head busters. Might get somewheres."

"Don't worry, Grammer will hear about us before the

day's out. Someone's probably already on the phone."

Their next stop was the Alhambra Saloon. There was a long bar at one side of the room, with a dice table and three blackjack layouts along the opposite wall. The bar was crowded with workers in rough garb, and knots of men were ganged around the gaming tables. When they inquired for the owner, one of the bartenders directed them to the rear. A stout man with a gold tooth and his hair parted down the middle stood at the end of the bar. He looked as though he sometimes acted as his own bouncer.

"Mr. Brannon?" Gordon said. "The barkeep told us you own the place."

Brannon sized him up. "Who's askin'?"

Gordon flashed his badge. "I'm Special Agent Gordon with the U.S. Bureau of Investigation. This is Deputy U.S. Marshal Proctor."

"You one of them Prohibition agents?"

"We all work under the same department. I'd like to ask you some questions about your business."

"Ask away."

"Do you purchase your liquor from Harry Grammer?"

Brannon managed a sphinxlike expression. "Never heard of him."

A door opened at the back of the saloon and a man motioned to Brannon. Through the door, Gordon saw a truck parked in the alley and two men unloading cases of whiskey. One man handed down the cases and the other carried them into the storeroom.

"Who's that?" Gordon asked.

Brannon suddenly appeared nervous. "He's the fella I buy from."

"What's his name?"

"John Ramsey."

Gordon and Proctor walked toward the storeroom. Ramsey backed away from the door, glancing past them at Brannon, and Gordon flashed his badge. He moved through the storeroom, inspecting the cases as the men continued to unload the truck. He tore open a case and removed a fifth of bonded bourbon.

"Only the good stuff," he said, nodding to Ramsey. "You must work for Harry Grammer."

"No," Ramsey said a little too quickly. "I run it in myself. From Kansas City."

"Where do you get your moonshine?"

"I don't sell moonshine. Never have."

"We could arrest you for what's on the truck."

"You could, but I'd be out on bail before sundown."

"John Ramsey?" Gordon hesitated, then took a shot in the dark. "Don't you supply the Hilltop roadhouse, outside Fairfax? I think I heard McSpadden mention your name."

Ramsey swallowed hard. "Burbank takes all my time and then some. Never been to Fairfax."

"Well, maybe I heard wrong. Tell Harry Grammer we plan to shut him down."

"Told you, I don't work for Grammer."

"Tell him anyway."

On the street, Gordon turned west on Osage Avenue. Proctor fell in beside him, and they walked along in silence a moment. Gordon finally glanced around.

"Did you see his face when I mentioned the Hilltop?"

"Damn sure did," Proctor said. "Sonovabitch turned pale as a ghost."

"Think he knows who killed Henry Roan?"

"Hell, he might've done it himself. Almost swallowed his tongue."

"Well, one thing's for certain."

"What's that?"

"Harry Grammer won't sleep good tonight."

Jack Spivey turned onto the road. Dusk had fallen and he switched on his headlights. He drove toward Pawhuska.

All day he'd been calling on Osages whose land was near Grammer's ranch. He started three miles east of the ranch, and early that afternoon he had driven three miles west and began working his way back. The home he'd just left was only a half mile from Grammer's fence line.

Spivey had met with mixed reception. In his guise as an insurance man, he'd jollied his way into homes and made his sales pitch on annuity plans. Over the course of the day, he had called on the heads of five Osage families, and actually sold one of them a twenty-year annuity. Although he wasn't allowed to keep the commissions, he'd begun to envy insurance men. He was making more than he earned with the Bureau.

Yet his good humor tonight was along altogether different lines. After his sales spiel, he'd subtly worked the conversation around to affairs in Osage County. Some of the men were more talkative than others, but they all had strong opinions on government run solely by and for the benefit of whites. Once he got them talking, he'd managed to steer the conversation around to the subject of the Osage murders. From there, it was only a short step to the matter of poisoned moonshine, and their nearby neighbor, Harry Grammer. Three of them had clammed up the moment Grammer's name was mentioned.

The other two spoke their minds. They were aware of the still on Grammer's ranch, and they were quick to speculate that the moonshine he produced might have been responsible for some of the deaths. No less quickly, they raised the possibility that white husbands had poisoned their Osage wives. Almost as an afterthought, linking Osage County's political boss to the moonshiner, Spivey casually asked if they'd ever seen Big Bill Hale at Grammer's ranch. The Osage he'd just left had pinned the tail on the donkey.

Luther Baxter was a simple man, with no gift for duplicity. He'd admitted seeing Big Bill Hale many times.

Hale's car was a maroon four-door Cadillac, known to everyone in Osage County. On several occasions, Baxter had seen the car driving in or driving out of the gravel driveway to Grammer's ranch house. Once, passing by in his chauffeured Pierce-Arrow, Baxter had seen Hale at the wheel of the Cadillac, pulling out into the road. He found nothing unusual in what he told Spivey, for Grammer couldn't operate without Hale's permission. Baxter had laughed and said: "Why else you think they call him Big Bill?"

Spivey was elated. As he drove away from Baxter's house, he couldn't wait to relay the news to Gordon and Proctor. Placing Hale at Grammer's ranch was hardly evidence of a conspiracy, and no proof at all that Hale was involved in the murders. But it was the first step in building a case, for it established an ongoing relationship between the political kingpin and Osage County's criminal element. There was no question in Spivey's mind that Gordon would devise some tricky maneuver to further incriminate Hale and Grammer. He thought he'd made a good start today.

A Reo truck passed Spivey at a high rate of speed. Directly behind, the headlights of a car flashed in his rearview mirror. The truck suddenly braked, skidding sideways in the road, and Spivey jammed on his brakes to avoid a collision. The passenger door of the truck opened and a man jumped out with a pump shotgun, aiming it at Spivey. The car behind skidded to a halt, and two men bailed out, hurrying forward to flank Spivey's Ford. The one on the driver's side put a pistol to his head.

"Gimme your gun!" he shouted. "Do it or I'll blow your fuckin' head off!"

Spivey carefully handed over his revolver. He had the unsettling feeling that the men weren't highway robbers. In short order, Spivey was transferred to the car behind, held at gunpoint in the backseat. The man with the shotgun climbed into his Ford, and the truck straightened itself on the road. Less than a minute had elapsed from the time Spivey was taken until the little caravan drove off. A short distance down the road, they turned into the driveway of Grammer's ranch.

The truck led the way past the house, where lights burned in the windows. On beyond the barn, the caravan disappeared into the trees along the rutted trail. A few moments later, the truck and the cars halted before the still, which blazed with lights. Spivey was roughly dragged out of the rear car, surrounded by the men, and marched through the wide double-doors. He took in the vats and boilers, intrigued by the sight of a still, even though he knew his situation was desperate. A short, stoutly built man was waiting for them off to one side of the room. He looked Spivey over with a crooked grin.

"Welcome to the party," he said in a mocking tone. "Guess you never thought you'd be the guest of honor."

"Who are you?" Spivey said, trying to sound indignant. "Why'd you bring me here?"

"I'm Bryan Burkhart, not that it'll do you any good. You might as well drop the innocent act, Mr. Jack Spivey."

"How'd you know my name?"

"Well, Jack, we've got friends among the Osages. Some of them Injuns purely love their moonshine. We got a call about you today."

Spivey looked bewildered. "I'm not following you. Call about what?"

"Why, one of them told us you're a mighty inquisitive fellow for an insurance man. Said you'd been askin' all kinds of questions about Mr. Grammer and Big Bill Hale."

"What's wrong with that? I'm new to Osage County and I'm trying to get the lay of the land. Pays to know who's who."

"No need lyin'," Burkhard said with amiable menace. "We're gonna get it out of you one way or the other. Might as well save yourself some grief."

Spivey realized the bluff wouldn't work. In a moment of stark clarity, he resigned himself to his fate. He knew he would never leave there alive, that Harry Grammer had already signed his death warrant. He resolved to tell them nothing.

"I haven't got the least notion what you're talking about. I'm just a working stiff trying to make a living."

Burkhart sighed heavily. "All right, boys, string him up."

The men stripped Spivey naked. Kelsey Morrison bound his hands, while Asa Kirby cinched his ankles together. A rope with a hook attached was suspended from an overhead rafter, and John Ramsay slipped the hook between Spivey's bound wrists. Joe Johnson heaved, hauling him a foot off the floor, and snugged the rope around a stanchion. Burkhart stepped in front of him with a thin-bladed skinning knife.

"This here's John Ramsey," he said, indicating Ramsey with the tip of the knife. "Over in Burbank today, he run across a federal agent name of Gordon and that old lawdog, Proctor. We think you're workin' with them."

"You're nuts," Spivey said, unable to take his eyes off the knife. "I don't know anything about that. I'm just a salesman."

"Well, Jack, here's the deal. You talk or I'm gonna flay you alive. What'll it be?"

"Honest to God, you've got the wrong man!"

"Guess we'll see."

Burkhart made a skin-deep incision across Spivey's chest. Spivey flinched, gritting his teeth, beads of sweat on his forehead. Still smiling, Burkhart made two vertical incisions down the stomach, forming a rectangle of seeping blood. He clipped the top incision between his thumb and the blade of the knife, and pulled. The skin peeled away in a strip of raw flesh.

Spivey's mouth popped open in a strangled scream.

Burkhart let the flap of skin dangle loose. "You can start talkin' anytime," he said impassively. "Believe you me, it's only gonna get worse."

Spivey closed his eyes, begged God for a quick death. But the torture went on and on, a strip at a time, as he thrashed and screamed and tried to avoid the knife. Burkhead skinned his chest and stomach with surgical precision, then began working on his back. Spivey moaned, barely conscious, his features contorted in a rictus of agony. Finally, reduced to a slobbering animal, the last vestige of his willpower was broken.

"Ahhh God!" he whimpered, hanging bloody and raw. "No more. *Pleeze!* No more."

"You're sure?" Burkhart pricked him with the knife point. "Waltz me around and I'll peel you like a grape. Ready to talk?"

"I will, honest to God! Just stop . . . stop."

"All right, let's try a question. You a federal man? Workin' with Gordon?"

Spivey told them everything. He confessed to his undercover role and the investigation of the murders, blubbering between gasps for breath. Burkhart peeled another strip off his back, just to make sure he hadn't held out. Spivey arched away from the knife, his eyes wild with terror and pain, flecks of spittle drooling from his mouth. He begged them to kill him.

Harry Grammer was called down from the house. When he came through the doors, Spivey hung limp from the rope, flayed to the bone, bleating pitiful little groans. Burkhart and the men stood around watching him with the detached interest of butchers studying a side of beef. Grammer halted beside Burkhart.

"Took long enough."

"Yeah, he was tougher'n most," Burkhart said with grudging admiration. "But, hell, in the end, they all talk. Nobody outlasts the knife."

Grammer nodded. "What's the story?"

"Just like you thought, boss. He's one of them federal agents, been workin' undercover. Anything he learns, he reports to Gordon."

"How much do they know?"

"Not a whole helluva lot," Burkhart said. "They think we're behind the killin's, and sorta halfway figure Uncle Bill's part of it. Haven't got a dime's worth of proof."

"Told your uncle we were moving too damn fast. Maybe he'll listen now."

"Well, you know how he is once he gets his mind set. No holdin' him back."

"'Fraid you're right." Grammer walked to the door, then turned and nodded to the body dangling from the rope. "Finish him off."

"Whatever you say, boss," Burkhart replied. "What d'you want done when we're through?"

"Think it's time we warned 'em off. Deliver him to Gordon."

Chapter Fourteen

Gordon stepped out of his room. A bright morning sun spilled through the street-side window of the hallway, and he saw no one about. He walked quickly to room 209 and knocked. He waited a moment, then knocked again. No answer.

A worried frown creased his features. Spivey hadn't reported in last night, and he'd slept fitfully, thinking the undercover agent would awaken him sometime during the night. He debated picking the lock to Spivey's room, then decided to wait until after breakfast. There would be fewer people around.

The clock in the lobby chimed seven as he came down the stairs. By now, he and Proctor had worked out a schedule for breakfast, and the old lawman came through the front door as he reached the bottom landing. He nodded to Proctor and started across the lobby. The desk clerk was leaning over the counter.

"Morning, gents," he said in a doleful voice. "Did either one of you know Mr. Spivey? The insurance man staying with us?"

Gordon stopped. "Something wrong?"

"Yessir, bad wrong. Somebody killed Mr. Spivey last night and left him outside. Terrible thing."

There was a moment of frozen silence. Gordon looked

as though he'd been struck a blow, but he quickly composed himself. "What did you mean, left outside?"

"Why, dumped him in the street, right in front of the hotel. Sometime during the night."

"You didn't see them?"

"No, must've been catching a nap," the clerk said. "First thing I know, the police showed up and then the sheriff. Not quite an hour ago."

"Street's clear now," Proctor said. "Where'd they take the body?"

"Newman's Funeral Home. Swear to God, why would anyone kill Mr. Spivey? He was a regular joe."

Gordon crossed the lobby. Proctor followed him out and they walked to the Chevy, two doors down from the hotel. Spivey's Ford ragtop was parked in the next space, and they inspected the interior, which appeared clean. Gordon's jawline tightened.

"They got on to him somehow, Will. The bastards killed him."

"Yeah, looks that way," Proctor said somberly. "Guess you know why they dumped him in the street? Could've just left him in his car."

"That wasn't good enough. They wanted to send the message loud and clear. Warning us to drop the investigation."

"Well, they sure as hell picked the wrong boys."

"Yeah, somebody just bought a one-way ticket to death row."

Ten minutes later they walked into Newman's Funeral Home. Gordon identified himself and an attendant escorted them to a dank mortuary in the basement. Daniel Newman, the funeral director, hovered by the door with a soulful expression. Sheriff Crowley and Dr. Tuttle were huddled across the room.

Spivey was laid out on a metal table used for embalming. He was naked, his eyes closed, his chest a suppurating mass of raw flesh. Dried strips of skin hung down over his genitals, and a small hole, caked with blood, was centered on his forehead. His limbs were stiffened in rigor mortis, and his features were twisted in a grimace of torment. He looked like an animal in a charnel house.

"What's this?" Crowley asked. "Somebody in my office call you by mistake?"

Gordon crossed the room and stared down at the body. A muscle ticced at the back of his jaw, his eyes cold as stone. "Was this how you found him?"

"Just like you see him," Crowley said. "Wasn't no sign of his clothes. You know this man?"

"His name's Jack Spivey," Gordon said tersely. "He was an agent of the U.S. Bureau of Investigation. Working undercover."

"Clerk at the hotel said he was an insurance sales-man. You saying he was working the Osage case?"

"Otis, get the wax out of your ears," Proctor said in a harsh tone. "What the hell happened here? How'd he die?"

Crowley glanced at the body. "Somebody peeled his hide off piece by piece. Doc says it took a while."

"Someone quite adept with a knife," Tuttle added. "Of course, the actual cause of death is gunshot. Not that he would have survived the—ummm . . . skinning."

"So he was tortured first," Proctor said, "and then they killed him. That it?"

"Yes," Tuttle said quietly. "Tortured by someone expert at his business. I've never seen anything like it."

Gordon thought that every man had his limits. The brutality of it was minor compared to a slow, agonizing form of suffering he could hardly imagine. He knew beyond doubt that Spivey had been broken, told them everything about the investigation. Then they'd shot him.

"Look here," Crowley said. "Why didn't you tell me about your undercover man? I thought we was workin' together."

Gordon fixed him with a hard stare. "Special Agent Spivey was investigating your local booze lord, Harry Grammer. I hear you take payoffs from Grammer."

"Whoever told you that's a gawddamn liar. I don't take payoffs from nobody!"

"Whether you do or don't doesn't much matter. But I want you to get word to Grammer."

"Word about what?"

"Tell him I know he killed Jack Spivey. Then tell him I'm going to put him in the electric chair."

Gordon walked out of the mortuary. Proctor followed along and they made their way back upstairs. Outside the funeral home, Gordon stopped, staring up at the pale blue sky, and drew a long breath. His face was an ugly mask of rage and sorrow.

Proctor cleared his throat. "Helluva way for a man to die. You think he talked?"

"Wouldn't anybody?" Gordon said, his features rigid. "From the look of it, he held out until he couldn't take any more. But, yes, I think he talked."

"So they know we suspect Big Bill Hale."

"If they don't, they will shortly."

"What're you gettin' at?"

"I intend to send Hale a message."

Ernest and Mollie Burkhart were having breakfast. Dorothy, their cook and maid, had prepared fried eggs, a steamy bowl of grits, crisp slabs of bacon, and fluffy buttermilk biscuits. Burkhart was tucking it away like he had a field of hay waiting to be baled.

Mollie picked at her food. Over the past few weeks her appetite had dwindled to nothing, and her slender figure was now almost boyish. She was haunted by memories of Anna, and her mother, and Henry, a cousin she'd loved like a brother. She couldn't reconcile herself to their loss, the overwhelming sense of grief that was with her night and day. She felt empty inside.

"Mollie, honey," Burkhart scolded gently. "You need to eat something before you dry up and blow away. You're skin and bones."

"I'm sorry," she said with sad eyes. "I'm just not hungry."

"Well, force yourself, maybe a few bites. Try one of Dorothy's biscuits with some of her peach preserves. You always said she makes the best preserves in the world."

"Omigod, everything in this house reminds me of Mama. She used to say the same thing. I miss her so much, Ernie."

"Of course you do," Burkhart said tenderly. "Only natural you would, and I do too. Your mother always brought a little laughter to the house. She was a fine woman."

Mollie's eyes glistened with tears. "Yes, she was fine, wasn't she? Everyone loved her."

"Look here, there's a dance at the club Saturday night. They're bringing in Teddy Rogers and the Bobcats, all the way from Tulsa. What say we get dressed to the nines and go trip the light fantastic? Sound good?"

"Oh, I don't know. . . ."

"Honey, you can't sit in this house forever. You've got to get back to living. Am I right, or am I right?"

"Yes, I suppose."

The doorbell rang. Dorothy bustled through the swinging door to the kitchen and sailed past them into the hallway. They heard voices from the vestibule, followed by a screech of indignation from Dorothy, and then loud footsteps. Dorothy came flying into the dining room.

"Told 'em you was havin' *breakfast*!" she shrieked. "Told 'em and *told 'em* and they jest wouldn't listen!"

Gordon and Proctor walked through the arched doorway. Burkhart rose from his chair and started around the table, but Proctor waved him down. "This is official business," he said bluntly. "Don't go buying yourself trouble."

Mollie looked bewildered and Burkhart slowly resumed his chair. He motioned to the maid. "It's all right, Dorothy," he said with a tentative smile. "Go ahead and finish up whatever you were doing. Don't worry about it."

"Well, I never!" Dorothy stormed through the kitchen door. "Jest come bustin' in on folks!"

Proctor took a chair at one side of the table and Gordon seated himself on the opposite side. Burkhart settled back in his chair, a tinge of irony in his voice. "We don't often have guests for breakfast. Help yourselves."

"No, thanks," Proctor said. "We're pretty picky where we eat."

"You'll have to excuse us, Mrs. Burkhart," Gordon said, turning to her. "A friend of ours was murdered last night."

"Oh!" She put a hand to her mouth. "I can't bear the thought of any more death."

"I'm not surprised," Gordon said. "Last time we were here, we talked about the murders of your sister and your cousin, and the untimely death of your mother. That must be a burden."

"You can't imagine what I've been through. Ernie was saying only a moment ago that I've turned to skin and bones."

"Well, there's always the money," Gordon said without inflection. "I mean, three and a quarter headrights buys a lot of solace. You have to think of it that way."

"Hold on now," Burkhart broke in. "You're out of line talking to my wife like that."

"Am I?" Gordon said. "You'll have to admit it's a lot of money. All death money."

"You're a *horrid,* despicable man!"

Mollie burst into tears. She jumped from her chair,

a hand clasped to her mouth, and ran from the room. They could hear her sobs as she hurried through the house, and a few moments later, the slam of a bedroom door. Gordon glanced across the table at Proctor.

"You know, Will," he said thoughtfully, "maybe we were wrong. I don't think she's in on it."

"Yeah, maybe," Proctor allowed. "'Course, women often as not fool you. Hide behind all them waterworks."

"In on what?" Burkhart demanded. "What the hell are you two talking about?"

"Murder," Gordon said icily. "One of our undercover agents was investigating the Osage murders. Last night he was tortured—*skinned alive*—and then killed. We think you know the men who did it."

"You're off your rocker!"

"Well, try this," Gordon said. "Yesterday he was talking to Osages who live near Harry Grammer, asking them questions about moonshine and illegal liquor. Last night he was dumped in front of the hotel—naked and dead."

"What does that have to do with me and Mollie?"

"Your brother works for Grammer. Osages don't have kind things to say about Bryan."

Burkhart went perfectly still. "You're accusing my brother of murdering your friend?"

"We think there's more to it than that. We hear your uncle is big pals with Grammer."

"You'll have to ask him about that. I'm not involved in his business."

"Aren't you?" Gordon said, his tone laced with skepticism. "Your brother works for Grammer. Your uncle's one of his cronies. Sounds like the whole family's crooked."

Burkhart flushed. "You're so high and mighty with your judgments. My uncle made this county what it is. Ask anybody."

"We have asked. Lots of people believe Grammer and

your brother are responsible for all these murders. Anna Brown, Henry Roan, and Lizzie Kile just add to the list. All killed for their headrights."

"You're nuts!" Burkhart protested. "My mother-in-law died of a heart attack. She wasn't murdered!"

"Wasn't she?" Gordon said. "We think you did it and we think your uncle was behind it. All for the money."

"So why haven't you arrested anybody?"

"We plan to arrest a bunch of people, real soon. You're first on the list."

"You know what I think? I think you're bluffing. All wind and no whistle!"

"Tell me that when they strap you in the electric chair."

"Get out of my house. Go on, get out!"

"Next time we'll come with a warrant. For you and your uncle."

Burkhart scowled, unable to frame a response, as they went through the door. Outside, they crawled into the Chevy and drove down the hill toward town. Proctor snorted a rough laugh.

"You damn sure sent a message to Big Bill. What d'you think he'll do?"

"Will, I don't know," Gordon said. "I'm just playing for time."

"Time for what?"

"A way to put the heat on Harry Grammer. He's the key to the case."

"What've you got in mind?"

Gordon told him.

The train pulled into Oklahoma City early the next morning. Jack Spivey's casket was unloaded from the express car and manhandled onto a large baggage cart. A hearse was waiting at the side of the depot.

Daniel Newman had been most obliging. The mortician had given Gordon a discount on a casket, then rushed the embalming of Spivey. He'd also made arrangements with a funeral home in Oklahoma City, and Gordon had caught the evening train out of Pawhuska. The Bureau would now take charge of delivering Spivey's body to his parents in Missouri.

Gordon touched the casket one last time as it was loaded into the hearse. He silently said a final good-bye and promised Jack Spivey that his death would bring swift and certain retribution. Then he caught a taxi in front of the depot and gave the driver the address of the Oklahoma Bureau of Investigation. A state agency, under the direction of the attorney general, the Bureau was charged with investigating major crimes in Oklahoma. To date, none of the Bureau's agents had appeared in Pawhuska.

The state capitol was located in a complex north of the downtown business district. Headquarters for the Oklahoma Bureau of Investigation was in a marble building across the street from the capitol. Colonel Robert Stroud, commander of the Bureau, was a taciturn man with close-set eyes and narrow features. Yesterday, on the telephone, he'd agreed to a meeting, even though Gordon had refused to divulge the reason. He rose from behind his desk, attired in a neatly tailored uniform, and exchanged a perfunctory handshake. He motioned Gordon to a chair.

"What can I do for you?" he said, bypassing the amenities. "You weren't altogether forthcoming on the phone."

Gordon disliked arrogant men in fancy uniforms. But he chose to overlook the officious manner. "Colonel, as you know, I'm investigating the string of murders in Osage County. I'm hoping you can provide some information."

"Get to the point, Mr. Gordon. Information about what?"

"A man named Harry Grammer controls the liquor

trade in Osage County. I'm specifically looking for criminal activities, anything of an incriminating nature. Something your Bureau might know that mine doesn't."

"You've come to the wrong place," Stroud said. "You
need to contact Carl Hager, chief of the federal Prohibition
agency for Oklahoma. I'm surprised that wasn't your first
stop."

Gordon shrugged. "I haven't seen a Prohibition agent
since I got to Osage County. Are you saying you have
nothing on Grammer?"

"Are you talking about his liquor operation?"

"No, Colonel, I'm talking about murder. Grammer
and his gang are reputed to have waxed eight or nine men
in their takeover of the county. I thought you would have
case files on the killings."

"Nothing of any use," Stroud said crisply. "We never
investigate mob rubouts, Mr. Gordon. We consider it good
riddance to bad rubbish."

"Colonel, since we're on the subject—" Gordon hesi-
tiated, his gaze direct. "I've never seen any of your agents
in Osage County either. Aren't you interested in the Osage
murders?"

"Osage County is the bailiwick of Sheriff Otis Crowley. We never intrude on a fellow officer's jurisdiction."

"Well, that certainly clears the air. I wondered why I
was assigned the case, when the state has its own Bureau.
Guess Injuns don't count."

"Save your sarcasm, Mr. Gordon. I don't need lessons
from you on law enforcement."

"Does Governor Trapp share your views about Osage
County?"

"The governor leaves the operation of various state
departments to the department heads. I answer only to the
attorney general."

"Colonel, as my Texas friends would say, that's a load
of horseapples."

Stroud stood. "I believe that ends our discussion."

Gordon left without a parting handshake. He recalled what Chief Lookout had said about Big Bill Hale's influence at the state capitol. He thought Stroud was a political hack, and probably crooked to boot. Graft often turned men blind.

In fact, Gordon told himself as he emerged from the building, Stroud was likely taking payoffs from Hale. That would explain why Stroud and his investigators stayed clear of Osage County, and had never looked into the murders. Even now, Stroud might be on the phone to Hale, or perhaps Harry Grammer. Which wasn't a bad thing from Gordon's perspective. The more pressure, the better.

Twenty minutes later he walked into the federal Bureau office. SAC David Turner knew he was returning Spivey's body to Oklahoma City, and he'd been informed as well of the meeting with Stroud. He evidenced no surprise when Gordon related the gist of the conversation, for his experience with the Oklahoma Bureau was less than rewarding. He wagged a hand back and forth.

"Stroud had three years to investigate the murders, and he sat on his thumb. That's why the Osage Council finally wrote Washington."

"Well, he was right about one thing," Gordon said. "I need to get hold of Carl Hager, the Prohibition chief. He might have something I could use as leverage over Grammer."

"You didn't tell me that on the phone," Turner said, somewhat taken aback. "Were you thinking Hager would have something incriminating on Grammer? Leverage enough to convert him into an informant?"

"Something like that, although I wouldn't let him skate. I want payback from the whole crowd for Spivey."

"Frank, I hate to be the bearer of bad news. Carl Hager and his Prohibition agents are born whores. They're on the pad of every whiskey peddler in Oklahoma."

"Jesus Christ," Gordon groaned. "I wondered why Osage County was so wide open. Thought maybe Hager just hadn't been there yet."

"Been there and gone," Turner said. "Sold his soul and his badge."

"Dave, things changed when they killed Jack Spivey. It's personal now."

"I share the sentiment a hundred percent. Jack deserved better."

"Then don't be surprised by what you hear out of Osage County."

"I'm not sure I want to hear whatever it is you're saying, Frank."

"You're right, we never had this conversation."

Gordon recalled all too vividly the sight of Spivey's body in the funeral home. He told himself there were no rules now, no limits. Only payback.

Chapter Fifteen

William Hale's ranch was twelve miles north of Pawhuska. The spread encompassed thirty thousand acres of tallgrass prairie, watered by a latticework of swift-running creeks. A herd of some five thousand cattle placidly grazed beneath a midmorning sun.

Sheriff Otis Crowley drove into the ranch compound shortly before ten o'clock. The main house was a two-story frame structure with a covered front porch, set in a grove of stately trees. There was a large bunkhouse and cook shack off to the north, with a corral and several equipment sheds scattered about in the distance. The driveway to the house was lined by a split-rail fence painted white.

Hale walked out onto the porch. His office was on the ground floor at the front of the house, which gave him a commanding view of the driveway. Visitors who dropped by on routine business were allowed in his office, where discussions could be conducted at leisure. But any business with the sheriff was of a private nature, and he studiously avoided his wife and daughter overhearing such conversations. He went down the porch steps as Crowley stepped from his car.

"Morning, Otis," he said genially. "What brings you around?"

"Got a call," Crowley said, glancing furtively over his

shoulder. "You remember our contact at the Bureau of Investigation? The one in Oklahoma City."

"Of course, the one I pay to let us know what's what."

"Well, he earned his pay this time, Mr. Hale. Special Agent Gordon called on Colonel Stroud yesterday. He was inquirin' about you and Harry Grammer."

Hale appeared unconcerned. "Try to be a little more specific, Otis. What sort of inquiry?"

"Worst sort there is, I'd reckon. He was lookin' to tie you and Grammer to the Osage murders. Didn't pull no punches about it neither."

Crowley didn't want to know if it was true. He was loyal to Hale, and he'd followed orders, suppressing investigation into the murders. But he never asked questions, and he kept his opinions to himself. He adhered to the dictum that knowledge could get you killed.

"Gordon's a real gadfly," Hale said. "What did Stroud tell him? Did our contact know?"

"Yessir, he got the straight dope. Stroud's pretty much in the dark himself, so there wasn't nothin' to tell. He gave Gordon the fast shuffle."

"Well then, no harm done. Stroud knows to stay clear of Osage County, and he's kept the bargain. I appreciate you coming by, Otis."

"Always glad to be of help, Mr. Hale."

Crowley got in his car and drove off. Hale returned to his office and settled into his chair, lost in thought. He glanced at the desk calendar, reflecting that Gordon had been nosing around the county almost a month. Contacting Stroud seemed to him the last straw, and he reached for the phone. Then he decided the matter was best discussed in person, and quickly. He went back to the kitchen and told his wife he wouldn't be home for dinner.

Outside, he crawled into his Cadillac and headed toward Pawhuska. A short while later, as he drove through town, he was reminded that Gordon and Proctor had called on Ernest day before yesterday and halfway accused him of killing Lizzie Kile. Gordon was determined and resourceful; and as Hale took the road west from Pawhuska, he thought he'd delayed too long in solving a problem that would only get worse. A few minutes before noon he pulled into the driveway of Grammer's ranch.

Grammer met him at the door, surprised by the unannounced visit. Hale was never comfortable talking in the house, and they took seats in the rockers on the porch. Hale lit a cigar, puffing wads of smoke, and related his earlier conversation with Crowley. When he finished, he was silent a moment, staring at the road. His eyes were cold behind his bottle-top glasses.

"I want it ended," he finally said. "Solve our problem with Gordon and Proctor once and for all. Do it soon."

Grammer appeared hesitant. "You sure you want the old man snuffed? He's no threat on his own."

"Don't go sentimental on me, Harry."

"No, it's not that exactly. We already whacked one federal man, and there'll be a big stink when another one gets dusted. Why make it any worse by poppin' an old man?"

"Because I say so." Hale flicked an ash off his cigar. "I want to send a message to the feds: Stay out of Osage County."

"That'll do it." Grammer paused, suddenly decided to speak his mind. "You ever think it could backfire on us and make things worse? Might piss 'em off so much they'll send an army in here."

"Harry, you never were much on strategy. The feds will cut their losses rather than risk losing face over a bunch of blanket-ass Indians. Just do what I tell you."

"Whatever you say goes. I'll put the boys on it right away."

"Fast and neat and no mistakes, Harry. Let's end it."

"Don't worry, it's as good as done."

Hale drove off in his Cadillac. Grammer watched him from the porch, still not convinced it was a smart move. Yet a deal was a deal, and his cut from the Osage murders was a tenth of the headrights, which was akin to a king's ransom. He hadn't gone wrong so far, and he wouldn't try to second-guess Hale now. Orders were orders.

Grammer walked down to the still. Friday was the day for weekend deliveries, and the trucks were parked out front, in the process of being loaded. When he came through the doors, Bryan Burkhart and the crew chiefs were talking and smoking off to one side of the building. He nodded as he approached them.

"Boys," he said amiably. "Things on schedule?"

"Sure are, boss," Burkhart said. "We'll be rollin' any minute now."

"Well, some of you will have to pull double duty on the deliveries. A situation's come up that won't wait till tomorrow. I need three of you for a job tonight."

None of them had to be told what he meant. He used the word "job" only in the context of someone having to be killed. They waited, their eyes alert, aware he was deciding who would be picked for the job. He nodded to Kelsey Morrison, Asa Kirby, and Joe Johnson.

"Kelsey, you'll be in charge," he said. "You know the federal agent, Gordon? And that old lawdog, Proctor?"

"Yessir, sure do," Morrison affirmed. "Known Proctor from way back when. Seen him with Gordon over in Pawhuska a couple times."

"You and Asa and Joe get on it. Find 'em and take 'em out tonight. Try to do it someplace quiet."

"We won't let you down, Mr. Grammer."

"And Kelsey?"

"Yessir."

"Don't leave any witnesses."

• • •

The sky was clear and black as velvet, bursting with stars. A cool breeze whipped through the windows as they drove into Gray Horse. The town was dark and still, no one about.

Gordon was behind the wheel. He'd returned from Oklahoma City on the afternoon train, infused with energy. He'd called Proctor, asking him to drive over from Hominy; later, at the hotel, he'd explained what he had in mind. He thought Ray Smith was the weakest link in the conspiracy, and he planned to brace the rancher, force him to talk. He wanted to do it tonight.

Proctor wondered at the rush. Ray Smith wasn't going anywhere and it could have easily waited until tomorrow. But then, on second thought, he noticed a change in Gordon, something oddly different. The younger man seemed on edge, his nerves tight as catgut, galvanized to get on with the job. Gordon had filled him in on the aborted meeting with Colonel Robert Stroud, but he didn't think that was it. He decided it was a delayed reaction to Spivey's death, a quiet rage at the brutality visited on a friend and partner. He'd seen it in other men.

"You're wound a little tight," he said as they passed through Gray Horse. "Got something on your mind?"

Gordon sat rigid and erect, his hands gripping the wheel. A car had been behind them at some distance, and he glanced in the rearview mirror as it turned off into Gray Horse. He hadn't spoken ten words since they'd left Pawhuska, and he wasn't sure what to say now. He finally decided on the truth.

"I've done a lot of thinking," he said. "Especially after I delivered Jack to Oklahoma City. You may think it's a little strange. . . ."

"Never know till you try me," Proctor said. "What've you been thinking, just exactly?"

"I can't get it out of my head how they killed Jack. I keep thinking it's changed the rules."

"You're talking about the way they tortured him."

"Yeah." Gordon's voice was vindictive. "Take no prisoners, that's what's been running through my head."

"Don't blame you," Proctor observed. "Bastards like that deserve whatever they get."

"What bothers me most is that I requested Jack for this assignment. Except for me, he wouldn't have died . . . not like that."

"Well, you shouldn't fault yourself too much. You didn't have no crystal ball when you started out."

"You ever lost a partner in the line of duty, Will?"

"Reget to say I lost two, Billy Suggs and Art Parnell. Those boys was salt of the earth."

"Did their killers get away?"

"Nope," Proctor said with a gravelly chuckle. "Tracked 'em down and shot 'em deader'n hell. Danced on their graves too."

"So you know what I mean," Gordon said. "About no reason to take prisoners."

" 'Course I do, but there's one little hitch."

"What's that?"

"You gotta give 'em an even break. Don't shoot a man like a dog even if he is one. You'd never be able to live with yourself."

"Sure, why not?" Gordon said, nodding to himself. "An even break and then shoot the son of a bitch. Sounds like justice to me."

Proctor laughed. "Frank, I think you would've done good back in Old Oklahoma. Brought most of our prisoners in feet first."

A few minutes later they pulled into the yard of the Smith ranch. The house was dark and Gordon left the headlights on as they stepped from the car. After knocking on the front door, they stood waiting for Smith or his wife to awaken. A light came on in the hallway, and a man opened the door, trousers hastily thrown on over dirty long johns. His eyes were gummed with sleep.

"Wha'cha want?"

"Lookin' for the Smiths," Proctor said. "I'm Deputy Marshal Will Proctor. Who're you?"

"Charlie Bohannon. Ray Smith hired me to look after the place."

"Are they gone?"

"Yep." Bohannon squinted into the headlights of the car. "Moved into Fairfax day before yesterday. Got a house on East Tenth Street."

Proctor frowned. "Why'd they move?"

"Didn't say and I didn't ask. Mr. Smith said he'd come by ever' day and gimme a hand with the stock."

"How long'd he hire you for?"

"Well, he said it'd be a month, anyway. Maybe longer."

"Obliged for your help, Mr. Bohannon. Sorry we woke you up."

"Yeah, me too."

The door closed and they walked back to the car. As Gordon turned the Chevy around, Proctor grunted, "What d'you make of that?"

"I don't like it," Gordon said. "They moved the day Jack's body was dumped in Pawhuska. I want some answers."

"Hell, let's go find 'em then. Hired man said it's a house on East Tenth. Smith's truck won't be hard to spot."

On the way back to Gray Horse, they came around a slight curve. A Studebaker sedan was parked across the road, and in the headlights, they saw three men with guns behind the car. The dirt road was barely wide enough for two vehicles, and trees on either side made it impossible to swerve onto the shoulder. Gordon jammed on the brakes, and as the Chevy skidded to a stop, the men behind the Studebaker opened fire. A shotgun exploded the right headlight and a pistol drilled a hole in the windshield.

Gordon hooked the gear shift into neutral and the Chevy rolled forward. He and Proctor bailed out the doors and ran for the trees, guns in hand. The Chevy slammed into the side of the Studebaker and stalled, one headlight still burning, the gunmen visible in the reflected glare. The shotgun boomed from the tail end of the Studebaker, buckshot skinning the bark off trees around Gordon. His Colt automatic extended at shoulder level, he aimed at the muzzle flash and fired three quick shots. A man lurched forward, dropping the shotgun, and fell facedown in the dirt.

Proctor knelt behind a tree on the opposite side of the road. The other men opened fire with pistols, slugs zithering past him with a dull whine. He took careful aim at the man nearest the hood of the Studebaker and feathered the trigger on his old Colt Peacemaker. The slug nicked the gunman in the left arm and he bellowed a curse, dropping his pistol and clutching at his bloody arm. The third man jumped behind the wheel of the Studebaker, grinding the starter, and swung the wheels onto the shoulder and back onto the road. Gordon and Proctor continued to fire, blowing out windows, as the wounded man hopped on the running board, clinging to the door frame. The Studebaker sped off into the night.

Gordon stepped from the trees. He walked forward as Proctor crossed the road, and they stopped in front of the fallen shotgunner. The man's shirtfront was pocked with blood and his eyes stared blankly at the starry sky. Proctor began shucking empties and reloading his Colt.

"Guess we know the score now," he said. "Tried to scare us off by killin' Jack and that didn't work. So they figured they'd better go on and kill us."

"Looks that way," Gordon agreed. "Damned near worked too."

"You shoot that automatic pretty good, pardner. Knew we had 'em when you knocked out the shotgun."

"Too bad he didn't live to talk."

"You got any doubt who sent 'em?"

"No, Will, none at all."

Later that night they delivered the body to the funeral home in Pawhuska. Sheriff Otis Crowley was awakened by phone and called down to the mortuary in the basement. He hemmed and hawed but finally identified the dead man as Joe Johnson. His next admission came ever harder.

He told them the dead man had worked for Harry Grammer.

The sun rose higher over hills studded with blackjack. Gordon and Proctor drove west on the main road from Pawhuska, wind whistling through the bullet hole in the windshield. The right front fender and headlight were riddled with buckshot.

They took it for granted that the sheriff had called Harry Grammer, or Big Bill Hale. Last night, after leaving the mortuary, they'd talked it over and concluded Crowley would try to cover himself with a phone call. But they didn't care one way or the other, for they finally had a reason to confront Grammer. The man they were certain had killed Jack Spivey.

Shortly before eight o'clock they pulled into the driveway. A man who fitted Grammer's description was talking with a younger man at the rear of the house. The younger man bore a striking resemblance to Ernest Burkhart, and they assumed it was Burkhart's brother, Bryan. The men stopped talking as Gordon and Proctor climbed out of the Chevy.

"Harry Grammer," Proctor called out as they approached. "Have to say you're as ugly as ever. Some things never change."

Grammer scowled. "What do you want, Proctor?"

"Where's your manners, Harry? This here's Special Agent Gordon, with the U.S. Bureau of Investigation. We're here to ask you some questions."

"Questions about what?"

"Joe Johnson," Gordon said in a level voice. "I'm sure you already know he was killed in a shootout last night. We understand he was one of your men."

"Not for a while," Grammer said with a smug look. "I fired Joe two, maybe three weeks ago. Got to be a real troublemaker."

"And I suppose you have witnesses?"

"Damn right, he does," Burkhart said with a grin. "I'm the foreman and I was standin' right there. Heard Mr. Grammer fire him myself."

Gordon looked at him. "You must be Bryan Burkhart. There's a definite family resemblance." He glanced down at Burkhart's feet. "Of course, Ernest doesn't wear cowboy boots."

Burkhart cocked his head. "Case you hadn't noticed, this here's a ranch. What's my boots got to do with anything?"

"A ranch?" Gordon said in mock disbelief. "I was told all the liquor in Osage County flows out of here. Heard you make your own moonshine."

"You were told wrong," Grammer countered. "Our only business is cows. Everybody knows that."

"Not everybody," Gordon said. "What we're looking for is a Studebaker sedan in pretty bad shape. Marshal Proctor and I shot it to pieces last night."

"Don't own one," Grammer said. "But even if I did, and even if it was shot to pieces, it wouldn't matter. Know why?"

"No, why?"

"There'll be icicles in hell before you convict a white

man of anything in Osage County. You're wasting your time."

"Don't bet on it." Gordon pointed off into the woods. "Heard you have a still hidden in those trees. Maybe we'll find the Studebaker down there."

"Show me a warrant," Grammer said. "Otherwise, get off my property."

"Well, don't you see, I think you're a blue-faced liar. Why not prove me wrong?"

"Watch yourself," Burkhart bridled. "You push it and I'll clean your plow. *Muy* damn quick."

Proctor laughed. "Sonny, you shut your trap or I'll arrest you. Just on general principle."

Burkhart started forward. The old Colt Peacemaker appeared in Proctor's hand and he whacked the younger man over the head with the barrel. The thunk of metal on bone stopped Burkhart in his tracks and the light went out in his eyes. He fell to his knees, then pitched forward to the ground.

Gordon studied him a moment, then looked at Grammer. "We know you killed Jack Spivey, and that was a big mistake. We'll come for you one of these days."

"Come ahead," Grammer said roughly. "You don't scare me."

"No, but I might bury you."

Gordon walked to the car. Proctor crawled into the passenger seat and they drove off down the road. Grammer watched them into the distance.

He wondered how he would explain it to Big Bill.

Chapter Sixteen

"You're a regular rooster with that old cannon."

"Lay it across a fella's noggin and down he goes. Never fails."

"You sure raised a knot on Burkhart's head."

"Never could stand a cock-o'-the-walk throwin' his weight around. Maybe it'll teach him some manners."

"I doubt anything would teach that bunch manners."

"Well, at least he's got a sore head."

Gordon thought it was small consolation. Burkhart had been laid out cold and Grammer had been put on warning. But apart from the personal satisfaction it brought, they had accomplished little. There was still no hard evidence.

On the way back to Pawhuska, they swapped ideas for moving the case along. Proctor finally suggested that they call on Ray Smith and pressure him to talk. They were both convinced Smith was involved, and his sudden move to Fairfax following Spivey's death further aroused their suspicions. Then too they'd been ambushed last night immediately after leaving Smith's ranch. The whole thing smelled fishy.

They arrived in Fairfax late that morning. The town was small, formerly a trade center for farmers and ranchers in the outlying area. But it was Saturday, and the main street was clogged with oil workers from rigs in the southwestern part of the county. Traffic was heavy, and it took some time to move through the business district and locate East Tenth Street. They found Smith's truck and his wife's Reo sedan parked in the driveway of a two-story frame house.

Nettie Brookshire, the Smiths' servant girl, met them at the door. She was plump and shy, her eyes downcast, and they could smell pork chops cooking in the kitchen. As she closed the screen door, Ray Smith came into the hallway from the dining room. His features were guarded.

"You've come at a bad time," he said. "We were just fixin' to have dinner."

"Sorry to bother you," Gordon said. "We need to ask you a few questions."

"I'm not up to your questions when food's on the table. Come back in an hour or so."

"Nossir, I reckon not," Proctor said brusquely. "We're here and we're gonna talk. Like to see your wife too."

Rita came in from the dining room, an apron over her dress. She said something to Nettie, and the girl looked relieved as she fled to the kitchen. Smith muttered a curse under his breath and led them into the living room. He dropped onto an overstuffed couch, with Rita beside him, and Gordon and Proctor took chairs. Gordon glanced around at the well-appointed furnishings.

"Nice place," he said. "You folks rent it?"

"We own it," Smith said sharply. "What the Sam Hill's that got to do with anything?"

"Just wondering why you moved into town."

"We're back and forth between the ranch and here whenever it suits us. What's with all the questions?"

"We went by the ranch last night," Gordon informed him. "Your hired man told us you'd moved into town indefinitely."

"Yeah?" Smith said in a surly voice. "That some of your business?"

"We're makin' it our business," Proctor said bluntly

"After we left your place last night, three men waylaid us on the road, and we killed one of them. Thought you might know something about it."

"What a crock!" Smith grated. "You tryin' to say I was in on it?"

"Good question," Gordon said. "Maybe you heard about the insurance salesman who was killed Tuesday night? His name was Jack Spivey."

"I read about it in the paper. What's your point?"

"Spivey was one of my agents. He was working undercover on the Osage murders. Didn't Ernest and Mollie tell you?"

Smith avoided his gaze. "We don't talk to them much."

"Why is that?" Gordon glanced at Rita. "You don't talk to your sister?"

"Not anymore," she said in a small voice. "We had a falling out when Mama died."

"Oh?" Gordon sensed he'd stumbled onto something. "What happened?"

There was a moment of oppressive silence. Rita finally placed her hand on Smith's arm. "Tell them," she said softly. "One of their agents was killed, Ray. We can trust them."

Smith hesitated, staring at her hand. "Didn't know who to trust," he said, looking at Gordon. "You popped up out of nowhere tellin' everybody you was investigating the murders. But the way it looked to us, you was workin' real close with the sheriff. That'd be the same as workin' with Hale."

Gordon played dumb. "What's Hale got to do with it?"

"Just about everything," Smith said. "He killed Rita's mother and sister, and her cousin, Henry Roan. Or at least he had 'em killed."

"What makes you think that?"

"Hell, it don't take a lot of brains. Kill off the whole family and all the headrights go to Mollie. Rita and me are next on their list."

"What makes you so sure?"

"Lost my temper after Miz Lizzie was killed. Accused Ernest of doping her moonshine with poison and he got plenty hot. 'Course he denied it."

"And what did Mollie say?"

"Why, what else, she sided with Ernest. Ordered me and Rita out of her house."

"So she didn't believe you?"

"Nope," Smith said dully. "Like to got hysterical when I accused Hale of masterminding the whole thing. Ernest's convinced her Hale hung the moon."

Gordon nodded thoughtfully. "That's why you turned your back on Hale at Mrs. Kile's funeral. I remember wondering about it at the time."

"No way Ernest wouldn't've told Hale what I said. So he knows I know, and that mean he's got his sights on me and Rita. Somebody's gonna try to snuff our wick."

"Is that why you moved into town?"

"Safer here than the ranch," Smith acknowledged. "I got a pistol and a shotgun, and we keep our eyes open. Anybody tries anything will wish he hadn't."

"I'm sure," Gordon agreed. "Tell me, what made you suspect Hale?"

"'Cause Ernest don't have brains enough to pour piss out of a boot. Saw the way things was headed after Miz Lizzie was killed, and put two and two together. Hale's the one pullin' the strings."

"For what it's worth, Marshal Proctor and I think the same way. We just haven't been able to prove it as yet."

Smith gave him a wooden look. "Wish t'hell you'd hurry things along. Rita and me feel like we're livin' on borrowed time."

"We're doing our best, Mr. Smith. Our level best."

Proctor was as amazed by what they'd heard as Gordon. On their way out of town, Gordon shook his head. "You ever see two people any more scared?"

"Got reason to be," Proctor said, staring at the bullet hole in the windshield. "You know what I think?"

"What's that?"

"I think Ray better keep his shotgun handy."

The Osage Grill was practically empty. Gordon and Proctor had stopped by for a late lunch after returning to Pawhuska. They were lingering over a last cup of coffee.

Proctor rolled a cigarette. He lit up, and in the flare of the match, his features appeared troubled. He dropped the spent match in an ashtray and exhaled a streamer of smoke. Gordon watched him a moment.

"Something bothering you?"

"Just thinkin' about Smith," Proctor said. "All this time, I had him pegged as one of the killers. Not usually that wrong about a man."

Gordon smiled. "Don't be so hard on yourself. I had him on my list too."

"You remember he said Hale knows he knows?"

"Sure, because he braced Ernest."

"Well, other side of the coin, Hale knows *we* know. Which mean he's got a lot of people to kill before he puts a lid on this thing. Bastard acts like he's God A' mighty."

"We'll get him," Gordon said with conviction. "All we need is a break. A solid lead."

"Still think Grammer's the key," Proctor said. "Maybe we oughta go back out there and search his still. Might find that Studebaker we shot up."

"Will, it wouldn't be there. Last night, his boys ditched that car someplace where it'll never be found. We wouldn't have found the man you wounded either."

"Yeah, I suppose you're right. Grammer likely has him hid out somewheres safe. Damn shame."

"Let's walk over to the hotel. I want to make some

notes on Smith while it's fresh in my mind. Especially the part where he accused Burkhart."

The desk clerk waved to them as they entered the lobby. "Mr. Gordon," he said, holding out a slip of paper. "I have a message for you. Chief Lookout called."

Gordon studied the slip. "You have here 'Come see me.' Was that all he said?"

"Yessir, he was sorta stingy with words. You know how these old Osages are. Every word's a pearl."

"When did he call?"

"Hour ago, maybe a little more."

Gordon nodded, turning toward the door. Proctor followed him out, and they walked to the Chevy, which was parked at the curb. As they drove away, Proctor started rolling another cigarette. His expression was quizzical.

"Don't sound like an invitation to supper. Wonder what he wants?"

"One way to find out," Gordon said. "We'll go talk to him."

Ten minutes later they pulled into the yard. Chief Lookout was seated beneath his favorite shade tree, watching his wife hang damp laundry on a clothesline. He smiled as they approached, motioning them to take a seat on the grass. He seemed in a jolly mood.

"Still kickin', huh?" he said with a little cackle. "Hear people been shootin' at you."

"Have for a fact, Chief," Proctor bandied right back. "So far, they missed and we didn't. We're still foggin' a mirror."

"Plenty good," Lookout observed. "Couldn't tell you if you was dead."

Gordon leaned forward, "Tell us what, Chief?"

"You 'member you asked me send out word? Find Osage willin' to talk?"

"You've found someone?"

"Somebody don't want name used. All same, figger you like to hear."

"What is it?"

"Big Bill Hale," Lookout said, a wicked glint in his eyes. "Took insurance policy on Henry Roan three months before he got shot. Made heap money on Henry."

"Hale was the beneficiary?" Gordon said, clearly astounded. "How much did he receive?"

"Twenty-five thousand."

"When?"

"Two days ago."

"You're sure about this? Whoever told you couldn't be mistaken?"

Lookout handed him a scrap of paper. "Guv'mint man like you find out easy enough. No mistake."

On the paper, laboriously printed in pencil, were the words "Capital Life Insurance Company in Denver." Gordon passed it across to Proctor, then turned back to Lookout. His mouth split in a grin.

"Chief, that's the best news I've had since I got here. Let's hope it's true."

"'Course it's true," Lookout said with a cockeyed smile. "Big Bill deposit check in bank yesterday. Citizen's National Bank, one he owns."

"How do you know?"

"How you think I know? Somebody with no name tell me. Now I tell you."

Gordon and Proctor left him sitting under the tree looking pleased with himself. They drove back to the hotel, hardly able to credit their sudden good fortune, and hurried up to Gordon's room. He got the operator on the line and placed a long-distance call to the Capital Life Insurance Company. After being transferred from operator to operator, he finally reached the company switchboard in Denver. He was connected with Herbert Wallace, chief claims adjuster.

Wallace was reluctant to divulge confidential information. Gordon advised him he could talk on the phone, or turn his records over to the Bureau's office in Denver. Though indignant, Wallace responded with alacrity to the threat, and revealed everything. Gordon took notes as he asked questions and listened intently to the answers. The call lasted some fifteen minutes, and when he hung up, he nodded with satisfaction. He turned to Proctor.

"They almost didn't pay the claim," he said. "When they found out Roan had been murdered, they sent an investigator here. He spoke with our friend Sheriff Crowley, who of course didn't tell us."

"Lemme guess," Proctor said. "Crowley didn't tell him boo about headrights, or our investigation, or anything else. Just another drunk Injun that got himself murdered after a bar fight over a woman. Did I miss anything?"

"That was the gist of it. Crowley told him Hale's a banker, the biggest rancher in the county, and an all-around pillar of the community. Too bad he didn't know about our investigation."

"Yeah," Proctor grouched. "Who took out the policy?"

Gordon smiled. "Hale paid the first year's premium in advance, by personal check. But the claims investigator authenticated Roan's signature on the policy. So they paid off."

"Hell's bells and little fishes, that'd raise the red flag for me!"

"Will, you took the words right out of my mouth."

"So what are we gonna do?"

"Let's go talk to Big Bill."

The sun dipped below the horizon in a fiery splash of gold. They drove into Hale's graveled driveway and stopped in front of the house. A brindle bulldog began barking as they got out of the car.

Hale pushed through the door onto the porch. "Hush there, Duke!" he ordered, and the bulldog obediently waddled around the corner of the house. "Agent Gordon. Marshal Proctor." He came down the steps, hand outstretched. "This is an unexpected pleasure."

Gordon ignored the handshake. "We're here on official business, Mr. Hale. We'd like to ask you some questions."

"Well of course," Hale said, dropping his hand. "I assume it must be important for you to call on a Saturday evening. How can I be of help?"

"You were the beneficiary on a life insurance policy taken out by Henry Roan. We understand the insurance company paid you twenty-five thousand dollars."

"As a matter of fact, I deposited the check just yesterday. Do you know someone in my bank?"

"How we came by the information isn't important. What does interest us is why Roan took out the policy only three months before he was murdered."

"I sold him some cows on credit," Hale said with a look of complete candor. "The insurance policy was my collateral."

"That's a lot of cows," Proctor said skeptically. "Sounds like about a tenth of your herd. Where'd Roan have grazeland?"

"I have no idea," Hale replied. "Trucks hauled them out of here, and I didn't ask. I can show you the bill of sale if you like. Why are you asking all these questions?"

"Henry Roan wasn't a rancher," Gordon said. "Why would he suddenly decide to go into the cattle business?"

"Who knows?" Hale said with an indifferent shrug. "The man came to me wanting to buy cows and I sold them to him. It's as simple as that."

"Roan had three headrights," Gordon noted. "He was earning a fortune in oil royalties. Why would he dabble in cattle?"

"Well, it wasn't my place to ask him his business.

He agreed to the terms and I sold him the cows."

"Don't make sense," Proctor said. "He could've paid for the cows a dozen times over with his oil money. Hell, if he wanted, he could've bought your whole herd."

"Marshal, he asked for credit, and as you are aware, that's the way many rich Osages operate. But he was a known drinker and drove fast cars, so I required some form of collateral. We decided an insurance policy was the simplest way."

"Still don't rhyme," Proctor persisted. "Why not just take a lien on his oil royalties?"

"Too cumbersome," Hale said. "If he defaulted, it would have taken a year or more to collect from the Bureau of Indian Affairs. Insurance was a better choice."

Proctor snorted. "'Specially if he was murdered."

"What the hell's that supposed to mean?"

"You paid the insurance premium," Gordon interjected. "Wouldn't it have been the natural thing for Roan to pay it? After all, he was the debtor."

Hale waved it off. "I included the premium in the price of the cows. And just so we're clear on this, that was at Roan's request. I told all this to the insurance investigator."

"Have all the answers, don't you?" Gordon's eyes hooded with disgust. "How'd you convince Roan to sign the insurance application? Was he blind drunk on Grammer's moonshine?"

"I don't care for your implications, Agent Gordon. It was a business deal, nothing more."

"Some deal," Gordon said. "Henry Roan signed away his life."

"Wait a minute now!" Hale protested. "Are you accusing me of Roan's murder?"

"No, not yet," Gordon replied. "But Grammer's already told you we're close. I think you're feeling the heat."

"Ridiculous," Hale scoffed. "I don't know what you're

talking about. Harry Grammer and I hardly ever see each other. You spouting pure hogwash."

"Call it what you like," Gordon said. "Hogwash or truth, it'll put you in the electric chair. Not just for Henry Roan either."

"Take your accusations and get out of here," Hale said in an aggrieved tone. "I'm going to file a formal complaint with my congressman. You haven't heard the last of this."

"We'll see you around," Gordon said with a stony look. "Your day's about done."

The threat rang hollow. On the drive back to Pawhuska, Proctor and Gordon knew they had failed to implicate Hale, either in insurance fraud or murder. Their failure was all the more onerous because they had yet to establish a link between Hale and Harry Grammer. They were stumped as to their next move.

Proctor glanced over at Gordon. He saw the muscles knotted at the back of the younger man's jaw, lines of frustration etched in his features. Nothing sapped a man's vigor like an investigation where every lead fizzled out like a burnt match. There were days when it all turned to smoke.

"What're you stewing on?" Proctor said. "You look like you could chew nails and spit tacks."

"I'm driving to Dallas tonight," Gordon said, as though he'd just made up his mind. "Haven't been home in two months, and that's way too long. I'll be back sometime Monday."

"Good idea," Proctor said. "Seein' your wife and kids will give you a breather. Get your head clear."

"You'll hold down the fort?"

"Not likely Hale'll kill anybody in the next couple days. Don't worry about it."

Gordon thought it was easier said than done. He knew

he would worry about Hale and Grammer and the Osages all the way to Dallas and back. But the old lawman was on the mark about one thing. He needed a breather.

A few days off from thinking about murder.

Chapter Seventeen

The night was dark and warm, stars sprinkled through the sky like pinpricks of fire. Cottony clouds scudded along on a southerly breeze, momentarily blanketing the land in dappled starlight. A bolt of lightning flickered and died far on the westward horizon.

A black Maxwell Roadster crested a rise through forested hills. John Ramsey was at the wheel and Asa Kirby rode in the passenger seat. Their faces glowed in the dim light from the dashboard, and their features were set in a sober cast. Kirby flipped a spent cigarette out the open window.

"Too bad about the girl," he mused. "She ain't exactly gettin' a fair shake."

"Wrong place, wrong time," Ramsey said. "Lots of people go under 'cause they're where they wasn't supposed to be. Happens all the time."

"Yeah, but she's hired help, for Chrissake. How'd you like your sister to get it just by accident?"

"I don't have a sister."

"C'mon, Johnny, you know what I mean."

"What d'you wanna do," Ramsey said, "sneak her out the bedroom window before the fireworks go off? Grammer'd ream us new assholes."

"Wasn't sayin' that," Kirby objected. "Just sayin' it's a damn shame. She's a cute little thing."

"She's fat as a goddamn sow! I wouldn't screw her with your pecker."

"Still say it ain't right."

Harry Grammer had picked them for the job day before yesterday. For the past two nights, they'd cruised past the house, sometimes parking across the street, inspecting the layout. Nettie Brookshire slept in a downstairs bedroom, and they'd watched her moving through the house, turning out the lights, before she went to bed. Kirby had seen her only a few times, but he kept wishing there was a way she might be spared. He liked fat girls.

The job was complicated by Ray Smith's wary manner. Smith and his wife never went out at night, and his wife never accompanied him when he went to check on the ranch east of Gray Horse. Sometimes they drove into downtown Fairfax for groceries, yet it was always in daylight—too risky to try shooting them. A car bomb might have worked, but no one in the crew knew how to rig such a device and escape alive. So Grammer finally decided there was only one solution. They would blow up the house.

Ramsey took a curve without slowing down. There was a metallic *clink* from the backseat and Kirby whirled around. "Take it easy!" he yelped. "You wanna get us killed?"

"Crap, I'm only doing thirty-five. Any slower and we'll be crawlin'."

"Any faster'n and our butts are mincemeat. Let's get there in one piece."

Explosives were readily available in the oil fields. When a well was drilled and the oil wouldn't flow, nitroglycerin bombs with dynamite detonators were used to free the oil from the paysand. In the backseat, cushioned in blankets, were three cylindrical tubes, each four feet in length and constructed of rolled tin. The bottom of each tube was packed with sand, followed by two quart bottles of nitro. Sand was then packed on top of the nitro, with a stick of dynamite and a long fuse, and the top of the canister crimped closed. The finished product was a bomb that would bring down a mountain.

Kirby thought three canisters was overkill. On Grammer's order, he had bought them in a no-questions-asked deal from a freelance demolitions man in the oil fields. He tried to tell Grammer that one canister was enough to demolish a house, only to be informed he'd missed the purpose of the job. Grammer wanted an explosion of such magnitude that there was no chance Ray and Rita Smith would survive the blast. Grammer was the boss, and Kirby had done as he was told. But he still thought it was a waste of nitro.

Shortly after midnight, Ramsey turned onto East Tenth Street and doused his headlights. All the homes were dark, and he parked one house down from the Smiths'. His job was to stay in the car and act as a lookout, just in case anyone happened along. The Maxwell's engine was tuned to a low murmur, and he left it running, the gear shift in neutral. He glanced in the rearview mirror as Kirby stepped out of the car.

Nothing moved along the street. Kirby spread the blankets aside and gingerly removed one of the canisters. He cradled it in his arms, careful of his balance, and walked to the rear of the house. He knelt down, tender as a gigolo with a new lover, and placed the canister on the ground by the back door. Twice more he returned to the car, watching his step, and positioned one canister at the east side of the house and the other on the west side. He realized his forehead was covered with cold sweat.

Timing was critical in the last step. The dynamite fuses were trimmed for three minutes, sufficient to get back to the car and take off before the blast. Kirby struck a kitchen match, lighting the fuse on the west side, then raced to the rear of the house, striking another match, and finally lit the fuse on the east side. He figured a minute or so had elapsed, but he wasn't taking any chances, and sprinted toward the car. He tripped, grabbing at a rose trellis by the front porch, and brought it crashing down as he fell to the ground. He jumped to his feet and ran for the car.

The front door burst open. Ray Smith, awakened by the noise, rushed out with a double-barreled shotgun. The car pulled away from the curb as he bounded down the steps into the yard. He threw the shotgun to his shoulder and fired, the earsplitting roar deafening in the still night. He fired again as the car gained speed and barreled off down the street. Out of the corner of his eye, he caught a flash of light and turned, still gripping the empty shotgun. He saw sparks on the ground at the side of the house.

"What the—"

The nitro bombs went off in a cyclonic blast. A towering fireball lifted the house from its foundation within a vortex of molten brilliance. For an instant the house sat uprooted and suspended, and then it disintegrated in a thunderous holocaust, blown apart in a tangled mass of boards and timber. The roof buckled, shredded to splinters in the next instant, and collapsed in a fiery shower of debris. As though some demonic force had scorched the earth, flames licked through the twisted pyre, leaping skyward. A billowing cloud of smoke blotted out the stars.

Ray Smith lay sprawled in the middle of the street.

Gordon arrived at the scene as night faded away to dawn. After the sheriff had called him at the hotel, he'd called Proctor and told him to drive over from Hominy. The old lawman was standing by his Model T.

The street was blocked by a truck from the Fairfax fire department. Firemen were hosing down the smoking rubble, and spraying cinders on the roofs of nearby houses. Windows were shattered in every house on the block, and neighbors, still dressed in their bedclothes, were gathered in the yards. They stared at the rubble in dazed disbelief.

The home of Ray and Rita Smith was gone. What remained was a smoldering ruin that looked more like volcanic ash, vaporous steam rising from where the fire hoses played over the debris. The concrete foundation had disintegrated beneath the force of the explosion, and in its place was a crater twenty feet in diameter and almost five feet deep. Here and there body parts were visible, and the charred torsos of two women, one headless, still lay in the wreckage. The stench of burnt flesh drifted on a dewy breeze.

Gordon was speechless for a moment. He stared at the devastation until finally he found his voice. "Will, what the hell happened here?"

"Blew 'em to kingdom come," Proctor said. "I only just got here myself, so I haven't talked with Crowley. Looks like somebody set off a big goddamn bomb."

"Were there any survivors?"

"Don't rightly see how there could be. Blowed a hole in the ground the size of a barn."

"Ray Smith said he and Rita were next. No question about it now."

"Wonder why Hale waited so long?"

The date was May 28, quickly dubbed by the newspapers as "Bloody Monday." Gordon had returned from Dallas a week ago, refreshed by a few days with his wife and children. He came back invigorated, his spirits restored, certain a break in the case lay hidden somewhere in the files. Every day for the past week, he and Proctor had combed through the files, discussing each murder in minute detail, searching for something they'd overlooked. They found nothing.

Sheriff Crowley was talking with a man in a rubberized

coat and a fireman's helmet. He saw Gordon and quickly excused himself, crossing the street from the fire truck. His features were slack and he appeared shaken. He shook his head.

"Never saw nothin' like it," he muttered. "Fire chief says it had to be nitroglycerin, and lots of it. Tornado couldn't've done no worse."

"Not from the looks of it," Gordon agreed. "Where would anyone get that much nitroglycerin?"

"Why it's common as dirt in the oil fields. They use it to bust open paysand that won't flow on its own. Call it 'shootin' a well.'"

"Maybe we can find somebody who sold nitro in quantity. That might be the lead we need."

"You'd be talkin' till your tonsils wore out. Probably a thousand men handles nitro on a regular basis."

"Anybody pull through?" Proctor asked. "I see a couple bodies there in the rubble."

"That's the women," Crowley said. "One without a head is Nettie Brookshire, the servant girl. Other one's Rita Smith."

"What about Ray?"

"Got his balls blowed off."

"His balls?"

"That and other things," Crowley said. "Neighbor saw Ray come out and fire a shotgun at a car drivin' away. Then the house exploded and something chopped off Ray's balls and his tallywhacker. Might as well chopped off his head."

Gordon looked at him. "Are you saying Smith's alive?"

"Yeah, leastways from what I've been told. They took him to the hospital before I got here."

"Who's the neighbor?"

"Clyde Simpson."

"I want to talk to him."

Simpson was an elderly man, still in his long johns and a frayed bathrobe. He was standing on the lawn of his house, his wife clutching his arm. Crowley signaled to him, calling his name, and he ambled forward in dog-earred house slippers. His features seemed dulled with terror.

Crowley made the introductions. Under Gordon's questioning, Simpson explained that he had a bladder problem, and sometime after midnight he got up to relieve himself. On his way to the bathroom, he heard a shotgun go off and hurried to the front window in the living room. He saw Ray Smith fire a second round at a car as it passed the streetlight on the corner. Then the house went up in a ball of fire.

"Knocked me down," Simpson went on, touching a gash over his brow. "Blew out my windows and flyin' glass come at me like sleet. Wonder I wasn't blinded."

"You're a lucky man," Gordon said, nodding in agreement. "Did you get a look at the car?"

• "Didn't see much but taillights. I was lookin' mostly at Ray."

"What happened after the explosion?"

"Well, first off, I called the fire department. Then I run out to where Ray was layin' in the street. Never saw nothin' like it in my life. Got him right between the legs."

Simpson was able to contribute little more. Gordon and Proctor left Crowley at the scene, and drove to the Fairfax hospital. There, outside the emergency room, they met with Dr. Amos Belton, the attending physician. He told them Smith had lost his penis and testicles, and suffered massive trauma to the groin. He'd staunched the bleeding, and administered morphine, but there was nothing else to be done. He was amazed that Smith was still alive.

Belton allowed them into the emergency room. Ray Smith was on a table, a sheet tented over his midsection, his face drained of color. His eyes were closed, and he looked curiously at peace, as though he'd dropped off for a nap. A nurse backed away as Gordon and Proctor moved to the table. Belton joined them.

"There's no pain," he said quietly. "Thank God for morphine."

Gordon nodded. "Any chance he'll regain consciousness?"

"Well, he's in and out. We're just trying—"

Smith's eyes fluttered open. He stared at the overhead light, then blinked, his gaze shifting to Belton and Proctor, and finally to Gordon. A faint smile tugged at the corner of his mouth.

"Told you . . . they'd . . . get . . . me."

"Yes, I remember." Gordon leaned closer. "Did you see the men in the car? Do you know them?"

"Got Rita . . . too."

"Ray, try to think about the car. Who were they?"

"Got us all."

"Listen to me—"

"Rita . . ."

A small rattling sound escaped Smith's throat. His jaw worked, then his eyes slowly closed, and his chest fell in a last sigh. His features went slack.

Gordon looked down at him with a stab of anger. He thought the dead man's final words were bleak summation. Anna, Lizzie, Henry Roan, Rita, and now Ray.

Got us all . . .

Gordon and Proctor had lunch at the Osage Grill. Afterward, they walked over to the hotel to check for messages. David Turner had called at 10:19 that morning.

Upstairs, Gordon placed a call to Oklahoma City. There was static on the line, but it cleared as the connection was completed. The secretary at the Bureau office buzzed him through to SAC Turner.

"Hello, Dave," Gordon said. "I'm returning your call. What's up?"

"We have a problem," Turner replied. "Or perhaps I should say, *you* have a problem. Deputy Director Hoover called me early this morning."

"What's he want now?"

"Your scalp, from the sound of it. Hoover got a call from a congressman in the Oklahoma delegation. He charged you with, and I quote, unwarranted and perfidious harassment of William Hale."

"Dave, there were three more murders this morning. A man and his wife and their servant girl were blown to hell with nitroglycerin. Hale is the one responsible."

A moment slipped past while Turner digested the information. "I'll try to cover for you," he said. "Hoover is steaming, and even these new murders might not cool him down. You know how politics work."

"Dave."

"Yes?"

"I don't give a damn about Hoover or his politics. Tell him he can stuff it or assign another agent to the case. I intend to keep the pressure on Hale."

"I'll try to be a little more diplomatic in how I say it."

"Handle it however you think best. Meantime, I'm going back to work."

Gordon hung up. "Hoover's on the warpath," he explained to Proctor. "Got a call from Hale's congressman and ordered me to back off. You heard what I said."

"For my money, it just proves Hale's our boy. So what d'we do now?"

"Let's try Ernest Burkhart again. Something tells me he went along to get along, and got in over his head. Maybe he'll talk if I offer him a deal."

Proctor looked surprised. "You authorized to make deals?"

"Will, if it means breaking the case, we'll get Burkhart a deal. Director Holbrook will back me up."

"After what we saw this mornin', I'd do most anything to stop these murders. Let's go try it on him."

A short while later the maid admitted them to the Burkhart residence. They found Ernest Burkhart seated in the living room, drink in hand, his features downcast. He told them Mollie was devastated by her sister's death and had taken to bed, her emotions shattered. He motioned them to chairs, his breath thick with whiskey.

"You don't look too good yourself," Gordon said. "I get the feeling you know your uncle's gone off the deep end."

"Told you before," Burkhart said with no great conviction. "I don't know what you're talking about."

"Ray Smith accused your uncle of planning to murder Mollie's family for their headrights. Doesn't it bother you, all those people dead?"

"Rita was blown to pieces," Proctor interjected in a draconian voice. "Ray had his balls blown off, *his balls!* He died cursing you and Big Bill."

Burkhart took a long slug of whiskey. "I didn't have anything to do with it. You're talking to the wrong man."

"No, we're not," Gordon said. "Look, it's only a matter of time till we nail Hale and Grammer. Why take the fall for them when you can save yourself? All you have to do is cooperate."

"What do you mean . . . cooperate?"

"Turn state's evidence. A sworn statement with everything you know about these murders. Details on the involvement of your uncle and Grammer."

Burkhart averted his eyes. He stared off into space a moment, then shook his head. "There's nothing to tell because I don't know anything. I can't help you."

"Help yourself," Gordon said evenly. "Otherwise you'll end up on death row—along with your uncle."

"You're wasting your time, Mr. Gordon. Why don't you show yourself the door? We're through here."

"You're making the mistake of your life."

"Then I guess I'll have to live with it."

Gordon seemed on the verge of saying something more. Abruptly he stood, nodding to Proctor, and they filed out of the room. Burkhart drained his glass, the whiskey raw at the back of his throat. He couldn't believe that it had gone so far, so fast. That he'd let himself be drawn into it ever deeper. A reluctant conspirator, more than an accessory.

A murderer.

Chapter Eighteen

A sickle moon hung lopsided in the sky. The night was clear with a freshening breeze out of the southwest. Fireflies blinked and darted in a flitting, aerial circus.

William Hale was seated on his front porch. He rocked back and forth in a cane-bottomed rocker, a cigar wedged in the corner of his mouth. His bulldog, Duke, lay at his feet, and he watched the fireflies with amused interest. He felt content with his world.

The plan was almost complete. Yesterday, with the deaths of Rita and Ray Smith, the months of plotting and maneuvering had come full circle. The mother, her two daughters, their cousin, and one of the daughter's husbands, a total of eight headrights. With Mollie's that meant nine, all under Ernest's control. And he controlled Ernest.

Hale was unconcerned that most people would consider him a monster. Life, in his view, was a journey of transforming ambition to reality. Money was the engine that generated power, and power enabled a man to shape the course of events. His power gave him control of Osage County, and the oil royalties from the headrights would allow him to broaden his horizons. He might one day buy himself a governor.

Harry Grammer thought they'd moved too fast. Five people killed in as many weeks, all from the same family, seemed to Grammer a dangerous enterprise. All the more so when Gordon, the federal agent, had arrived in Pawhuska the week these last murders began. But Hale believed there was an orderly manner to such things, and once he evolved a plan, he saw no reason to change it. There were state and national elections in the offing, and the oil royalties would broaden his power base. Politics was an expensive vice.

Nor was Hale overly concerned about the U.S. Bureau of Investigation. Yesterday afternoon Ernest had dropped by and related how Gordon had offered him a deal. Ernest was a little jittery, but nonetheless dependable, and Hale had dismissed it out of hand. His political connections in Washington were working behind the scenes, and in any event, no one cared about a bunch of dead Indians. In the unlikely circumstance he was charged, there would never be an indictment, much less a trial. He owned the law in Osage County.

"Bill."

His wife, Ethel, opened the screen door. She waited until the rocker stopped. "It's late," she said. "Aren't you coming to bed?"

"Not for a while yet," Hale said, gesturing with his cigar. "I've got to meet with some folks."

"In the middle of the night?"

"Honey, it's still shy of ten."

"Well, even so, it's almost bedtime. Honestly, you work too hard, Bill. What's your meeting about?"

"Just a political matter that has to be resolved. Nothing serious."

"If it's not serious, you should have made them wait until tomorrow. You need your rest."

"I won't be too late."

"Alright, sugar, I'll see you in bed."

The screen door closed. Hale set the rocker in motion, puffing lazy eddies of smoke. At times, he was reminded that he was the most fortunate of men. He and Ethel had been married twenty-four years and he still considered her a prize. She was a good homemaker, a woman of Christian principles, and a fine mother. His daughter, Rebecca, was the mirror image of her mother, and he had plans to marry her off to a financier or a wealthy oil man. Someone who shared his interests in politics and power. A pragmatist.

One thought triggered another, and Hale was reminded that a legacy was forever at peril. He was called "The King of the Osage" by white men and Osage alike, and he reflected on the adage that uneasy lies the head that wears a crown. Someone always wanted to overthrow the king, for power was coveted, and there were men of daring, or fear for their own fiefdom, who would risk it all in a bold play. Whoever wore the crown had to safeguard it against those who might betray him to their own ends. Tonight, he meant to rid himself of one such man.

A car turned into the driveway shortly after ten. The bulldog roused himself with a low growl, and Hale shushed him into watchful silence. Bryan Burkhart got out from behind the wheel of the car, followed by Kelsey Morrison from the passenger seat. Asa Kirby and John Ramsey crawled out of the backseat, and the four men stood waiting in the silty starlight. Hale left the bulldog on the porch, went down the steps, and crossed the yard. He nodded to the men.

"Evening, boys," he said pleasantly. "See you found your way all right."

"Yessir," Bryan said. "Waited till it was good and dark. Nobody saw us."

Apart from Bryan, none of the men had ever been to the ranch. They knew Hale was his uncle, but they had no idea why they'd been summoned here tonight for a secret meeting. They waited to be told.

"You boys do good work," Hale said. "I was real impressed by that bombing over in Fairfax. Nitro takes a special touch."

"That was Asa and John," Bryan said with a note of pride. "Nobody'll forget that job for a while."

Hale chuckled. "I just suspect you're right."

The men shifted uncomfortably. They knew that Harry Grammer operated under the protection provided by Hale. But until now, they were unaware that Hale had knowledge of the murders. The meeting was off to a strange start, and they wondered why they were here. All the more so since Bryan had sworn them to secrecy.

"Guess you're wondering why you're here," Hale said, as though reading their minds. "The plain fact of the matter is, I've decided it's time for a change. Harry Grammer's become a liability."

Bryan squared his shoulders. "What Mr. Hale's sayin' is that Grammer's on his way out. I'll be taking over the liquor operation."

"With my full approval," Hale added, looking around at the men. "Under the new arrangement, each of you boys will have a two percent share in the profits. Every month, after expenses, you get your share in cash." He paused with a broad smile. "Anyone object to making a lot of money?"

The men were too astounded to say anything. Yet they understood that their newfound wealth was in exchange for their loyalty and their silence. After a moment, Kelsey Morrison found the nerve to express a concern that was on all their minds. He addressed the question to Hale.

"We're with you all the way," he said. "But there's liable to be a problem with this takeover. What'd we do about Grammer?"

"I want you to kill him."

Starlight reflected off Hale's bottle-top glasses. Grammer could link him to the murders, and unlike Bryan and Ernest, who were blood relatives, he wasn't to be trusted. Loyalties changed with time and circumstance, and eliminating Grammer seemed to Hale the only recourse. He spread his hands in a sweeping gesture.

"Make it look like an accident," he said. "The sporting crowd and the bootleggers will get the message. Keep it simple."

"Leave it to me and the boys," Bryan said confidently. "We'll give Harry a proper send-off and nobody the wiser."

"One other thing," Hale said. "Take care of a man named Wayne Vaughn. He lives in Pawhuska."

Bryan appeared surprised. "Who's Wayne Vaughn?"

"A lawyer too nosy for his own good. Arrange for him to have an accident."

"Good as done," Bryan said. "We've got some unfinished business with Gordon and Proctor. How you want that handled?"

Hale brushed it off. "I'm working a political angle to take care of them. Let's concentrate on Grammer and Vaughn."

"Anything else?" Bryan asked, motioning to the men. "These boys are all ears."

"Just a reminder," Hale said, his eyes cold behind his glasses. "Anybody who talks out of school won't live to regret it. Our business is nobody else's business. Understood?"

The men dutifully bobbed their heads. A few moments later, as the car pulled out of the driveway, Hale rejoined the bulldog on the porch. He took a seat in the rocker, puffing on his cigar, staring out into the night. He was satisfied everything would go as planned.

Grammer and Vaughn were the last of it. Their unfortunate accidents would write an end to his excursion into murder. What they knew would die with them, and the prospect of it made him grin. He chuckled softly to himself.

Long live the king.

Bright morning sunlight streamed through the windows. Gordon sat in the armchair, watching the wood-bladed fan stir languid air around the ceiling. Proctor was seated in one of the straight-back chairs, paring his nails with a pocketknife, a cigarette dangling from his mouth. Neither of them had spoken for several minutes.

Three days had passed since the explosion in Fairfax. Rita and Ray Smith had been buried in a cemetery plot near Rita's sister, Anna Brown. The funeral was attended by Mollie and Ernest Burkhart, and Big Bill Hale was there with his wife and daughter. Gordon and Proctor were uninvited guests, standing back away from the grave, and largely ignored by the mourners. At the time, Gordon thought of them as ghouls rather than mourners, for Hale and Burkhart looked anything but sad. Mollie was the only one who cried during the graveside service.

The funeral had occupied only part of a day. The other two-and-half days had been spent by Gordon and Proctor in a fruitless investigation. They had toured the oil fields throughout Osage County, searching for anyone who might have sold nitroglycerin in quantity. The purpose of their search was to tie one of Grammer's men to the purchase of nitro, and thereby establish a connection to the bombing. They spoke with "shooters," the demolitions men who exploded paysand, and the managers of equipment stores that supplied the rigs. They came away with nothing for their efforts.

Proctor was of the opinion that one of the shooters was lying. The man's name was Arnie Fitzgerald, and they'd questioned him at length on two separate occasions. But he denied selling nitro, denied knowing any of Grammer's men, and he stubbornly stuck to his story. What he couldn't hide was a look of nervous fear, and they were convinced he knew the identity of the men who had killed Rita and Ray Smith. Still, in the end, like the rest of their investigation, it went nowhere. Fitzgerald wouldn't budge.

"Aren't we a pair?" Proctor said, folding his pocketknife. "Bunch of killers out there runnin' around loose and we're sittin' here feeling sorry for ourselves. It's down-right pathetic."

"I'm open to suggestion," Gordon said, still watching the wobbling turn of the fan. "I've been sitting here wait-ing for a brainstorm to point me in the right direction. So far, I've drawn a blank."

"Pardner, I think we're at the proverbial dead end. Anywhere you turn, you've been there before."

"Amen to that."

"So what're we gonna do?"

"Will, I don't have the least damn idea."

The phone rang. Gordon stretched, still seated in his chair, and snagged the receiver off the hook. "Hello."

"Agent Gordon?"

"Speaking."

"This is Deputy Edwards, over at the sheriff's office. Sheriff Crowley called and asked me to call you."

"What about?"

Deputy Edwards explained in some detail. As he talked, Gordon rose from his chair and motioned Proctor to his feet. When the conversation ended, Gordon jammed the receiver on the hook. His mouth split in a grin.

"We're back in business, Will."

"What the hell happened?"

"Harry Grammer's dead."

"Dead or murdered?"

"Let's go find out."

Thirty minutes later they drove past Grammer's ranch. Two miles farther along, Deputy Noah Perkins was stand-ing on the shoulder beside his patrol car. He motioned them south onto a backcountry dirt road; a half mile or so farther on the sheriff's car, a black Ford, and an ambulance blocked the road. They parked behind the Ford.

The ambulance driver directed them to an old wagon trail that angled southwest off the road. A short distance down the trail, they saw the trunk of a dark blue, four-door

Buick upended over the lip of a shallow ravine. Sheriff Crowley and Dr. Orville Tuttle were standing by the left rear fender of the Buick. Crowley greeted them with a curt nod.

"Just for the record," he said, "I'm still tryin' to cooperate. I know you've been investigating Harry Grammer and his moonshine operation. So I had my office call you."

"Cooperation noted," Gordon said. "What happened here?"

"Why, it appears Grammer got drunk and drove off into that gully. The crash caved in his skull pretty bad. He's deader'n hell."

"Fairly recent," Dr. Tuttle added. "I'd say within the last twelve to fourteen hours. That's a guesstimate, of course, based on the state of rigor mortis."

"Timing sounds right," Crowley said. "While we was waitin' on you to get here, I drove back to the ranch and notified Grammer's wife. She was some broke up, but I finally got her to talk a little. She said he left home last night about eight."

"Was he drinking?" Gordon asked.

"She said he'd had a couple."

"So he managed to get drunk in a hurry. This is less than three miles from his house."

"Who knows?" Crowley said lamely. "Maybe he was drunk as a skunk when he drove off from home. Wouldn't be the first time a wife fudged the truth about her husband."

"We'll talk to her later," Proctor broke in. "Where'd she say Grammer was headed?"

"Burbank," Crowley replied. "Told her he had some business to tend to."

Proctor raised an eyebrow. "Must've been powerful drunk. Drove off the Burbank road and down here, then swerved onto this trail and crashed in that gully." He paused with a skeptical frown. "Went out of his way to find the right spot, didn't he?"

"Will, he was drunk," Crowley protested. "You think a sober man'd drive his car in here?"

Gordon climbed down the side of the gully. Proctor followed him and they moved to the front door of the Buick, which hung open. Harry Grammer was slumped forward, his arms dangling loose, his head on the steering wheel. A deep depression was gouged in his forehead and his left eye protruded from the socket. On the seat was a half empty bottle of bourbon.

"Something funny here," Gordon said. "His head supposedly hit the steering wheel hard enough to kill him. But where's the blood?"

Proctor studied the body. "What're you seein' I'm not? There's blood on his forehead."

"Yeah, but only a little. A fracture that serious should have produced lots of blood. His head's split open."

"What is it you're sayin'?"

"Hit a corpse and you don't get blood. I think he was already dead when the car crashed."

Gordon noticed a spot of dried blood on the side of Grammer's suit jacket. The location puzzled him, for it seemed unlikely blood would have splattered so far from the forehead. He examined the suit jacket closer, then took a grip on the dead man's left arm. The body was stiff with rigor mortis and he pried the arm outward to shoulder level. A small hole, encrusted with blood, was centered below the armpit.

"Look at this," he said. "Somebody shot him."

"I'll be damned," Proctor said, peering at the ragged hole. "Likely got him square in the heart."

"Took more than one man for the job. They had to force his arms overhead and hold him still. Then someone shot him at just the right angle."

"Probably run his car off the road after he left home. Brought him here, got him in a viselock or some such, and shot him. Wouldn't be no trouble to push his car into this gully."

"No question he was murdered," Gordon said. "Then they staged it to look like a drunk in an automobile accident."

"Why go to all that trouble?" Proctor wondered out loud. "Why not just shoot him and have done with it?"

"My money's on Big Bill Hale. Grammer was the only direct connection to the murders, so he had to be silenced. But Hale didn't want it to look like a killing, probably because we were investigating Grammer. He ordered someone to rig an accidental death."

"Someone like Bryan Burkhart. He's Hale's nephew, and with Grammer dead, he'll likely take over the liquor operation. Keeps it in the family."

"We need to talk with Mrs. Grammer," Gordon said. "She might know more than she told the sheriff, or maybe more than he told us. Then we'll buttonhole Bryan Burkhart."

Proctor snorted. "I don't figure him to spill the beans."

"Never know till we try."

They climbed out of the gully. Crowley and Tuttle were still standing at the rear of the Buick. Gordon stopped, dusting off his hands, Proctor at his side. He looked at Tuttle.

"Don't rush to sign the death certificate," he said. "Grammer was shot underneath his left arm."

Tuttle's mouth dropped open. Crowley stepped away from the car with a look of consternation. "Are you sayin' he was murdered?"

"Why don't you ask Big Bill Hale? I just imagine he could tell you who pulled the trigger."

Gordon and Proctor drove back toward Grammer's ranch. Some minutes later, as they turned into the driveway, Gordon was reminded of that day at the Oklahoma City train station. The promise he'd made over Jack Spivey's coffin.

He halfway hoped Burkhart would pull a gun.

Chapter Nineteen

The locomotive chuffed steam at trackside. Passengers rushed to catch the last train of the evening out of Oklahoma City. Departure was scheduled for ten o'clock.

The Midland Valley Flyer provided overnight service through the northeastern part of the state. The terminus was the town of Bartlesville, where the Flyer turned around and provided day service back to Oklahoma City. There were three passenger coaches, a sleeper coach, and a dining car. A club car was attached to the end of the train.

"All aboard!"

The conductor sounded the last call for boarding. Wayne Vaughn hurried from the depot, a ticket in one hand and his briefcase in the other. His homburg hat was askew, glasses perched on the end of his nose, and his shirt collar was damp with sweat. He handed the conductor his ticket.

"Yessir," the conductor said, glancing at the ticket. "You'll be in berth 4A on the sleeper. Porter will show you where it is."

"Can I still get something to eat?"

"Dining car's closed on our overnight run. You can get a sandwich in the club car."

"A sandwich will do just fine. Maybe a whiskey too."

"Nothing like a drop or two to help you sleep. You'll be in Pawhuska before you know it."

"Six in the morning, right?"

"Yessir, you can set your watch by it."

Vaugh stepped aboard. The sleeper was between the dining car and the club car, and he debated dropping his briefcase in his berth. Then, on second thought, he decided the contents, particularly the papers of his deceased client, were too valuable to risk theft. He turned right and made his way through the passenger coaches, the deserted dining car, and the sleeper. The train lurched into motion with a blast of the engineer's whistle.

The club car was almost empty. A few people were seated at banquettes on either side of the car, watching out the windows as the train pulled away from the station. There was a bar, which hadn't served liquor since the advent of Prohibition and now functioned as the late-night kitchen. At the end of the car was a door leading to an open observation platform. Passengers often stepped outside for a breath of fresh air.

Vaughn took a seat at a banquette in the middle of the car. He was exhausted, having caught the train from Pawhuska late that morning; he thought his wisest decision of the day was to book a sleeper berth for the return trip. A waiter appeared with a menu, and Vaughn ordered a roast beef sandwich with coleslaw, and a ginger ale. He'd missed supper at the hospital, what with his client dying and the need to console the family. He suddenly realized he was famished. The waiter returned directly with his order. Vaughn removed a hammered silver flask from his briefcase and poured a dollop of bourbon into the ginger ale glass. The law prohibited both the sale and consumption of alcoholic spirits, whether in a public place or in private. But the ubiquitous flask was carried by men and women across America, and waiters in the club car were under standing order to look the other way. Vaughn wolfed down the sandwich, pausing between bites for sips of the laced ginger ale. The alcohol, more than the food, helped relieve the tension of a long and trying day.

The long-distance call had come into Vaughn's office that morning. George Braveheart, one of his Osage clients, was in the Wesley Hospital in Oklahoma City, and the prognosis wasn't good. The doctors doubted he would last the night, and his wife, her voice choked, begged Vaughn to come as quickly as possible. He canceled his appointments for the day, then called his wife and told her he had no choice but to rush to Braveheart's bedside. On the run, he'd hopped the late morning train out of Pawhuska.

The urgency was due to Braveheart's messy personal affairs. Heavily in debt to the Citizen's National Bank, the Osage had signed over management of his oil headright to the bank's president, William Hale. The contract gave Hale an annual 20 percent fee, and allowed him to disburse funds in such a way that Braveheart was constantly taking new loans with the bank. Just a month ago, to reduce the loan debt, Braveheart had deeded to Hale a parcel of tallgrass prairie in northern Osage County. All of the transactions had taken place without Vaughn's knowledge.

Ten days ago Braveheart's family had committed him to the hospital in Oklahoma City. The Osage was dying of cirrhosis of the liver, brought on by a lifetime of drinking cheap whiskey. The family contacted Vaughn, desperate to straighten out the financial tangle, and provided him with copies of the contracts. Vaughn's legal opinion was that Hale had concocted a fraudulent scheme to bilk Braveheart of more than fifty thousand dollars. He planned to depose Braveheart as to Hale's methods, and create a document that could be used to overturn the bogus contracts. But other clients, and a prolonged court case, had prevented him from taking the deposition. The call that morning, with the news that Braveheart would not last the night, had galvanized him to action. He'd caught the train to Oklahoma City.

Vaughn's nerves were frayed from the ordeal of watching Braveheart die. After the sandwich, he'd had another ginger ale and bourbon, then another, and he was now on his fourth drink. Though the whiskey relaxed him, Braveheart was still very much on his mind, and he wondered how many Osages William Hale had duped with similar schemes. As the train pulled into Chandler, he glanced out the window and saw two men waiting to board. He checked his pocket watch, surprised that it was already eleven-thirty, and remembered the club car closed at midnight. He ordered a last ginger ale.

John Ramsey and Asa Kirby came into the club car as the train got under way. They seated themselves at a banquette, ordering frosty bottles of Coca-Cola, as Vaughn topped his ginger ale with bourbon. Vaughn took a long sip, gazing out the window, and contemplated the thicket of corruption in Osage County. He knew the chances of successfully charging Hale with fraud were practically nil. Like everyone else in Pawhuska, he'd heard of the federal investigator, Frank Gordon. Tomorrow, he intended to contact Gordon and request federal assistance in the case. He thought he might yet find justice for George Braveheart.

Vaughn finished his drink. The club car was empty except for the two men across the way, and he nodded to them as he gathered his briefcase and walked toward the door. They watched him go through the vestibule, steadying himself against the rocking motion of the train, and enter the sleeper coach. Ramsey glanced at the bar and saw the waiters preparing to close for the night. He kept his voice low.

"Think our boy finished off that flask. He oughta sleep like a baby."

"That ain't the half of it," Kirby said with a coarse chuckle. "Before long, he'll sleep like the dead."

"Wonder what he done?" Ramsey said quizzically.

"You know *who* wanted his clock stopped real quick."

"Who cares what he done? You know who says do it, so we'll do it. End of discussion."

"You're sure he's in sleeper 4A?"

"How many times I gotta tell you? I followed him to the station and stood right behind him when he bought the ticket. Heard it myself."

"Hope you heard right."

"'Course I heard right. You think I'm deaf?"

"Just askin', that's all."

Their meeting with Hale had taken place two nights ago. Burkhart had assigned them to Vaughn, while he and Morrison took care of Harry Grammer. Yesterday, they had tailed Vaughn around Pawhuska, looking for a way to make it appear an accident. Then, just that morning, they'd stumbled upon a plan that seemed to them providential. Wayne Vaughn was going to commit suicide.

They finished their Cokes as the club car closed. Then, with wide yawns, they walked through the sleeper coach and the empty dining car to the last passenger car. The overhead lights were dimmed and the other passengers asleep when they found vacant seats near the lavatory. Their plan was to wait until the train crossed the bridge spanning the Arkansas River, into Osage County. The likelihood of the sheriff investigating a suicide was almost nonexistent.

The train rattled across the bridge around four in the morning. The next stop was a half hour away, and the conductor and the porter were catching a nap. Ramsey and Kirby left their seats, careful not to wake anyone, and stealthily made their way back through the dining car and into the sleeper. They paused, waiting for the rush of wind to die down from the vestibule door, then walked quietly to 4A. The berth was a lower bunk.

Their moves were orchestrated in advance. Ramsey slid the curtain aside and tapped Vaughn roughly on the chest. As the lawyer jerked awake and sat up, Kirby bashed him across the head with a lead-loaded blackjack. Vaughn collapsed in the bunk, out cold, clad only in his shorts and undershirt. His other clothing, as well as his glasses and briefcase, was in a web netting attached to the wall. Ramsey pulled him from the bunk and hefted him over his shoulder.

Kirby led the way, opening and closing doors in the vestibule. They moved through the darkened club car, the lawyer hanging limp across Ramsey's shoulder. At the rear of the car, Kirby unlatched the door and they stepped onto the observation platform. The train was traveling at top speed, and the *clackety-clack* of steel wheels on steel rails was almost deafening. A quarter-moon faintly lighted the countryside as Ramsey tossed the lawyer over the platform railing. They watched the body bounce and roll across the studded roadbed.

"Whatta way to go," Kirby said with a foxy smile. "Never felt a thing."

Ramsey nodded. "Yeah, that last step's a killer."

They returned to their seats in the passenger car.

Gordon pushed his plate away. Proctor began rolling a cigarette as the waitress came to clear the table. The lunch crowd had thinned out, and only a few people were still seated at tables. Neither of the men felt any compunction to rush their last cup of coffee.

The newspaper had run a sensational article on the murder of Harry Grammer. Everything people had known for years, but never spoke of openly, was published with the hyperbole normally reserved for distant typhoons and earthquakes. Grammer was reputed to have operated a million-dollar liquor empire and killed a dozen men in his rise to power. Speculation was rampant that the Kansas City mob had executed Osage County's homegrown gangster.

Gordon and Proctor speculated on nothing. Yesterday,

after leaving the murder scene, they had driven to Grammer's ranch. There, they spoke with the widow, Naomi Grammer, who repeated what she'd told the sheriff. Then, down in the woods, they'd gotten their first look at the still, and braced Bryan Burkhart. The new lord of the moonshine operation had feigned shock at the thought that he would kill his beloved boss and mentor. The men working the still had alibied not only Burkhart, but themselves as well. The whole crew had played poker the night of Grammer's murder.

The story rang as false as a lead nickel. Gordon and Proctor knew they were talking with Grammer's killers, and that Burkhart had engineered the half baked accident. But breaking an alibi required a turncoat, someone willing to betray the others, and the men had all but laughed them out of the still. They briefly toyed with the idea of confronting Hale, and just as quickly discarded the notion. Accusations were cheap, and without hard evidence, it was nothing more than hot air. Big Bill would have laughed loudest of all.

After lunch, they walked across to the hotel. As they entered the lobby, the desk clerk gestured to the grouping of chairs by the front window. A wisp of a woman rose from her chair and hurried forward, carrying a briefcase. Her features were gaunt, and her eyes were red and puffy from crying. She stopped in front of them.

"Mr. Gordon?"

"Yes," Gordon said. "Can I help you?"

"My name is Alice Vaughn. May I speak with you . . . in private?"

"About what?"

"Murder."

The desk clerk was craning his neck to hear. Gordon introduced her to Proctor, then led the way upstairs. In his room, he offered her the armchair, and he and Proctor seated themselves in straight-back chairs. He nodded to her.

"You were saying something about murder?"

"I've just come from the funeral home," she said softly. "Sheriff Crowley asked me there to identify the body of my husband."

"Was your husband Osage?"

"No, but he was investigating the fraud of an Osage. A man named George Braveheart."

Gordon looked interested. "Your husband was murdered because of his investigation?"

"Yes, he was." Her chin jutted defiantly. "Dr. Tuttle and the sheriff ruled it a suicide. They said he jumped off the back of a train."

"But you don't think so?"

"Wayne wouldn't have committed suicide."

"Why not?"

"Because he was on his way to see you, Mr. Gordon."

"Me?" Gordon said with some surprise. "Perhaps you'd better explain, Mrs. Vaughn."

Alice Vaughn quickly related her husband's story. She told them how George Braveheart was being defrauded, and how her husband was gathering proof against William Hale. She went on to recount how her husband had been summoned to Oklahoma City, so that he might take a deathbed deposition. She noted that Braveheart had died early yesterday evening.

"Wayne called me from the hospital," she said. "He had the deposition, and he was hurrying to catch the train. He told me he planned to contact you this morning."

"I see," Gordon commented, "And what was in this deposition?"

"It was Mr. Braveheart's account of how he'd been tricked by Hale. How he'd been defrauded of fifty thousand dollars or more."

"And where is the deposition now?"

"Gone." She snapped open the briefcase on her lap. "This is my husband's briefcase, recovered from his sleeper berth on the train. They gave me this and his other effects at the funeral home. The deposition is missing."

"Uh-huh," Gordon said. "And you think his murderers stole it?"

"Well, it could just have easily been Sheriff Crowley. Everyone knows he works for Hale."

"Mrs. Vaughn, I don't mean to sound skeptical, but I need something more to go on than a missing deposition. Why are you so certain your husband was murdered?"

"Because he was only wearing his underclothes."

"Pardon me?"

"No one jumps off a train in their underwear. Wayne's other clothes were neatly folded in his sleeper berth."

"Believe me, Mrs. Vaughn, stranger things have happened. Anything else?"

"Yes." She removed a pair of horn-rimmed glasses from the briefcase. "Wayne's glasses were found in his berth. He couldn't see three feet in front of him without his glasses."

"Frank, she's right," Proctor interjected. "How'd he get from the sleeper to the club car if he couldn't see? Don't make sense."

"No, it doesn't," Gordon agreed. "But without that deposition, it's a blind alley. What he told Mrs. Vaughn on the phone is hearsay."

"But these aren't." She took a sheaf of documents from the briefcase. "I went by Wayne's office before I came here. These are copies of the contracts between Hale and George Braveheart. The proof is here."

Gordon accepted the documents. "Your husband apparently felt the deposition was critical to his case. If the proof is here"—he tapped the contracts—"why did he need the deposition?"

"What's the matter with you?" Her voice was clogged with emotion, "You know very well my husband didn't commit suicide. Those contracts are why he was murdered. Why won't you believe me?"

"I do believe you," Gordon said. "But proving it is another thing entirely. Tell you what, give us a moment to look these over."

The moment stretched into a half hour. There were two contracts, one involving George Braveheart's oil headright, and the other the deed of prairie grazeland to Hale. Gordon and Proctor read through the documents, handing them back and forth, and then read them again. They finally looked up at Alice Vaughn.

"Stripped of legalese," Gordon said, "the contracts are fairly straightforward business agreements. On the other hand, they *indicate*"—he paused to underscore the word—"that Hale's intent was to swindle George Braveheart. All we have to do is prove it."

"You see it, then," she said, staring at him intently. "You see why Wayne was . . . killed?"

"Oh, there's no question Hale had your husband murdered. Finding the men he hired to do it will be the tough part."

"But you'll try? You'll go after Hale and the men who did it? You promise me?"

"We'll do everything in our power to bring Hale to justice. You have my word."

"Thank you," she said with a bleak smile. "Wayne was such a good man, and he tried so hard to help Mr. Braveheart. Justice is the very least he deserves."

"Don't you worry," Proctor assured her. "We won't quit till the job's done."

"I knew I did the right thing in coming here. Thank you, thank you so much."

Proctor showed her to the door. When he turned back into the room, his features were knotted in a quizzical expression. "That woman thinks we're gonna have it solved by suppertime. Hope you've got an ace up your sleeve."

Gordon scratched his jaw thoughtfully. "You know how a magician uses misdirection? Now you see it, now you don't"

"Why sure, makes things appear outta puff of smoke. What're you gettin' at?"

"Let's go show Hale our magic act."

Chapter Twenty

"So you have the deposition?"

"Yessir, got it right in front of me. Signed by George Braveheart."

"Otis, I often think the government made a big mistake in teaching Indians to write. Education has its limits."

"I wouldn't know one way or another about that. What should I do with this deposition?"

'Stick it in an envelope and put it in your safe. I'll pick it up tomorrow."

"Whatever you say, Mr. Hale."

"Do I detect something in your voice, Otis? You sound a little snippy today."

"Well, you know." Crowley hesitated, then rushed on. "Nobody much cared about Grammer. Wayne Vaughn's a different kettle of fish. One of the few honest lawyers in town. Folks respected him."

"Correct me if I'm wrong. Vaughn did commit suicide, didn't he? Wasn't that Tuttle's ruling?"

"Yessir, but nobody's gonna believe it. That's all I'm sayin'."

"Your job is to make them believe it. Isn't that right, Sheriff?"

"Yessir."

"So do your job."

Hale hung up. He was seated in his office, and he sat staring at the phone a moment. He had an uneasy feeling that Crowley was developing a nervous condition, maybe a conscience. He thought the sheriff should be retired at the next election. Or perhaps have an accident.

The afternoon was early. Hale resolved he wouldn't waste it worrying about nervous sheriffs. Spring roundup was under way, and all across the ranch, cowhands were dragging roped calves to the branding fire. His foreman was on top of things, but he'd always enjoyed roundup, the sharp smell of the branding iron. He decided to saddle a horse and ride out to some of the camps.

A Chevrolet sedan turned into the driveway. Hale let out a groan as he rose from his chair and stood looking out the window. He watched Gordon and Proctor step from the car, and some inner voice told him they were there about Vaughn's suicide. There was nothing for it but to put on his mask and play whatever role the situation demanded. He walked out of the house.

"Back again?" he said as he came down the porch steps. "You boys are getting to be regular pests. What is it now?"

"Just a few questions," Gordon said. "A forthright man like you shouldn't mind a few questions."

"Save your sarcasm and get on with it. What's the burning question of the day?"

"Where were you the night Harry Grammer was murdered?"

"Oh, come on," Hale said, incredulous. "Are you serious?"

"Just answer the question."

"I was right here, with my wife and daughter. Where else would I be?"

"Bryan did better'n that," Proctor said with gruff mockery. "Him and his gang was playin' poker all night. 'Course them boys are natural born liars."

Hale laughed. "Quit trying to get me to rise to the bait. You're wasting your time."

"Mighty convenient," Proctor said. "You know, the way Grammer got himself killed. Lots of money in liquor."

"What are you driving at?"

"Why, it's a cozy arrangement, what with your nephew runnin' the operation. You and him splittin' the take, are you?"

"You ought to turn in your badge, Proctor. You're starting to go feeble-minded."

"Some folks are sayin' the same thing about you. Wonderin' if Big Bill lost his marbles."

Hale flushed with anger. "I don't allow people to call me by that name. I've never liked it."

"Like it or lump it, you're stuck with it. They'll carve 'Big Bill' on your headstone."

The plan was for Proctor to take the lead and nettle him with accusations about Grammer's murder. Gordon was to await the opportune moment before he pulled the rabbit out of the hat. He wanted Hale distracted, thoroughly off guard.

"What is it?" Hale said sullenly. "You came here to insult me?"

"You'd be hard to insult," Proctor said with a wiseacre grin. "C'mon now, don't take it so personal, Big Bill."

"I told you not to call me that!"

"By the way," Gordon interrupted. "We have Braveheart's deposition."

Hale blinked, thrown by the sudden switch. He was on the verge of denying it, a word away from saying the deposition was in Crowley's safe. But then, biting back the denial, he got control of himself. He gave Gordon a bemused look.

"I don't understand," he said. "Are you talking about George Braveheart?"

"No need to pretend," Gordon said. "There were two

copies of the deposition, and we have the second one. Your killers missed it."

Hale caught himself again. He was about to mention Wayne Vaughn, and stopped just in time. "What's this about killers?" he said, acting confused. "Braveheart died of a liver disease."

"We're talking about Braveheart's lawyer, Wayne Vaughn. Your men killed him on the train from Oklahoma City."

"You're out of your mind. I hadn't even heard Vaughn was dead. When did this happen?"

Gordon ignored the question. "We also have copies of your contracts with Braveheart. Along with the deposition, that establishes motive for murder. Vaughn was going to charge you with fraud."

Hale kept a straight face. He wondered if Crowley had missed a copy of the deposition while searching Vaughn's briefcase. Even more, he asked himself, how had Gordon gotten copies of the Braveheart contracts? He decided to bluff it out.

"Go ahead and bring charges," he said. "You'll just end up with egg on your face. I haven't done anything."

"So you say," Gordon retorted. "Once we prove fraud, I think we'll get you for murder. You went one step too far with Vaughn."

"I'm through talking to you, Gordon. Get off my property."

Proctor grinned. "See you in court, Big Bill."

Hale watched them drive off. He didn't know if they had a case or not, but it was a risk he couldn't afford to take. He wished now he'd gone ahead with the original plan, rather than contacting his congressman. Some things were better resolved with direct action, which was certain and final. Gordon and Proctor proved the point.

He went inside to call Bryan.

. . .

"You reckon he bought it?"

"Will, you saw the look on his face. He's convinced we have the deposition."

"So what d'we do now?"

"Wait for Braveheart's wife to get back from Oklahoma City. I want to depose her."

"What'll that accomplish?"

"Couple things," Gordon said as they drove toward Pawhuska. "She was a witness to her husband's deposition. That's almost as good as Braveheart himself talking."

"Yeah, almost," Proctor said. "What's the other thing?"

"She can testify as to how Hale misled Braveheart and duped him into taking additional loans. A widow's words in court carry a lot of weight."

"Awright, let's say we've got enough to charge him with fraud. How do we convict him on murder?"

"No guarantee we will," Gordon admitted. "At this point, I'd be satisfied to send him away on fraud. Braveheart's contracts, and his wife's testimony, should do it."

"Sure as hell won't satisfy me," Proctor grumped. "Not after all the people he's killed."

"Look at it this way, Will. With him in prison, we'll probably save a lot of lives. Murder won't seem so profitable anymore."

"Well, like they say, an ounce of prevention is worth a pound of cure. Maybe it'll do some good."

"Certainly won't do any harm."

They rode along in silence a while. Proctor stared out the window, watching a bank of snowy clouds framed against a westerly sun. He seemed lost in thought, mulling over something he wasn't quite ready to put into words. He finally turned back to Gordon.

"Know what I think?"

"What's that?"

"Hale's more'n likely gonna try and kill us. He's probably callin' Bryan Burkhart right now."

Gordon considered a moment. "That'd be a dumb play on his part. But if he does . . ."

"Yeah?"

"Whoever he sends, let's take one of them alive. Get a witness and we get him."

"Damn tootin'!" Proctor whooped. "Wire him straight to hell ridin' Old Sparky. I'd pull the switch myself."

"What say we share the honors?"

"Got yourself a deal."

Sometime after three o'clock they parked in front of the hotel. Gordon wanted to call Alice Vaughn and find out how to contact Braveheart's widow. Upstairs, the phone rang as they walked into the room. Gordon caught it on the second ring.

"Hello." He listened a moment, then nodded. "Yes, Martha, he's right here. Hold on." He extended the phone to Proctor. "It's your wife."

"She don't hardly ever track me down when I'm workin'. Somebody must be sick."

Proctor took the phone. After he'd answered, his wife cut him short and began talking. He listened, nodding rapidly, and motioned to Gordon for pencil and paper. He wrote down a number, repeated it to be sure, and hung up. He looked puzzled.

"Odd thing," he said. "Warden of the state prison called the house. Wants me to call him back."

"Did he tell Martha what it's about?"

"Nope, just said it's important. Told her to try and get hold of me."

"Sounds like you'd better call him."

"Yeah, reckon so."

Proctor placed the call. The line clicked as he was

transferred from operator to operator through several local exchanges. Some minutes later, he was connected to the state penitentiary, at McAlester. Warden Elmer Carter came on the line.

"Warden, this Deputy U.S. Marshal Will Proctor. I'm returnin' your call."

The conversation was one-sided. Proctor listened, bobbing his head, and asking a few questions that elicited short replies. He finally agreed he would leave right away, and hung up. He turned to Gordon with a bewildered smile.

"Miracles never cease," he said in an awed voice. "There's a con down at the state pen name of Blackie Thompson. Wants to talk to me."

Gordon nodded. "Who's Blackie Thompson?"

"One of the sorriest sonsabitches you'd ever hope to meet. Year ago August, I sent him to death row for shootin' his wife's boyfriend. He's set to be executed next week."

"Any idea what he wants?"

"Well, don't you see, he was workin' for Harry Grammer at the time. One of Grammer's thugs, rough as they come."

Gordon stared at him. "Are you saying he knows something about the murders?"

"I just suspect so," Proctor allowed. "He asked Warden Carter to call me and relay a message. Says he can break the case wide open."

"How close was he to Grammer? Would he know that much?"

"Him and Bryan Burkhart were pretty thick. Way I heard it, he was like Bryan's second-in-command."

"Sounds too good to be true," Gordon said with a note of skepticism. "I'm always suspicious about cons who pop up with a story."

Proctor grunted. "Don't look a gift horse in the mouth. Anything he says will be more'n we know."

"Yeah, we have nothing to lose by listening. Where's the prison?"

"Little town called McAlester."

"How far?"

"Day's ride south of here."

"So we could be there in the morning?"

"Well, sure, if we drive all night."

"You'd better call Martha," Gordon said. "Tell her to pack your bag."

Proctor looked surprised. "You aim to leave right now?"

"Just as soon as I throw some things together."

"Thought you wanted to talk to Braveheart's wife."

"Will, I'd rather get Hale on murder than on fraud. Let's hope this Thompson has something worth saying."

Ten minutes later they went out the door. Neither of them knew if it was a fool's errand or a sudden stroke of good fortune. But they were willing to toss the dice.

Blackie Thompson's story might be for real.

McAlester was located in the heart of the old Choctaw Nation. Before statehood, when the Five Civilized Tribes still governed Indian Territory, rich deposits of coal had been discovered in the surrounding countryside. The mines had supplied homes and trains with fuel for four decades.

Apart from coal, the town's principle claim to fame was convicts. The Oklahoma State Penitentiary was situated on a level plain outside the community, and housed over a thousand felons. There, in a stark room painted gunmetal gray, some of the most infamous outlaws in recent history had met their end. The electric chair, with no humor intended, had been dubbed "Old Sparky."

Gordon and Proctor drove into town a few minutes before six the next morning. Their clothes were rumpled and their eyes bloodshot, even though they had taken turns driving through the night. They had breakfast in a café on the highway that catered to truck drivers and unwary tourists. Afterward, carrying what Proctor referred to as their "warbags," they used the restroom to shave and change into fresh shirts. They were presentable if not the picture of sartorial fashion.

Shortly after seven o'clock they pulled into the parking lot of the penitentiary. The stone walls were twenty feet tall, joined in a massive quadrangle, with machine gun towers at the four corners. A guard at the front gate took their names, checked their identification, and called inside before they were admitted. Life began early in a prison, and another guard escorted them through the halls of the administration building. He left them at the warden's office.

Elmer Carter greeted them with a firm handshake. He was an austere man, impassive as an owl, with the no-nonsense attitude of someone who dealt in harsh, impersonal discipline. After a round of introductions, he took a seat behind his desk and waved them to chairs. His expression was curious.

"Heard about the Osage murders," he said. "Guess you wouldn't be here if you'd made your case."

"That's a fact, Warden," Proctor acknowledged. "We're hopin' Thompson's got the straight goods."

"Maybe he does, maybe he don't. Thompson's scheduled to be executed in five days. He'd probably say anything to avoid the chair."

"You think he's lookin' to make a deal?"

"Hasn't said one way or the other. But I doubt he's suddenly got religion. Him and God don't have much in common."

"What's your opinion?" Gordon asked. "Do you think he's trying to run a scam?"

"That's the way of things in here," Carter said.

"Every con runs a scam of some sort or another. Thompson's got more incentive than most."

Proctor shrugged. "No harm in hearin' him out. Worst he can do is lie."

"I assume you're armed," Carter said. "You'll have to leave your guns with me. That's the rule."

Proctor surrendered his old Peacemaker and Gordon his automatic. A guard was summoned and escorted them through a maze of steel-barred gates leading to the inner prison. Inmates dressed in blue fatigues were mopping the hallway floors with water that reeked of disinfectant. They were finally shown into a small interrogation room.

"I'll be right outside," the guard said. "You need me, just give a yell."

Blackie Thompson was seated at a scarred table. His wrists were handcuffed, and he had manacles on his ankles, the manacles secured to a bolt in the floor. He was stoutly built, with broad features and hard eyes, his hair trimmed short. His mouth quirked in a tight smile.

"Howdy, Marshal," he said. "Long time no see."

"Near a year," Proctor replied. "How's prison life treatin' you?"

"Three squares a day and a private cell. Boys on death row even get the newspaper. I've been readin' about the killin's back home."

"One thing we're not short on is murders. This here's Special Agent Gordon, with the U.S. Bureau of Investigation. He's the man in charge."

Thompson nodded as they took chairs on the opposite side of the table. "Nothin' like talking with the top man," he said. "Gets us from here to there all the quicker."

"We're here to listen," Gordon said. "Do you know something about the murders?"

"Oh, hell yes! I can deliver it to you in a pink ribbon. 'Course, I gotta have a deal."

"What kind of deal?"

"Well, I know they ain't gonna pardon me. But I figure they'll commute the death sentence to life. 'Specially if I hand over your killers."

"Anything's possible," Gordon observed. "Let's hear what you have to say."

"Hey, I didn't fall off the turnip truck. Show me a deal and I'll talk."

"Doesn't work that way, Mr. Thompson. What you say here is worthless unless you agree to testify in court. Convince me you've got the goods and I'll get you the deal. I have the connections in Washington to make it happen."

Thompson searched his eyes a long moment. "Hell, why not?" he said with a fatalistic laugh. "You know I worked for Harry Grammer?"

"Yes, we know."

"A week or so before I was arrested, Grammer took me and Joe Johnson aside. Offered us a thousand bucks apiece to kill Anna Brown."

"That was a year ago," Gordon said. "Why would he wait so long to have her killed?"

"Damned if I know," Thompson said. "Maybe he waited to see if I was gonna rat him out."

"Why haven't you talked before now?"

"State Supreme Court turned down my last appeal three days ago. I'm facin' Old Sparky."

"Grammer and Johnson are dead," Gordon pointed out. "How do we know you're telling the truth?"

Thompson grinned. "'Cause Bryan Burkhart told me it was all for his brother. Bryan and me was real tight, and he said the idea was to kill off Mollie's whole family." He hesitated, his grin wider. "That way Ernest would end up with all the headrights. Him and Bryan'd be filthy rich."

"You'd testify to that in court?"

"On a goddamn stack of Bibles."

"Did you ever speak with Ernest about this?"

"Funny thing," Thompson said. "Saw him in town the very day I was arrested. Told him what Bryan'd said and he just gave me a little nod. Never said a word."

"What about William Hale? Do you have any knowledge of his involvement?"

"Nothin' I'd swear to. But hell, he's Bryan and Ernest's uncle. Used to drop by Grammer's place couple times a week."

Gordon looked disappointed. "You'll have to sign a written statement and an agreement to testify in court. Break the agreement and you'll be back on death row. Understood?"

"I ain't no welcher," Thompson said, grinning. "Get me the deal and I'll sign anything you want."

By eleven that morning the deal was struck. Gordon called Director Holbrook in Washington, who in turn called Governor Martin Trapp. The governor commuted Thompson's death sentence to life in prison without possibility of parole. Thompson then signed a sworn statement and a separate agreement for his court testimony. He was moved from death row to an isolation cell for informers.

Gordon and Proctor took possession of the sworn statement. They jumped in the car, elated by the turn of events, and drove north toward Pawhuska. A mile or so up the road Proctor broke out laughing.

"Big Bill's gonna wet his drawers!"

"Especially when he hears who's waiting for him."

"Waiting? You lost me there, pardner. Who's waiting?"

Gordon smiled. "Old Sparky."

Chapter Twenty-One

A half moon lit the countryside in a fuzzy glow. The two-lane highway stretched endlessly into the night, empty except for an occasional trucker operating on caffeine. The speedometer on the Chevy hovered around fifty.

Gordon had been unusually quiet for most of the trip. They'd stopped along the way for supper, and again on the outskirts of Tulsa for coffee. Proctor now and then tried to engage him in conversation, but was met with monosyllabic answers. He'd finally lapsed into silence himself.

A few miles out of Tulsa Gordon seemed to recover his sense of speech. His features were sober, lit in the shadow of the moon. He glanced around at Proctor.

"I've been thinking."

"No kiddin'," the old lawman said. "I figured you'd just drifted off into a trance of some sort."

"Something like that," Gordon admitted. "I was working out our strategy."

"You should've asked me instead of strainin' your brain. We arrest the whole bunch and toss 'em in jail. How's that for strategy?"

"That's what had me stumped," Gordon said. "We don't have enough on Hale to arrest him, much less get a conviction. Thompson's statement only implicates the Burkharts."

"Somebody'll break," Proctor insisted. "We sweat 'em hard enough, somebody's gonna squeal on Hale. You can bet on it."

"But if they don't, we're up the creek without a paddle. When we arrest Hale, I want it rock-solid, so he'll never wiggle free. I'd rather take it a step at a time."

"So what are you sayin'?"

"I've always thought Ernest Burkhart's the weak sister of the bunch. Bryan strikes me as the kind of man who wouldn't talk if you held his feet to fire. I think we should start with Ernest."

"You're right about Bryan," Proctor conceded. "We'd probably have to kill him just to arrest him. He's tough as they come."

"And Thompson's statement nails Ernest to the cross for premeditated murder. I think he'll crack."

"You know, I'm likin' it better all the time. We always suspected he'd slipped Lizzie Kile poisoned moonshine. Wouldn't it be the cat's whiskers to hear him confess!"

"Will, I think we're in business."

They reached Proctor's home in Hominy a little before midnight. Neither of them had slept much in the last day and a half, and they agreed they needed their wits about them tomorrow. They left it that they would meet for breakfast at eight in the morning.

Gordon drove on to the hotel in Pawhuska. In his room, he stripped out of his soiled clothes, threw them on a chair, and crawled into bed. He was so exhausted he thought he'd drop off when his head hit the pillow. But instead he lay there, staring at the ceiling fan, searching for chinks in his strategy. He went to sleep wondering if he'd overlooked anything.

Proctor met him for breakfast at the Osage Grill. Neither of them noticed the man who had trailed Gordon across the street from the hotel. Nor were they aware that Asa Kirby ducked out after spotting Proctor and hurried to a pay phone. He placed a call to Bryan Burkhart, who had been searching for the lawmen since they'd disappeared two days ago. Burkhart's orders were to kill them, but he decided now to wait until nightfall, rather than risk witnesses in broad daylight. He told Kirby to keep him informed of their movements.

Gordon and Proctor arrived at the house on Twelfth Street shortly before nine. The maid opened the door at their knock, and they brushed past her into the hallway. Ernest Burkhart heard the maid's shriek of alarm and hurried out of the dining room with a napkin still tucked in his shirt collar. Mollie was a step behind, dressed in a pale blue silk peignoir. Ernest stopped with a puzzled scowl.

"What's the meaning of this?" he demanded. "You interrupted our breakfast."

"You're under arrest," Gordon said flatly. "The charge is accessory to murder."

The maid let out a little yelp. She scurried past them through the door to the dining room. Mollie looked like she might faint, but she recovered herself and clutched Ernest's arm. He glared at Gordon.

"You've got your gall! What's this about an accessory? Whose murder?"

"Your sister-in-law, Anna Brown."

Mollie wilted, her legs rubbery. Ernest caught her, supporting her around the waist; she seemed unable to catch her breath. The lawmen moved them from the hallway into the living room, and got them seated on the couch. Proctor remained standing and Gordon took a chair across from them. He fixed Ernest with a stare.

"We had a long talk with Blackie Thompson yesterday."

"Thompson?" Ernest said blankly. "I don't know any Blackie Thompson."

"Bub, you're a poor liar," Proctor said, cocking an eyebrow. "Thompson remembers you and Bryan like it was yesterday."

"Here." Gordon pulled the sworn statement from inside his suit jacket. "Read this and see if it refreshes your memory."

Ernest accepted the two-page typewritten document as if it were a hand grenade. He started reading and before he got to the bottom of the first page, his face went chalky. By the time he got to the end of the statement, his features were rigid and his hands were shaking. He let the pages flutter to the floor and Gordon picked them up, leaning back in his chair. There was a moment of leaden silence.

"What is it?" Mollie said in a frightened voice. "Ernest, what's wrong?"

Ernest dropped his head to his hands. When he didn't answer, Mollie looked at Gordon. "I'm sorry, Mrs. Burkhart," Gordon said. "Your husband was involved in Anna's death. There's no question of it."

"Nooo!"

Mollie recoiled to the end of the couch. Ernest reached for her, mouthing silent words, and she saw the guilt stamped in his features. She jumped to her feet with a strangled cry of anguish and ran toward the bedroom. The door slammed and Ernest slumped back on the couch. Gordon pinned him with a look.

"We're going to offer you a deal," he said in a measured tone. "Talk to us today and we guarantee you a grant of immunity. If you refuse, the offer's off the table. You'll stand trial for murder."

"And you'll be convicted," Proctor added. "They'll strap you in Old Sparky and fry your brains to mush. Helluva way to die, gettin' electrocuted."

"Immunity?" Ernest said weakly. "Immunity from what?"

"Everything you've done," Gordon said. "Except the murder of Lizze Kile. You'll have to serve time for that."

"I didn't—"

"Don't start with a lie," Gordon warned him. "We

know you poisoned your mother-in-law. Tell us the truth or you're headed for the electric chair. There's no other way."

Ernest went numb. His mind suddenly flashed back to the trenches in France. He saw again the men maimed by artillery shells and choking out their lungs on mustard gas. The sight had sapped his courage then, and it was still vivid in his nightmares. He'd been awarded medals not for heroism, but because he was a survivor, always looking to his own safety. He knew he lacked the strength to have survived the horrors of France only to face a grimmer death. He couldn't let himself be strapped in the electric chair.

"All right," he said in a hollow voice. "What do you want to know?"

"Start at the beginning," Gordon said. "Who killed Anna Brown?"

"Bryan was there, but Kelsey Morrison shot her. Katherine Cole was with them."

"Who's Katherine Cole?"

"Morrison's girlfriend."

Ernest folded once he'd betrayed his brother. He confessed to murdering Lizzie Kile with arsenic, and then convincing his wife it was a heart attack. He told them John Ramsey shot Henry Roan, and Ramsey and Asa Kirby bombed the home of Rita and Bill Smith. Under prodding from Gordon, he admitted his brother was responsible for the death of Jack Spivey, as well as the murder of Harry Grammer. The lawyer, Wayne Vaughn, had been killed to silence him about the fraud of George Braveheart.

"Let's finish it," Gordon said when he stopped talking. "What part did your uncle play in the murders?"

Ernest seemed to withdraw, fear evident for the first time in his eyes. He swallowed hard, took a grip on himself. "All of it was his idea," he said, forcing the words. "You have to understand, nobody says 'no' when he gives an order. It was all about the headrights."

"We're talking about William Hale, correct?"

"Yes."

"And you're saying he was the ringleader? The man responsible for the murders?"

Ernest slowly nodded. "That's what I'm saying."

"Good, you've bought yourself a new lease on life. Just sit where you are a minute."

Gordon signaled Proctor, who followed him into the hall. He kept his voice low. "We can't risk putting him in Crowley's jail. They'd find a way to kill him."

"No doubt about it," Proctor said. "So what're you thinkin'?"

"There's a train to Oklahoma City this morning. We'll take him there and hold him in the federal lockup. I'm arresting Mollie as a material witness."

"What for?"

"Hale might take her hostage and use her as leverage on Ernest. He wouldn't hesitate to kill her."

"What're we gonna do about Hale?"

"Let's get Ernest and Mollie out of town alive. I'll worry about Hale later."

"How you want to handle this?" Proctor asked, looking back into the living room. "Him and Mollie aren't exactly lovebirds anymore."

"I'll stay with Ernest," Gordon said. "You tell Mollie she's under arrest and have her pack a bag. Make sure there's not a gun in the bedroom. She might shoot him."

"Don't know as I'd blame her. How the hell do I get her out of that negligee and into a dress?"

"You'll think of something."

"Guess I can always cover my eyes."

Proctor walked off toward the bedroom.

The train was scheduled to depart at eleven o'clock. Gordon parked the car on the street, near the front of the depot. Ernest was handcuffed in the passenger seat, and Proctor was in the backseat with Mollie. The time was ten-thirty-one.

Gordon escorted Ernest into the depot. Proctor followed behind with Mollie, carrying a small suitcase. The waiting room was only about half full, and they got the Burkharts seated on a bench. Gordon left Proctor to guard them and walked to the ticket counter. He nodded to the agent.

"I'd like four tickets to Oklahoma City."

"One way or round trip?"

"One way."

"That'll be twenty dollars," the agent said, opening the ticket drawer. "Aren't you that federal man?"

Gordon looked at him. "Why do you ask?"

"I see you've got Ernest Burkhart in handcuffs. Arrested him and Mollie, have you?"

"I'm not at liberty to say."

Gordon placed a twenty on the counter. The agent passed across the tickets, waiting until Gordon turned away, then reached for the telephone. He gave the operator a number, all the while watching the Burkharts, nervously tapping his fingers on the counter. A voice answered and he spoke rapidly, his voice pitched low. He nodded a couple times, fielding questions, and hung up. He told himself he'd done the right thing.

The train pulled into the station at ten forty-three. A few passengers got off, and those in the waiting room hurried across the platform to board. There were three passenger coaches, a dining car, a sleeper coach not in use on the day run, and a club car. Gordon delayed, inspecting the train, waiting for the platform to clear before he took the Burkharts outside. He wondered if the club car was the same one used to throw Attorney Vaughn to his death. Today, no irony seemed too small.

Five minutes before departure, Gordon nodded to

Proctor. They walked the Burkharts through the waiting room and out the door. As they started across the platform, a patrol car screeched around the side of the depot and skidded to a halt. Sheriff Otis Crowley and three deputies piled out of the car and rushed onto the platform. Crowley put up a restraining hand.

"Hold on!" he called out. "What's going on here?"

"Hell's fire," Proctor cursed under his breath. "Somebody called him and tipped our hand."

Crowley stopped, the deputies ganged around him. He was breathing hard. "What's the meaning of this, Gordon?"

"Official business," Gordon said. "These people are under arrest."

"What's the charge?"

"You'll be advised in good time."

"By God, I'll be advised right now! I'm askin' you again, what's the charge?"

"Murder."

"Don't try dancin' me around. Murder of who?"

"Lizzie Kile," Gordon said evenly. "I've formally charged Ernest Burkhart with her murder."

"Have you?" Crowley said with a frown. "And what about Mrs. Burkhart? You charged her too?"

"She's under arrest as a material witness."

"Witness to what? Mollie didn't see nothin'."

"Sheriff, I have a train to catch. You'll be informed of the particulars no later than tomorrow. That's the best I can do."

"Not by a damnsight!" Crowley barked. "You don't haul people out of my jurisdiction without a court hearing. You're not takin' 'em nowhere."

The deputies spread out, hands loosely poised over their pistols. Proctor flipped his jacket aside, revealing the holstered Peacemaker at his beltline. Ernest and Mollie Burkhart stood rooted in place, their eyes darting from Crowley to Gordon. No one moved.

"Here's the drill," Gordon said, his gaze fixed directly on Crowley. "Let it go or I'll charge you with obstruction of justice. I'll arrest you right here."

"You'll arrest me!" Crowley squawked. "You'd play hell makin' that stick."

"Try me and see. You'll be charged and tried in a federal court, a long way from Pawhuska. I'd say it's good for five years."

Crowley glowered at him. A beat in time slipped past as they stood locked in a staring contest. Then, with a muttered curse, Crowley waved his deputies back. His face was mottled with rage, but suddenly his eyes went beyond Gordon. He chortled a sour laugh.

"Forget about me," he said. "You got real troubles now."

Bryan Burkhart stepped through the depot door. He was followed by Kelsey Morrison, John Ramsey, and Asa Kirby. They started across the platform.

"Whole gang's here," Proctor mumbled. "How the hell'd they know?"

"Will," Gordon said.

"Yeah?"

"Get the Burkharts on the train."

"You can't handle them bastards by yourself."

"Don't argue with me—do it."

Proctor let out a gusty sigh. He handed Mollie her suitcase, then took hold of Ernest's arm, and marched them toward the train. The conductor, who was about to sound the last call for boarding, watched the scene unfold with an open mouth. Gordon turned to face the four men.

"Far enough," he said. "You're too late."

"Hell we are," Bryan said coarsely. "Where you think you're takin' my brother?"

"Your brother is under arrest, Burkhart. That's all you need to know."

"Get the fuck out of my way. You're not arrestin' anybody."

"You're interfering with an officer of the law in the discharge of his duties. Take another step and I'll stop you."

"How you figure to do that?"

"If necessary, I'll kill you."

Bryan snorted a rough laugh. "We got you a little outnumbered. You gonna kill us all?"

"No, just you." Gordon brushed his jacket back to clear the holstered automatic. "Your men will get me, but you won't be around to see it. You'll be dead."

"You're blowin' smoke out your ass."

"One way to find out."

There was an instant of frozen silence. Bryan almost pulled the revolver stuck in his waistband. But as he looked into Gordon's eyes, something stayed his hand. A gut instinct told him that if he moved, he was dead. It wasn't a bluff.

"All balls, huh?" he said. "I halfway think you mean it."

Gordon gave him nothing. "Do it or don't."

"We're not done," Burkhart said in a clipped voice. "There'll be another time."

"Sooner than you think," Gordon said. "I won't be gone long."

"We'll be right here waitin' on you."

"Yeah, you do that."

Gordon backed away, never taking his eyes off them. He stepped aboard the train, and found Proctor waiting in the vestibule with the Burkharts. The conductor signaled the engineer, then swung aboard, and a moment later the cars lurched forward. The train slowly eased away from the depot.

"God A'mighty," Proctor said. "You tryin' to get yourself killed?"

"You play poker, Will?"

"What's that got to do with anything?"

"I raised the stakes on him."

"What kind of raise you talkin' about?"

"Too big for him to call."

Gordon glanced out the window as the train gathered speed. Crowley and his deputies were walking toward their patrol car at the end of the platform. But Bryan Burkhart and his gang were still standing by the door to the depot. He stared at them until they were out of sight.

Next time, he promised himself, it wouldn't end with a standoff. He hoped they would resist arrest.

Jack Spivey deserved to have the account closed.

Chapter Twenty-Two

Gordon and Proctor drove into Pawhuska late the next night. They were accompanied by Walter Horton and Eugene Ludlow, two of the Bureau agents who had worked with Gordon on the Ku Klux Klan investigation. They checked into the hotel a little before midnight.

Yesterday evening, in Oklahoma City, Ernest Burkhart had given a sworn statement. Mollie Burkhart had been detained as a material witness, and was being held under protective custody. Special Agent in Charge David Turner had assigned Horton and Ludlow to Gordon's command, and provided a Bureau car for their return to Pawhuska. Then he'd wired J. Edgar Hoover that arrests were imminent in the Osage murders.

Proctor left the agents at the hotel and drove on to Hominy. On the way from Oklahoma City, they had discussed the case at length, and evolved a step-by-step strategy. The temptation was to raid Harry Grammer's ranch, and arrest every gang member found at the still. But Proctor had observed that the gang would almost certainly fight, and dead men make poor witnesses. His logic prevailed, and they'd decided on a tactical approach. Their first arrest would be Katherine Cole.

Gordon believed Bryan Burkhart was the linchpin. The fact that he was responsible for Jack Spivey's death put him at the top of the list. But over and above personal feelings, Bryan was the only man who could corroborate Ernest's testimony against their uncle, William Hale. Grammer was dead, and according to Ernest's statement, Hale never dealt directly with the other gang members. That targeted Bryan as the key witness.

To make it airtight, they needed corroboration that Bryan and Kelsey Morrison had murdered Anna Brown. Ernest's statement identified Katherine Cole as an eyewitness to the killing, and Gordon argued she was the critical first step. She was Morrison's girlfriend, and if she turned on him, her testimony would send him to the chair. Morrison might then be persuaded to play songbird against Bryan, and the end result seemed inevitable. Bryan, to save his own skin, would sing the sweetest song of all. The one that convicted Big Bill Hale.

The following morning, Proctor met the agents at the Osage Grill. Gordon wanted to move fast, before anyone suspected their true plan of attack. He was somewhat amazed that Katherine Cole was still alive. Morrison and Bryan Burkhart were cold-blooded murderers, and they had every reason to silence her. But Ernest had assured the agents that whatever else he was, Bryan was a man of his word. He'd agreed not to kill Katherine, and he trusted Morrison to keep her quiet. Gordon was wary that it might all unravel unless they moved quickly and quietly. He intended to take her that morning.

Katherine's home was at the corner of Eighth Street and Lynn Avenue. She was a fullblood Osage, and her oil royalties allowed her to live in relative comfort. The house was a two-story frame structure, with a broad front porch and a gabled roof. A Buick Roadster, waxed and shined, was parked in the driveway, and tall hedges blocked the view of the house next door. The neighborhood was quiet and clean, with tall, stately trees lining the street. There was no sign of activity in the house.

Gordon parked three houses down. They knew Morrison didn't live with Katherine, but there was no way to determine if he'd slept over last night. To cover any contingency, their plan assumed Morrison was there and that he would fight rather than be taken prisoner. Gordon and Proctor took the front of the house, and Horton and Ludlow, circling through a neighbor's backyard, took the rear. They approached with caution.

Katherine answered the door. She wore a yellow sundress, her hair hanging loose, a look of surprise on her face. Gordon flashed his badge, and Proctor moved past her, covering the hall and the stairway with his pistol. Her surprise quickly turned to shock.

"Tell us the truth, Miss Cole," Gordon ordered. "Is Kelsey Morrison in the house?"

"No," she stammered. "I . . . I'm alone."

"We'll just make sure."

Proctor searched the lower floor. He let Horton and Ludlow into the kitchen through the back door, and they performed a search of the second floor. By the time they returned, Gordon had Katherine seated on a couch in the living room. Proctor joined him, leaving the agents to watch the street, and Gordon took a chair across from the girl. She looked terrified by the sight of so many men with guns.

"Miss Cole, you're under arrest," Gordon said sternly. "The charge is accessory to murder."

"Me?"

"Yes, ma'am, specifically the murder of Anna Brown. We know you were there the night she was killed."

"Omigod!" Her eyes went round with tears. "Am I in trouble?"

"As bad as it gets," Gordon informed her. "We have irrefutable proof that Morrison and Bryan Burkhart killed Anna Brown the night of April 25. We can also prove you were an eyewitness."

"No, I wasn't!"

"You deny you saw her killed?"

"Yes, I didn't see it," she said hurriedly. "Kelsey and Bryan took her down to the creek and I heard a shot. They came back without her . . ."

"Go on," Gordon prompted. "What happened then?"

"Bryan said I'd be killed if I ever told anyone. He meant it too."

"So you never reported the murder?"

"I didn't want to be killed!"

"By law, Miss Cole, that makes you an accessory. You are as guilty as the men who pulled the trigger. You could go to prison for the rest of your life."

"No," she breathed. "You don't understand. I didn't do anything."

Gordon felt sorry for her. She'd been threatened, and had she talked, Burkhart or one of his men would have killed her. But his sympathy was eroded by the quickened urgency to apprehend the murderers. He kept his tone severe.

"You will go to prison," he said. "You'll be convicted by your silence and sentenced to life—unless you cooperate."

"Cooperate how?" she said, imploring him with her eyes. "What is it you want me to do?"

"Testify against Morrison and Burkhart."

"But they'd kill me! You know they would."

"We'll protect you," Gordon reassured her. "Morrison and Burkhart will go to the electric chair, and you'll be freed. You have my word on it."

"I won't have to go to prison?"

"You'll never serve a day."

She struggled briefly with her feelings for Morrison weighed against life in prison. She offered a small shrug. "You promise you'll protect me?"

"No one will harm you, Miss Cole. I guarantee it."

"All right, then . . . I'll testify."

"You won't regret it," Gordon said confidently. "Now, our first order of business is to take Morrison and Burkhart into custody. Are they still at Grammer's ranch?"

"Yes, Bryan is," she said. "He and Kelsey had a big argument after you arrested Ernest. Bryan doesn't believe his brother could ever betray them. Kelsey's not so sure."

"Bryan doesn't know it yet but he lost that argument. Where's Morrison?"

"Hiding in the oil field at Burbank. He said he'd wait and see if Ernest turned on them. He took a job as a roustabout."

"There's hundreds of oil wells over there. Do you know where he's working?"

"Marland Well Number 34," she said. "I asked him how I could reach him and he told me. Then he made me promise I wouldn't tell anyone."

Gordon considered a moment. "Just as a formality," he said, "we have to arrest you and prefer charges. We'll also hold you in protective custody."

"You're putting me in jail?"

"Only until we round up Morrison and the others. Our first concern is for your safety."

She made a face. "How long will I be in jail?"

"Four or five days at the most."

"God, I wish I'd never met Kelsey Morrison. I'll never live down the embarrassment."

"Well, Miss Cole, it's better than going to prison."

Gordon had her pack a bag. Twenty minutes later they escorted her into the county jail beneath the court-house. The jailor called the sheriff, and Crowley rushed downstairs from his office. He came through the door with a look of consternation.

"What's this?" he demanded, glancing from the girl to Gordon. "You want to put a woman in my jail?"

"Just for a few days," Gordon said. "Make sure she has a cell with privacy."

"Who do you think you are, giving me orders? I'm not obliged to hold your prisoners."

"I could call a federal judge and have the order issued over the phone. Would that satisfy you?"

"Always throwin' your weight around," Crowley grumped, backing off. "What are you chargin' her with, anyway?"

"Accessory to murder," Gordon said. "Sheriff, I'd like you to meet Special Agents Horton and Ludlow. They'll alternate shifts guarding Miss Cole."

Horton and Ludlow stepped forward. Crowley looked them over as though suddenly confronted by lepers. He glared at Gordon. "You don't trust me?" he said. "You're puttin' your own men in *my* jail?"

"Otis, nobody trusts you," Proctor chimed in. "Anybody tries to hurt her, these gents are ordered to shoot 'em dead. Better watch your step."

"Are you threatening me, Will Proctor?"

"Take it anyway you see fit."

The three male prisoners in jail were moved to the far end of the cell block. Katherine Cole was provided a cell near the holding room door, and Horton and Ludlow were assigned to stand four-hour shifts. Crowley stormed out of the jail, and Gordon and Proctor were only a moment behind. On the street, they walked toward the car.

"Takes care of that," Proctor said. "Who's next on the list, Morrison?"

Gordon nodded. "Let's go find that oil well."

Marland Oil Company had wells all over the Burbank field. The company was small compared to such giants as Standard and Dutch Shell, but it was an aggressive bidder on drilling leases. The wells were randomly scattered across the vast underground pool.

Locating the well proved more difficult than expected.

Gordon and Proctor arrived in Burbank around midmorning, and discovered there was no central listing for oil holdings. Tracking an independent producer, such as Marland, was like tracing threads through an intricate patchwork quilt. The owner of an underground pipe company finally steered them in the right direction.

Early that afternoon, four miles south of Burbank, they found the rig. The well was in the process of being drilled near a creek on the flat, windswept prairie. A huge bull wheel groaned, playing out rope thick as a man's wrist, and the crown block at the top of the derrick set up a grinding wail of protest. On the derrick floor a massive beam mounted atop a post bobbed and rose in a teeter-totter motion as the rope lowered a string of drilling tools over the well head. A sign was nailed to the side of the rig.

MARLAND #34

Three cars were parked along the bank of the creek. Gordon brought the Chevy to a halt, hooking the gear shift into reverse, and switched off the engine. The well was perhaps thirty yards from the creek, several men were working on the derrick floor. Gordon and Proctor stepped out of the Chevy and stood for a moment, studying the faces of the men. They knew Morrison was one of the men they'd seen at the train station two days ago, but they didn't know which one. They were looking for a familiar face.

"Don't see him," Proctor said. "Think we got the right well?"

"Marland 34," Gordon noted. "That's what Katherine Cole told us."

"Scared as she was, I tend to doubt she was lyin'. Maybe Morrison lied to her."

"I sure as hell hope not. Let's talk to the boss of this operation. He'll know one way or the other."

They walked toward the rig. A tall, rangy man,

powerfully built from a lifetime of physical labor, came down a ladder at the side of the derrick. He pulled out a packet of Mail Pouch, and stuffed his mouth with a fresh quid of tobacco as he waited for them to approach. His features were grizzled and ruddy, burned dark as saddle leather from working in the sun. He gave their street clothes a slow once-over.

"Afternoon," Gordon said. "Are you in charge here?"

"Larry Scullin," the man said agreeably. "What can I do for you?"

"I'm Frank Gordon, U.S. Bureau of Investigation. This is Deputy U.S. Marshal Proctor."

"Guessed you wasn't in the oil business. What brings you out here?"

"We're looking for a man named Kelsey Morrison. Does he work for you?"

"Just hired him yesterday," Scullin said. "Don't tell me he's in trouble with the law?"

"We believe he can assist us with an investigation. Isn't he working today?"

"Yeah, he's on today. Sent him to town for a load of cable. Oughta be back in an hour or so."

"We'll wait," Gordon said. "It's important we talk with him."

Scullin spat a wad of tobacco juice onto the ground. He shifted the cud to his other cheek, his eyes curious. "You don't mind my askin', what's Morrison done?"

"I'm not able to say, Mr. Scullin. It'll have to wait till he returns."

"Way you fellers look it must be serious."

Proctor started to roll a cigarette. Scullin frowned, shook his head. "No smokin', Marshal," he said. "Enough gas hereabouts to blow us all to hell and gone. Could I offer you a chew?"

A driller's cardinal rule was that cigarettes and matches were forbidden around a rig. Casinghead gas, escaping from the well, collected in pockets low to the ground. A single spark could detonate the volatile gas, destroying the derrick and killing anyone nearby. Oil men, wary of an explosion, either chewed tobacco or dipped snuff.

"Thanks all the same," Proctor said. "Never had much taste for chewin' tobacco. How far down you drilled?"

"Twelve hundred feet," Scullin replied. "Hopin' to bring her in by the end of the week. Maybe sooner."

"Ever hit a duster around these parts?"

"Haven't drilled a dry hole since I came to Burbank. Whole field's floatin' on a bed of oil. Never seen nothin' like it."

"Makes a man's job easier, don't it?"

"Does for a fact, and I gotta get back to work. Morrison oughta be along directly."

Scullin climbed the ladder to the derrick floor. The lawmen were forced to wait, and to pass the time, Proctor launched into an explanation of the drilling operation. He pointed to an inch-thick steel cable strung over the crown block as it lowered a string of tools into the well head. The drill bit was a steel bar some five feet in length, shaped like a blunt wedge with rounded sides. Hung from stems and sockets, weighing a couple of tons altogether, the bit was jerked up and down in the hole by the seesaw motion of the walking beam. The rocking action imported a jarring impact to the tools, pulverizing underground rock formations. The bit literally pounded its way through the earth.

After an hour or so, the tools were pulled from the well and swung aside. Proctor continued his explanation as a roustabout threw the ropes of the tug wheel, quickly engaged the band wheel, and ran a bailer into the well. A short while later, the bailer was lifted out of the hole, full of pulverized cuttings and water, which were dumped in a slush pit off to the side of the derrick. The dulled bit was manhandled to the engine house, where it was hammered back into the shape over a large anvil. All the while, the bailer went up and down in the hole, dredging out what drillers called a "screw"—some eight feet of pulverized rock.

"Gotta drill down to the cap rock," Proctor went on. "That's like a shield just above the oil pocket. Then they're into paysand."

"Paysand?" Gordon said. "Does that mean they've struck oil?"

"Not unless they're damned careful."

Oil was embedded in sand at various depths in the earth. Above and below these beds were formations of rock and clay, generally impregnated with water. The trick was to tap the oil at its upper level, but not to drill so deeply that the hole went beyond paysand. A driller drilled foot by foot at that point. And prayed.

"One foot too far," Proctor observed, "and they got a water well 'stead of an oil well. Water's not fit to drink, neither."

Gordon smiled. "Scullin looks like he knows his business."

"Yeah, not too likely he'll—"

Proctor stopped. A truck turned off the road and lumbered toward the derrick. The bed of the truck was loaded with spools of cable and the driver was Kelsey Morrison. They moved away from the car.

Morrison saw them as he drove past. His face registered surprise and anger quickly mixed with fear. He jammed the accelerator to the floorboard, rapidly gaining speed, and swerved away from the derrick. In his panic, he was thinking only of flight, and he tried to muscle the truck back onto the road. But he misjudged the turn, and the rear wheels hit the muddy edge of the slush pit. The truck went into a violent skid, precariously tipped sideways on two wheels. The spools of steel cable rolled ponderously in the direction of the skid.

The truck toppled over on the passenger side and slammed to the earth. Gordon and Proctor ran forward as Morrison scrambled out the driver's door, an automatic pistol in his hand. He jumped to the ground, winging a quick snap-shot at them, and scurried around the front of the truck. The lawmen separated, their guns drawn, cautiously flanking the truck from opposite directions. Morrison stepped past the crumpled front fender and fired.

Gordon shot him three times. The heavy slugs stitched bright red dots up his shirt front, the last one centered on his chest. He lurched backward, his feet tangled, and sank to the mud on his rump. His features went rigid in an amazed look, and a trickle of blood leaked out of the corner of his mouth. He slowly keeled over on the ground, the pistol slipping from his hand. His eyes were open and empty.

Proctor came around the truck from the other side. They stood looking down at the body, and Gordon cursed softly. "Wish he hadn't fought," he said. "Lost our best link to Bryan."

"Word'll spread," Proctor remarked. "Maybe we oughta collar him before he gets wind of this."

"By the time we got to the ranch it would be dark. That increases the risk he'll be killed if he fights. I want him alive."

"So you're thinkin' daylight's better?"

"We'll get there first thing in the morning."

Larry Scullin walked forward from the oil derrick. He surveyed the overturned truck, and then moved around for a look at the body. "First time I ever saw a man shot," he said. "You'd think he would've give up against the two of you."

"Just never know," Proctor commented. "Some men

are bound to get theirselves killed. Odds don't mean nothin'."

Gordon spotted the pistol on the ground. He recognized it as a Colt .32 caliber automatic, and remembered the first murder. The shell casing he'd found beside the body of Anna Brown. A woman shot and left for animals to gnaw on.

She would have applauded the killing of Kelsey Morrison.

Chapter Twenty-Three

The alarm clock went off. Gordon rolled over, jolted from a sound sleep, and saw that it was still dark outside. He whacked the knob on top of the clock and the hammering ring abruptly stopped. It was five in the morning.

A groggy moment passed before he levered himself out of bed. He hitched up his boxer shorts, padded barefoot across the room, and switched on the overhead light. His eyes flared in the sudden brightness, and he walked to the bathroom, tripping the light switch. The tiled floor was cool beneath his feet.

The mirror over the sink blazed with light. He turned on the hot water tap, cupping water in both hands, and splashed his face. After brushing his teeth, he took a shaving mug and brush and lathered the stubble along his jawline. As he shaved, using one of the new safety razors with a double-edged blade, his thoughts turned to Bryan Burkhart. He wondered again if he'd made a mistake.

Last night, after checking on Katherine Cole at the county jail, he'd returned to the hotel. He was all too aware that Bryan would have learned of her arrest, probably by way of the sheriff calling Big Bill Hale. There was the possibility as well that Bryan would hear of Morrison's death, even through he and Proctor had left the body with a

Burbank undertaker. He began wondering if they should have arrested Bryan first.

Still, even with the benefit of hindsight, he wasn't sure he would have revised the plan. Katherine Cole was a crucial witness, for she could place Bryan at the scene of Anna Brown's murder. All the more so since Morrison, the only other witness, was now dead. There was some likelihood that Bryan would have fled, or gone into hiding, after learning of Katherine's arrest. But on the other hand, Bryan probably thought himself immune to arrest, and certainly to conviction. His belief, never yet proven wrong, was that Big Bill could fix anything in Osage County.

Thirty minutes later, dressed and shaved, Gordon admitted Proctor to the room. The old lawman carried a paper bag with ham and egg sandwiches, prepared by his wife, and a thermos of strong, black coffee. As they ate, they reviewed their plan for taking Bryan Burkhart alive. There was always the possibility that Bryan would fight rather than submit to arrest. Yet he might surrender in the firm belief that his uncle would spring him from jail and call in political chits to preclude an indictment. They saw it as a tossup.

Shortly after sunrise, they turned into the driveway of the Grammer ranch. There were lights on in the house, and they parked out front, then knocked on the door. They knew Bryan occupied the foreman's quarters in the bunkhouse, and their thought was to gather whatever intelligence possible from Naomi Grammer. She answered their knock, still dressed in a housecoat, and evidenced no surprise to find them on her doorstep. She invited them inside.

Though recently widowed, she looked no worse for the experience. She insisted they take chairs in the living room and seated herself on an overstuffed couch. Gordon got the impression she was too hospitable by half, and wondered if there was something on her mind. But the thought was fleeting, and quickly gone. He went straight to the point.

"We're here to arrest Bryan Burkhart," he said. "Can you tell us if he and his men are still on the ranch?"

"Bryan is," she said in a whispery voice. "Ramsey, Morrison, and Kirby haven't been around for three days. They left just after you arrested Ernest."

"How'd you know about that?"

"Why, it's no secret, Mr. Gordon. Everyone knows you want them for these murders."

Gordon exchanged a sideways glance with Proctor. He decided not to tell her about Morrison. "We need your help, Mrs. Grammer," he said, trying a shot in the dark. "Do you have any idea where the other men went?"

"Yes, I do," she said, surprising him. "Harry owned a cabin in the hills outside Barnsdall. He kept it for men who were in trouble with the law. I think you'll find them there."

"That's more than I expected." Gordon hesitated, taken aback by her candor. "Any particular reason you're being so helpful?"

"I want a favor in return."

"What sort of favor?"

"The truth," she said, holding his gaze. "Did Bryan and the other men kill my husband?"

"We think so," Gordon said honestly. "Ernest says they did, and we believe him. Why do you ask?"

"Bryan hasn't been the same since Harry was killed. He's taken over the place like he owns it and I'm a poor relative. You'd think he inherited the ranch instead of me."

"Figures," Proctor cut in with a baleful frown. "He'd probably like to get rid of you and have it all to himself. The ranch *and* the still."

"The way he looks at me sometimes, I wouldn't be surprised. I get the feeling I'm next on the list."

"Mrs. Grammer—" Gordon waited until he had her

attention. "Assist us and we'll remove Bryan from your life. Where can we find him?"

"Bryan's schedule doesn't vary." She smiled a wicked little smile. "Every morning, he pretends he's a ranch foreman and rides out to check on the cowhands. If you hurry, you can catch him."

Gordon and Proctor went through the house and out the back door. Fifty yards from the rear of the house, on the west side of the barn, they saw Bryan lead a sorrel gelding from the corral. They took off running, their guns out, trying to close the distance. Bryan spotted them and vaulted into the saddle, pulling a revolver holstered on his hip. He fired as he booted the sorrel into a gallop.

Proctor slammed to a halt. He assumed a marksman's stance, the Colt Peacemaker extended at shoulder level. The long seven-and-a-half-inch barrel tracked the galloping horse, then he swung the sights a horse-length ahead and feathered the trigger. The horse went down, folding like an accordion from front to rear, shot through the head. Bryan was thrown from the saddle, flung through the air as though fired from a cannon, and hit the ground with a jarring impact. He lay perfectly still.

Gordon and Proctor walked forward, covering him with their guns. As they approached, he groaned, flopping onto his back, the skin peeled raw on the right side of his face. The horse was sprawled motionless, blood seeping from a wound just below its left ear. Gordon wagged his head in amazement.

"Will, that's the damnedest shot I ever saw."

"Helluva note," Proctor grouched irritably. "Aimin' for the man and all I killed was a good horse. Don't know how I missed."

"Yeah, too bad about the horse. But look on the bright side and be glad your aim was off. Told you I wanted him alive."

"Guess you got your wish."

Proctor stood guard while Gordon brought the car down from the house. They handcuffed Bryan, who was still dazed and limp, and dumped him into the backseat of the Chevy. Naomi Grammer was outside the house as they drove by, and she waved with a broad smile. She looked somehow triumphal.

Bryan came to his senses a short way down the road. Proctor told him with considerable exuberance that he'd been betrayed by his own brother. He then elaborated on the sworn statement, signed by Ernest to save himself. Bryan's skinned features contorted in a grimace.

"You're full of shit!" he raged. "Ernest wouldn't sell me out. Not in a hundred years!"

"Don't you understand English?" Proctor said. "I just told you we got it in writin', the whole shebang. You've got one foot in the grave."

"You're tryin to trick me, you old coot. Might as well save your breath."

"Save yours, sonny. You're gonna need it when they sit you down in the electric chair. 'Course, we might strike a deal if you was to open up about Big Bill."

"Turn it sideways and stick it up your ass. I got nothin' to say."

Bryan refused to say anything more. In Pawhuska, they parked in front of the courthouse and marched him into the jail. The jailer got on the phone, calling upstairs, as they moved toward the cell block door. Walt Horton rose from a chair outside Katherine Cole's cell as they came into the lockup. Bryan saw her, and even though he was handcuffed, he strained to break loose. His face was dark with anger.

"You stupid bitch!" he snarled. "You're gonna get yours. Just wait and—"

Gordon twisted the handcuffs and he howled with pain. They locked him in a cell at the end of the corridor and left him to consider the gravity of his situation. Horton was waiting as they walked back to the front of the lockup. His features were set in a sardonic smile.

"Thought you should know," he said. "Sheriff Crowley skipped town with his family. Apparently happened during the night."

"Huh!" Proctor laughed. "Rats are desertin' the ship."

"Looks that way," Gordon said. "Who's the new sheriff?"

Noah Perkins appeared in the doorway. "I am," he said with a clown's grin. "Chief Deputy takes over in an emergency. That's the law."

"Congratulations," Gordon said, deadpan. "I have an assignment for you, Sheriff."

"Well, you're gonna find a new spirit of cooperation now that I'm in charge. What can I do for you?"

"You'll notice we have Bryan Burkhart in custody."

"Yessir, I sure do."

"When you report to his uncle—"

"Hold on!" Perkins protested. "Don't go thinkin' I'm Hale's man."

"But you will call him, won't you?"

"Well, yeah, I suppose."

"Then give him a message."

"What's that?"

"Tell him he's finished."

"Finished with what?"

"Osage County."

Gordon hung up the phone. He and Proctor were in his room at the hotel, and he'd just finished talking with SAC David Turner in Oklahoma City. He was pleased with Turner's response.

"All set," he said, turning from the phone. "Two more agents will be here by tonight. We'll take over the jail."

"Damn good thing," Proctor said. "I don't trust Noah Perkins any more'n I did Crowley. Maybe less."

"No telling which way he'll jump. I think he's already looking ahead to the next election."

"Sure as hell won't get my vote."

Their concern was that Perkins might somehow engineer the escape of Bryan Burkhart. Ambition robbed men of common sense, and from what they'd seen, Perkins wasn't yet convinced that Big Bill Hale was through in Osage County. David Turner shared their concern, and had agreed to provide two additional agents to reinforce Horton and Ludlow. By tonight, they would control the jail.

"So what's next?" Proctor asked. "Time to put the collar on Hale?"

"I've been thinking about that," Gordon said. "Until Bryan talks, we don't have a solid case against Hale. Ernest's testimony might convict him, and then again, it might not."

"Bryan don't show no signs of spillin' the beans. He figures Hale's gonna get him off someway or another."

"And Hale likely knows he'll dummy up."

"Which sorta leaves us betwixt and between."

Gordon deliberated a moment. "John Ramsey and Asa Kirby are unknowns in the mix. Who knows how much they know?"

"You're thinkin' we oughta bring 'em in? Maybe offer 'em a deal?"

"We have to bring them in sometime. Why not today?"

"All we have to do is find 'em."

"I know who to ask."

Gordon placed a call to Naomi Grammer. He outlined the situation, and reminded her of her comment that morning about the cabin outside Barnsdall. She saw it as further revenge for her husband, and quickly agreed to help. Proctor was more familiar with the backcountry of Osage County, and Gordon put him on the phone. He listened as she gave directions, and sketched a crude map. He hung up after she wished them good hunting.

"Shouldn't be hard to find," he said. "Off Bird Creek, three or four miles south of Barnsdall."

Gordon checked his watch "Only nine o'clock and we've already put in a full day's work. How far to Barnsdall?"

"Twenty miles as the crow flies."

"What say we hit the road?"

"Like they say, time's a-wastin'."

Proctor spent the drive relating one of his war stories. In 1896, he'd trailed a gang of horse thieves along Bird Creek, which angled through much of the old Osage Nation. He was leading a squad of Osage Lighthorse Police, and the chase had ended some eight miles south of Barnsdall. The horse thieves were captured while taking a siesta, and not a shot fired. On a summer day much like today.

"Way I like it," he said. "Take 'em nice and peaceable. Nobody gets hurt."

"Like this morning," Gordon ragged him good-naturedly. "When you unlimbered that old cannon."

"Well, any man worth shootin', he's worth killin'. Still wish I'd got Bryan 'stead of the horse."

The sun was high overhead when they found the wooden bridge described by Naomi Grammer. Beyond the bridge, just past Bird Creek, there was a chain of hills studded with blackjack. They stopped on the road where a rutted trail curled through the trees to the top of a hill. There were tire tracks imprinted in the loose dirt of the narrow, winding trail. Proctor judged them to be three days old.

They separated, their guns drawn, one on either side of the trail. The trees were dense, affording cover as they moved on, birds flitting through the branches. Halfway up the hill, a downdraft brought the scent of woodsmoke, and they paused, testing the wind. The trail might have been walked in ten minutes, but they took their time, careful of noise and branches underfoot. Some thirty minutes passed before the trees opened onto a clearing at the crown of the hill. A log cabin, ancient with age, occupied the center of the clearing. Parked nearby was a Reo truck.

The hood of the truck was latched open, and John Ramsey was tinkering with the radiator. Asa Kirby came through the door of the cabin with two steaming mugs of coffee and walked toward the truck. Gordon and Proctor stepped out of the treeline, silent as ghosts, and stopped at the edge of the clearing. Kirby caught movement out of the corner of his eye and turned, looking at them with an expression of stunned disbelief. Then something in his face changed and he dropped the mugs, black streams of coffee floating in midair. He clawed at a pistol holstered on his belt.

"Don't!" Proctor shouted.

Kirby brought the pistol to bear. Proctor fired, the roar of the Peacemaker reverberating through the trees. The slug dusted Kirby on both sides, splotching his shirt pocket and exiting along his spine. His legs went haywire and he fell like a scarecrow suddenly ripped clean of stuffing. His bowels voided as he hit the ground.

Ramsey banged his head on the hood as he jerked back from the truck. Gordon stared at him over the sights of the automatic. "Let's see your hands!" he ordered. "I don't want to shoot you."

Proctor crossed the clearing, checking to make sure Kirby was dead. He then relieved Ramsey of a bulldog revolver and handcuffed his hands behind his back. Gordon holstered his automatic and walked forward.

"You're under arrest," he said. "The charge is murder."

"Got the wrong man," Ramsey croaked. "I haven't killed nobody."

"Hell you haven't," Proctor said sharply. "We've got Ernest and Bryan in jail, and they both gave you up. Told us you was Grammer's main shooter."

"That's a gawddamn lie! Bryan's just tryin' to save his own ass."

"You sayin' he was in on it?"

"Bet your butt I am."

"Maybe we oughta talk."

They took Ramsey into the cabin. Gordon offered him a deal to turn state's evidence, a chance to escape the deadly embrace of Old Sparky. Over the next hour Ramsey confessed to killing Henry Roan and the lawyer, Wayne Vaughn. He identified Bryan Burkhart and Kelsey Morrison as the men who had killed Anna Brown. When asked, he also admitted that he and Kirby had bombed the home of Rita and Ray Smith. He told them the murders had been carried out at Harry Grammer's instructions.

"So it was murder for hire?" Gordon said. "You were paid a thousand apiece to kill people?"

"That's the way it worked," Ramsey replied. "Grammer gave us the names and we did the job."

"How about Jack Spivey? Was that your work too? Did you torture him?"

"Swear to Christ, that wasn't me! I could barely stand to watch what Bryan did to him. Almost got sick at my stomach."

"Bryan tortured him?"

"Yeah, with a skinning knife."

"And who killed him?"

"Bryan did," Ramsey said. "Grammer told us to kill him and Bryan shot him in the head. Then we dumped him in front of your hotel."

Gordon forced himself to take a deep breath. "Let's move on," he said. "Who killed Grammer?"

"Bryan and Kelsey Morrison. Run his car off the road and shot him. Tried to make it look like an accident."

"And who ordered that?"

"Why, Big Bill Hale. Nobody would've touched Grammer without Big Bill's say-so. That's the straight of it."

"How did it happen?"

"Big Bill called us all out to his ranch. Bryan, Kelsey,

Asa, and me. Told us Bryan would take over the liquor operation and we'd all get a piece of the action. Shook hands on it right in his front yard."

"You'll swear to that in court?"

"Sure as hell will."

"Understand me," Gordon said in a hard voice. "You renege on the witness stand and our deal's off. You'll get a quick ride to the electric chair."

"Hey, I ain't that dumb," Ramsey blurted. "You put me on the stand and I'll tell it just like it was. Big Bill's the man."

Gordon and Proctor exchanged a mutual look of relief. The admission was unexpected, and from an unlikely source, but nonetheless welcome. The words they thought they might never hear. *Big Bill's the man.*

They took Ramsey's written statement that night in Pawhuska.

Chapter Twenty-Four

A full moon washed the land in a spectral glow. Somewhere in the distance an owl hooted and then the night went still. High overhead, a shooting star flashed through the heavens.

Hale sat in the rocker on his front porch. His bulldog, Duke, lay at his side, snoring peacefully. Inside the house, his wife and daughter were listening to the radio, and he heard the music of an orchestra from a studio in New York. He couldn't place the tune.

Noah Perkins, Osage County's new sheriff, had called not quite an hour ago. In a troubled voice, Perkins had informed him that Asa Kirby was in the funeral home, shot dead, and John Ramsey was in jail. Earlier in the day, Perkins had called and told him that Bryan had been taken into custody that morning. The county jail was now under the control of federal agents.

Hale thought it ironic that Otis Crowley had fled the state with his family. Of all those involved, Crowley had the least to fear, for there was no blood on his hands. But in the end, it made little difference because the Crowleys of the world were dispensable, and easily replaced. Noah Perkins, though hardly more than an ambitious clod, was nonetheless bright enough to realize that nothing had really changed. He wanted to be the next sheriff, and his phone calls indicated that he understood the truth of the situation. One man was still the boss in Osage County.

The immediate problem was more a matter of inconvenience. Hale knew, from his last conversation with Perkins, that Gordon and Proctor were on the way to arrest him. He assumed Ernest had talked, and while that angered him, he wasn't overly concerned. Ernest hadn't been involved in the killings, apart from murdering Lizzie Kile, and most of what he knew bordered on hearsay. Grammer was dead and Hale was confident Bryan would never betray him; a smart lawyer could easily impeach Ramsey on the witness stand. He wasn't worried.

Headlights turned into the driveway. The car came to a stop in front of the house, and Gordon and Proctor stepped out. They were exhausted, for they'd been on the move since before sunrise, fought two gunfights before the sun went down. Yet for all their weariness, they were energized by what they saw as the final link in their investigation. The thing they'd so often despaired might ever happen. They were here to arrest Big Bill Hale.

Hale shushed his bulldog into silence. He rose from his rocker, crossing the porch, and went down the steps. Gordon had turned off the headlights, and the two lawmen stood bathed in a pool of moonlight. Proctor couldn't resist a smile.

"Your clock's run out," he said. "We're placin' you under arrest."

"I can't stop you," Hale said without rancor. "But when all's said and done, you'll make fools of yourselves. I'm an innocent man."

"Not accordin' to Ernest," Proctor remarked. "You nephew says you're the ringleader, the top dog. We've got it in writin'."

"I wouldn't put too much stock in that, if I were you Ernest won't make a very credible witness."

"We only need one charge to stick," Gordon noted.

"We're also arresting you for the murder of Harry Grammer."

"You'll never prove that."

"I think we will. You stood here in your yard and ordered Bryan, John Ramsey, Kelsey Morrison, and Asa Kirby to kill Grammer. Ramsey will swear to it in court."

Hale shrugged it off. "Bryan will contradict him and so will I. And you've shot the other two so-called witnesses. Sounds pretty weak."

"Don't depend on Bryan," Gordon said. "He'll be convicted fast and hard by the testimony of Ernest and Blackie Thompson. Or maybe we hadn't told you about Thompson."

"Thompson's in prison, on death row. What's he got to do with anything?"

"Quite a bit, since he and Bryan were best pals. Bryan told him everything before he was arrested. The A to Z of how you planned to kill off Mollie's family."

Hale just stared at them, clearly startled. Proctor was so pleased that he laughed out loud. "Care to confess?" he said. "Always heard it's good for the soul."

"I have nothing to confess to."

"Well, you'll have lots of time to think about it in jail."

"I'd like to tell my wife I'm leaving. Give me a minute."

"Make it quick," Proctor said. "Don't go any further than the door. We got our eye on you."

Hale mounted the steps and crossed the porch. "Ethel," he called through the screen door. "Would you come here?"

Ethel Hale appeared at the door. Her eyes went past her husband and fixed on the lawmen a moment. She stepped onto the porch. "What is it, Bill?"

"I've been arrested," he said with a sanguine air. "Some nonsense or another involving Bryan. Nothing to worry about."

Her mouth parted in a perfect oval. "Good Lord, Bill,

what's Bryan done? Why are they arresting you?"

"A mistake of some sort. But on the off chance I'll need a lawyer, call Tom Lyman. Tell him to meet me at the county jail."

"Do you mean they're going to hold you overnight?"

"No, nothing like that. I'll be home in no time. Don't worry yourself."

Hale kissed her on the cheek, then turned back across the porch. As he came down the steps, Proctor held out a pair of handcuffs. He flushed with humiliation. "Is that necessary?"

"Yep." Proctor spun him around and cuffed his hands behind his back. "Wouldn't want you to try nothin' stupid."

"Bill!" Ethel Hale hurried to the edge of the porch. "Are you all right?"

"I'm fine," Hale reassured her. "I'll be back soon."

"Don't bet on it," Proctor muttered. "You're long gone and then some."

They put him in the backseat of the Chevy. Proctor slid into the passenger seat and Gordon cranked the engine, turning around in the driveway. Ethel Hale was still standing on the porch, watching with a forlorn expression as they drove away from the ranch. Hale let out a sigh as though he'd been holding his breath. His voice was ripe with indignation.

"You could've waited to handcuff me. There's no reason to belittle a man in front of his wife."

"Tonight's just the start of it," Gordon said without inflection. "Wait till she sees you convicted for murder."

Thirty minutes later they walked him into the county jail. Big Bill Hale in handcuffs brought conversation in the cell block to a stop. Horton and Ludlow, and the two agents just arrived from Oklahoma City, nodded to Gordon with sober smiles. Proctor uncuffed Hale and placed him in a cell across the aisle from Bryan. The door clanged shut with steely finality.

Katherine Cole sat on the cot in her cell, and John Ramsey couldn't bring himself to look at Hale. Bryan gripped the bars of his cell as though he wanted to tear the door off. He shook his head, his gaze on his uncle.

"Who'd ever thought it'd come to this?"

Hale offered him a lame smile. "We'll be out of here in no time. Trust me."

"Hear that!" Bryan glowered at the girl, then turned his stare on Ramsey. "You and that Injun bitch won't never live to see the witness stand. Tell 'em, Uncle Bill!"

"That's enough," Hale admonished him. "Anything you say only makes it worse. Keep your mouth shut."

"Hell, let him talk," Proctor said with a chuckle. "You've both got a date with Old Sparky, anyway. Don't matter what he says."

A sudden silence settled over the cell block. Hale sat down on the cot in his cell, elbows on his knees, staring at the floor. His confidence seemed to wane, and he looked somehow old and defeated. Gordon spoke with the Bureau agents, instructing them to split shifts and stand guard around the clock. No one was to be allowed into the cell block without his permission.

The moon was at its zenith when Gordon and Proctor came out of the jail. Pawhuska lay quiet and still, the empty streets bathed in shimmering light. They started toward the car and Proctor lit a cigarette with a kitchen match. He exhaled a wad of smoke.

"Something botherin' me," he said. "Hale knew we had the goods on him six ways to Sunday. Why you reckon he didn't run?"

"Too arrogant," Gordon said. "Power makes some men think they're invincible. Above the law."

"Wish he'd been carryin' a gun. We could've shot him and saved the state the trouble."

"I have a feeling Jack Spivey would have voted for the electric chair. Shooting a man's too quick."

"You ever seen anybody electrocuted?"

"No, but I'm planning to, Will."

"When they fry Hale?"

"We could meet at the prison and watch it together. Care to join me?"

"I wouldn't miss it for all the tea in China."

Gordon smiled. "Neither would Jack."

Chief Lookout declared the next day a day of celebration. A special session was called at the old council house on Main Street, and over a thousand Osages turned out for the occasion. The street was clogged from one end to the other with shiny Pierce-Arrows.

Gordon and Proctor, the honored guests, arrived at ten o'clock. The crowd spilled out onto the sidewalk, and men and women shouted their names and heartily pummeled them across the back as they were escorted inside. The interior of the council house had been stripped bare for the occasion, and a mass of people were wedged shoulder-to-shoulder around the walls. A wide open space was left clear in the center of the throng.

Chief Lookout, in tribal regalia, stood waiting with his eagle-wing fan. He was surrounded by the members of the Tribal Council, all of them dressed in traditional finery. Gordon and Proctor were ushered into the open circle, still not sure why they were there or why the atmosphere seemed so ceremonial. The crowd stilled as they were led into the circle within a circle formed by the council members.

"Today special day," Lookout said in a sonorous voice. "We here to honor the men who brought peace back to the Osages. Their names Frank Gordon and Will Proctor."

The crowd muttered approval. Lookout waited until the murmur subsided, then lifted his eagle-wing fan. "From this day on," he said clearly, "these men are one of us, one of the people of *Wah' Kon-Tah.*" He touched first Gordon and then Proctor with the eagle-wing fan. "We give you greatest gift we have to give. You are now Osages."

Gordon felt a lump in his throat. Proctor, for the first time in his life, was speechless. Before either of them could respond, members of the council stepped forward and placed colorful mussel-shell gorgets around their necks. The crowd chanted in unison and stamped their feet in acclamation. Chief Lookout raised his fan for silence.

"Osage needs Osage name," he said, nodding to Gordon. "After today, wherever you walk among your new people, you will be *No Pah Sha*—Man Not Afraid."

"Thank you," Gordon said humbly. "I'll try to carry the name with honor."

"Already have, long time now." Lookout turned his gaze to Proctor. "You old friend of Osages and we name you *Ho Lah Go Ne.*"

"*Ho Lah Go Ne,*" Proctor repeated. "Got a nice ring to it, Chief. What's it mean?"

"Good Voice," Lookout said with a grin. "Means man who talks a lot."

"You pegged me," Proctor said, laughing. "I've been known to outtalk a magpie."

"Good Voice good name for magpie."

The Osages broke ranks and crowded around to congratulate them. Few white men had ever been adopted into the tribe, and they were lauded with praise for having solved the murders. Yet they were pressed for time, and just as they were about to leave, Chief Lookout took Gordon aside. His voice was unusually sober.

"Osages never forget you," he said. "You ever get tired Texas, come back here to our hills. Always big welcome for *No Pah Sha.*"

"I'll be back," Gordon said. "Even if it's just for a visit. Depend on it."

"We look for you then."

Gordon and Proctor slowly made their way through the crowd. Outside, after another round of handshakes, they crossed the street and walked uphill to the courthouse. Noah Perkins and several deputies were waiting in the holding room of the jail. Perkins all but snapped to attention.

"Mornin', Sheriff," he said, beaming at Proctor. "Got any orders for me and the boys?"

Overnight, Governor Martin Trapp had appointed Proctor to the post of interim sheriff. He was to serve with full authority, and a mandate to clean up Osage County, until the election next year. He thought his first official act would be to demote Perkins.

"Get the boys outside," he ordered. "There's liable to be a crowd when we bring the prisoners out. Keep 'em at a distance."

"Yessir, we'll handle it, Sheriff."

Perkins led the deputies out the door. Gordon was across the room, talking with Horton, Ludlow, and six other Bureau agents. Last night, he'd called SAC David Turner at home and reported the case closed. After discussing the situation, Turner had agreed to have four more agents in Pawhuska by early morning. The prisoners would be transported by car to the federal lockup in Oklahoma City.

The agents listened intently as Gordon again instructed that the four cars were to travel in convoy, never more than a car length apart. "Any questions?" he asked, looking from one to the other. "All right, let's get the show on the road."

Gordon and Proctor went outside. A large crowd of Osages was gathered across from the courthouse, and the deputies were holding them on the opposite side of Grandview Avenue. Feelings were running high, and Gordon's major concern was that someone would attempt to shoot Hale. By now, everyone in town knew that Big Bill was behind the murders.

The prisoners were brought out one at a time. John

Ramsey and Bryan Burkhart were restrained with handcuffs and leg irons, and each of them was accompanied by two agents. The crowd watched impassively as they were marched to the first and second cars parked at the curb. Katherine Cole came out next, handcuffed but without leg irons, and was escorted to the last car in line. Gordon's Chevy was the third car in the convoy.

"Guess it's time, Will," he said extending his hand. "Thanks for watching my back through all this. I couldn't have done it without you."

Proctor clasped his hand. "Hope it's not the last time, Frank. We made a pretty good team."

"Maybe I'll swing by during the elections and watch you campaign for sheriff."

"Who said I was runnin' for sheriff?"

"Old warhorse like you, how could you resist?"

Proctor laughed. "You got me there, pardner."

A roar went up from the crowd. Big Bill Hale, squeezed between the last two Bureau agents, came out of the jail. The Osages surged forward, shouting jeers and catcalls as he was marched to the Chevy in handcuffs and leg irons. The deputies held the crowd in check while Hale was loaded into the backseat with one of the agents. The other agent got behind the wheel and Gordon climbed into the passenger seat. He waved to Proctor as the cars pulled away from the curb.

Beyond the business district, the convoy took the highway leading south from town. On the crest of a hill, Gordon looked back and recalled the day he'd first seen Pawhuska. Nothing then had prepared him for the savagery and corruption he'd found in a lawless land.

Yet his most distinct memories were of the living rather than the dead. A noble people who walked their own path in their own way.

The Osages who followed *Wah' Kon-Tah* westward into the sun.

Epilogue

The federal government moved expeditiously to halt the violence in Osage County. Following the rash of murders in 1923, Congress enacted legislation that prohibited an Osage headright from passing to the person responsible for a murder. The law further stipulated that Osage headrights, specifically oil leases and royalties, could be inherited only by another Osage. No white man ever again acquired control of a tribal headright.

The system of judges appointing white guardians over fullblood Osages was abolished. In 1924, the Interior Department filed twenty-five lawsuits against corrupt guardians to recover land and oil royalties stolen from Osage wards. To avoid criminal prosecution, the accused guardians agreed to out-of-court settlements, and none of the lawsuits went to trial. The murders of dozens of Osages by their guardians never resulted in a criminal conviction.

William "Big Bill" Hale was tried for murder in the Federal District Court at Oklahoma City. He was convicted, and after an appeal was denied, the court sentenced him to life imprisonment. He spent the next twenty-four years behind bars under maximum security in the federal penitentiary at Leavenworth, Kansas. The Osages, the prosecutors, and Frank Gordon believed he escaped justice by not being sentenced to the electric chair. In 1947, Hale was paroled at the age of seventy-two on condition that he never return to Oklahoma.

Ernest Burkhart was tried for murder in the State Court of Osage County and sentenced to life in prison. He served fourteen years in the state penitentiary at McAlester, and in 1937, was paroled on condition that he not return to Osage County. John Ramsey was convicted of murder in the Federal District Court at Oklahoma City and sentenced to life imprisonment. He was paroled from the federal penitentiary after serving twenty-four years, and moved to a remote section of Idaho. Bryan Burkhart, in a travesty of justice, turned state's evidence, testifying against his brother, Ernest, and his uncle, Big Bill Hale. He escaped imprisonment in Oklahoma, only to be convicted of counterfeiting in Texas. He was sentenced to federal prison.

Will Proctor won election as sheriff of Osage County. After serving one term, he discovered that an honest sheriff was no match for corrupt politicians and Roaring Twenties mobsters in the oil fields of Oklahoma. He retired to his home in Hominy, retaining his commission as a Deputy U.S. Marshal, and spent the rest of his life as an honored member of the Osage tribe. In 1924, upon the retirement of Forrest Holbrook, J. Edgar Hoover was appointed Director of the U.S. Bureau of Investigation. Eleven years later, in 1935, the name of the agency was permanently changed to the Federal Bureau of Investigation. Hoover, with files on every politician in Washington, retained his post as Director of the FBI.

Frank Gordon returned to his family in Dallas. As recognition for his role in the Osage murders, President Warren G. Harding awarded him the Medal of Valor for distinguished service to his country. His future with the Bureau was assured, despite his adversarial relationship with J. Edgar Hoover, and an uneasy truce lasted between them for almost three decades. He ended his career as Special Agent in Charge of the FBI field office in Houston, Texas.

The Osages forever called him *No Pah Sha*—Man Not Afraid.